# *Undertow*

## By Leigh Talbert Moore

This book is a work of fiction. Names, characters, places, and incidents are products of the author's imagination or are used fictitiously. Any resemblance to actual events or locales or persons, living or dead, is entirely coincidental.

*Undertow*
Copyright © Leigh Talbert Moore, 2013
www.leightmoore.com
Printed in the United States of America.

Cover design by Jolene B. Perry.

*To my faithful readers and friends.*

*To my Mammaw and my Bobie, who loved to read and loved romance. I wish you could have read this one.*

*And to my husband, Richard, who keeps me believing in my big dreams.*

# *Anna* – December 26

Day after Christmas, and it was eighty degrees out. Everyone was complaining about the heat, but not me. I loved that it was still warm enough to venture into the ocean in only a swimsuit—even if it was a one-piece.

I lay back on my board, trying hard to hold my eyes closed against the glare of the sunlight. The breakers crashed behind me, and I let the gentle rocking of the waves relax my shoulders. Yesterday I'd been at Nana's all day with my parents, exchanging gifts and having Christmas dinner, and when I got home late last night, all I could think about was getting out here today.

One more week and semester break would be over. Then we'd be back, flying to the end of senior year with all that entailed—prom, graduation, leaving for college... But right now I could hold onto this quiet, savor the calm. It was a welcome relief after the last six months.

My best friend Gabi moved away in August, and instead of solitude, I'd stepped onto a roller coaster. It started the minute Lucy Kyser invited me to her enormous home for a study date. I met her brother Jack, had a mini-sexual revolution, started to fall in love with him, then lived through four months of drama as he pushed me away only to pull me back again.

And I let him.

I cringed in shame at the memory, and my mind flooded with the images. Every touch, every kiss, every fight, every make-up leading to a make-out. My stomach twisted, and I sat up fast on my board, crossing my arms over my waist. I hated how that stupid longing tried to creep back in when I didn't expect it. How it meant there was still the tiniest possibility I had feelings for him. That I wasn't completely sure what would happen if he showed up here wanting me back.

It made me mad. I'd spent the whole break focused on conquering these emotions. This was not helping me find my calm.

I closed my eyes and flexed every muscle in my body—I even held my breath. It was silly, but I imagined pushing him out of my heart and my head by sheer force of will, as if I could somehow focus so hard, I could send that stupid last bit of longing flying out of me like the cork from a shaken champagne bottle…

At that very second, a body shot through the quiet water with a loud yell. My eyes flew open, and I screamed even louder. All the breath I'd been holding blasted out, and I gripped my board so I didn't fall off.

Julian could barely speak for laughing. "Gotcha!"

"Julian!" I yelled.

Adrenaline surged through me, making me trembly and weak, and I curled forward to rest my head on my fists, trying to hide my smile. Julian, my funny, gorgeous, incredibly talented friend did get me, and I was so glad.

After a moment, I felt his warm hand on my shoulder. "Hey," he said, still fighting laughs. "I didn't give you a heart attack, did I?"

"You wish," I said, turning my head to slant my eyes at him. Then I stretched forward to lie on my stomach.

His blue eyes sparkled like the waves. "Admit it. You freaked."

I sighed, pretending to be annoyed. "You are so mature."

He crossed his arms on the end of my board, and his face was close enough that I could feel his breath against my skin. Every kiss we'd shared danced through my mind, and I pictured myself sliding off the board and into his arms. This last week as he'd taught me to surf, our bodies pressed together in only swimsuits, he'd managed to be very respectful of my request for time. But it was getting harder to fight my own feelings.

Still, I had to. I couldn't let Julian be some stupid rebound thing. He meant so much more than that. I had to be sure I was over Jack first.

"It's a terrible day to surf." He looked around the water with a frown. "Didn't I teach you anything? What are you doing out here?"

"Trying to have some alone time, thanks."

"Okay." He let go of the board and moved like he would swim to shore.

"Wait," I rose to my elbows. "Julian. Don't be like that. How was your Christmas?"

He turned back with a smile and warmth traveled all the way to my toes. "Same as always," he shrugged. "New art supplies, a few tools. Just me and Mom. I didn't expect to see you out here. You were very deep in thought. What's on your mind?"

I studied my palm, not wanting to tell him what I'd been doing before he burst through the water.

"I don't know. School starts next week," I said. "I was thinking about the end of senior year."

"It's gonna be great. We'll do everything."

My nose wrinkled as I squinted at him. "Everything?"

"Sure! If it's happening, we're doing it. You still working at the paper?"

"All the way to May." I loved my internship at the city paper. It had been my one constant through the emotional mess of last fall, and it made my college applications look *so* good. "And possibly some during the summer."

"You should." He smiled, holding the end of my board again. "You're a natural. Anyone who could get Mom to talk about her art career... I never thought that would happen."

My eyes flickered away from his. He didn't know why his mom had offered to talk, that her interview had been in exchange for my silence after I'd discovered her secret—that Julian was the son of Bill Kyser, the ultra-rich, most powerful developer in town. That he and Jack were half-brothers.

It was *not* a deal I'd asked for. I told her I'd never tell Julian what I'd discovered, although now that promise felt like it was becoming harder to keep. I was afraid of what Julian would say if he found out I knew and didn't tell him. And I couldn't help thinking how this secret could change his life.

As the son of Bill Kyser, Julian could take his place beside Jack and Lucy as one of the leaders in our town, possibly even beyond. Every door would fly open to him.

The way things now stood, he and his mom lived in a tiny cottage a block off the beach road in Dolphin Shores. His mom ran a local art and souvenir shop a few blocks east of that, and he'd had to work so hard for everything he'd achieved, even his scholarship to the Savannah College of Art and Design.

I wanted him to have everything he deserved. I wanted him to know the truth. But Bill Kyser said no. He insisted their connection had to remain a secret, and he'd even given me three journals to convince me to trust him. Journals that still lay under my bed just waiting for me to read them.

"What are you thinking, Anna? You're not even listening to me," Julian said, his voice softer.

I glanced up at his blue eyes, and again I remembered the few times he'd kissed me. I longed for the day when I could reach out and touch him, pull him close without having to worry.

"Just… working at the paper," I said. "What did you say?"

"I *said* I have to go to Darplane next month. They're putting my runner at the National Athletic Center, remember? I figured if it weren't for you, they wouldn't even know about me, so you should be my date to the unveiling."

"I'd love to go!" I said. "But I thought the ring was my thank you gift for that."

My mind drifted to the delicate, sparkling dragonfly ring he'd made for me. It was unique and beautiful, and I kept it wrapped in tissue and hidden safely in my drawer.

Without thinking, I reached for his hand, which rested on the board beside my arm. I turned it so I could see the tiny, matching dragonfly tattoo he'd inked above his thumb. Warmth filled my chest as I ran my finger across it.

He shrugged, watching my movements. "That wasn't a thank you. It was something special. Just for you."

"I love it." I smiled, picturing us together. *Soon*, I thought. "And I'd love to go with you to the unveiling. But let's paddle in now. I need some lunch."

"My house?"

"Sure." I slid off the board and swam with him back to shore.

* * *

Last-minute instructions were given, kisses and emergency numbers handed out, and my parents were off for their annual, post-Christmas, long-weekend getaway. It was their tradition, following the month my mom spent organizing Christmas on the Coast, the huge fundraiser for the arts association in Fairview where she worked.

The house was finally quiet, and I was finally alone with the journals. The story.

It was a complete accident that I had walked in on Jack's dad locked in an embrace with Julian's mom. They'd said they were simply old friends, but working at the paper, I'd discovered their deeper connection hidden in the dusty files and old pictures.

Nothing was in writing, but when I'd asked Julian's mom, she'd told me the truth. She'd also nearly had me fired — until Mr. Kyser intervened. And did the unthinkable. He put the whole story in my hands in the form of three private journals, and he made me promise to tell no one about them. Not even Ms. LaSalle.

I couldn't wait to dig into their contents, but so far, every time I'd pulled them out to read, something or someone had interrupted me. Now I had an entire weekend alone to immerse myself in the story, to try and understand.

Breathless with anticipation, I slid the first one off the bed and slowly opened the cover. It belonged to Margaret Weaver Kyser, Meg for short. She was Will,

Jack, and Lucy's mom, and she died in a car crash when they were babies.

My fingers trembled as I gently turned the pages. There were gaps in the timeline, I noticed, and I wasn't sure what I would discover here.

But I was ready to know.

# Book 1 – Meg

*May 31, 19 –*

*Margaret Louise Kyser. Mrs. William S. Kyser. William and Margaret Kyser. Bill and Meg Bill and Meg Kyser. Bill and Meg Kyser cordially invite you to their estate on Hammond Island…*

Nothing's more exciting than a new journal. The blank pages just waiting to be filled with all the interesting and amazing things about to happen to me. I'm starting a new life. It's almost as fun as planning a wedding. And planning a wedding is *so* much more fun than going to high school.

I've actually been planning my wedding since I was a little girl dressed up in my grandmother's chiffon nightgowns and scarves. Meeting Billy provided the face to my mystery groom, and what a perfect face. I knew the minute I saw him our first day at Fairview High School that he was the one. Tall and slim with soft brown hair and beautiful blue eyes — it was love at first sight.

We'll be together forever, of course, with little Will, John, Lucy, and Megan. Will will be named after Billy and John for my daddy. Lucy is for my best friend Alexandra Marie LaSalle, who has the coolest name ever. We all call her Lexy for short, and I know, Lucy's not the same as Lexy. But it reminds me of Lexy, and I want my little girl to be just like her — creative, beautiful, full of flair, and loyal to the end.

Megan's for me, but that's just my safety. Billy hasn't said if he wants four babies, but I can probably change his mind. And I know, my given name is Margaret. But everybody calls me Meg. That's why I chose Megan. It's a cute little variation and will give her her own personal style.

Our wedding is set for June 15. The perfect date for the most perfect day of our lives. We'll be married on the beach, of course. The beach Billy is always talking about filling with high rises. I don't want to be disloyal, but I think blocking up the East End Beach skyline is a terrible idea. Of course, Billy knows best.

He and his best friend Bryant Brennan have a plan for taking the barren landscape of South County and turning it into a high-end tourist destination. I don't care about that. I'm only interested in our perfect house and our three (or four) perfect children. He can take care of the rest.

Lexy is my maid of honor. We've been best friends since she moved to Port Hogan to live with Mrs. Stella Walker and go to the Magnolia School with me. Miss Stella has a big old Victorian home down on Port Hogan Road, and she's famous for helping the Sisters of St. Joseph with their orphans. Before she lived here, Lexy lived with the sisters at the Little Flower Convent in Sterling. Her mother's mentally ill and can't take care of herself, much less a baby.

I think growing up in a place called Little Flower must've had some influence on how artistic and imaginative she is. But we don't ever talk about that. I'm sensitive to Lexy's feelings.

When we started kindergarten, she had the biggest brown eyes of any little girl I'd ever seen. She was very shy, but she was certainly eye-catching with her long dark hair and olive skin. I knew immediately we'd be best friends. With my long blonde hair and blue eyes we were like night and day together. The complete set.

Lexy is the most talented artist I've ever met, which I guess isn't saying much because I don't know any other artists. Still, her brilliant oil paintings fill a room, just like her personality now that we're grown up, and she's already been accepted to the Savannah College of Art and Design. That's the best art school around.

Everybody calls it SCAD, which I think is crazy because it sounds like SCAB, but whatever. I told her she'd get in. Gallery owners all over Newhope and East End Beach have been carrying her works since she set up an easel outside the marina where Billy keeps his boat. She would sit out there and slap brilliantly colored paints on huge canvasses and in a few hours she'd be signing off on massive images of sailboats waiting to go out, brown pelicans sitting atop pier posts, even piles of blue crabs stacked after emptying a day's trap. Tourists and locals would wait for hours to pay her for a finished piece, and she was only in high school.

In a month she'll move to Savannah, but before she leaves, she's going to walk down the aisle in front of me to celebrate the most perfect day of my life.

My mother, Mrs. Georgiana Weaver, is on practically every volunteer board and committee in South County. That's because my daddy, Dr. John Weaver, is the best surgeon at the hospital in Fairview, and he's a founding member of the hospital expansion committee.

When the county commissioner's wife had to have her gall bladder removed, she insisted on having my daddy perform the surgery. It means we have a lot of money, and it tends to make people take notice of us.

Anyway, my mother wasn't too keen on the idea of me getting married right out of high school. Those were her exact words, "not too keen." But once I explained to her the only thing I wanted to do was marry Billy and start having the most beautiful children this county's ever seen, she laughed and said I should follow my dreams.

Everyone acts like your dreams should be something earth-shaking and huge. When I was South County's contestant for the State Junior Miss competition in Sterling, all the other contestants would talk about how they were going to be ambassadors or newswomen or actresses — things that would take them far away from their homes and families.

I'm glad I didn't win. I can't imagine living anywhere besides here. I know everyone in South County. I know where everything is and who owns what, and once Billy sets his plan in motion, he's going to put East End Beach on the map, and we'll be rich. He's told me that a hundred times, and if anybody does what they say they will, it's Billy.

We're perfect for each other, Billy and me, because I'll be his patient, loving wife making his home and taking care of our beautiful children while he's out conquering the world. I'm used to husbands who work a lot from my daddy. He's always on call or at the hospital late or on Saturdays and Sundays. Billy's working won't bother me a bit because in the end we'll just be two old people sitting on our front porch surrounded by our grandbabies. And we'll smile and pat each others' hands and reminisce about how hard we had to struggle and how happy we are together.

It also helps that Billy's daddy owns a good-sized horse ranch in Midlind, so even if my future husband's master plan doesn't pan out, we'll still land on our feet.

Lexy's coming over to try on her maid of honor dress in a few hours, and I can't wait. Miss Sensory Ocean-Mystic "You shouldn't be getting married so young" is going to flip when she sees it—dark maroon strapless bodice with a white tulle skirt. She'll look amazing next to me in my all-white, strapless dress with matching tulle skirt.

I went with all-white even though I've got a secret that only Billy and I know. I'm expecting little Will before Christmas.

We'll tell everyone just as soon as the honeymoon's over. And after that, we'll be on our way to living happily ever after.


*June 10, 19—*

Of course Lexy loved her bridesmaid's dress. My wedding is going to be perfect, and it's only five days away. I'm having trouble eating, sleeping, concentrating on anything. I'm so excited. A cruise this evening was the perfect idea. Billy's so clever.

Going out on Billy's boat is one of my all-time favorite things in the world. It's so perfectly Gulf Coast. We load up in the marina at East End Beach and set out to feel the breeze on our faces and watch the sun set. Speaking of watching, watching my future husband batten the hatches and tighten the lines as he puts us out to sea is almost as exhilarating as the sunset. He's typically shirtless, and Billy has a perfect physique. I expect all of our sons to inherit their daddy's good looks. Of course, the girls will all look just like me. The model family.

Lexy arrived just a few minutes after us. She drives a funny Jeep-like vehicle, a sidekick or something. I'm pretty sure it was recalled by the manufacturer a few years ago, which is the only way she could buy it. Miss Stella is good to her orphans, but she can't afford many luxuries. Lexy was able to use her painting money to lift this heap off some old-timer. God, how I love our group. How I hate that we'll all be separated soon.

Bryant is bringing Donna Albriton with him. She's a nice girl. A little thick around the ankles, but she has a sweet face. And anyone who can put up with Bryant's boisterous personality deserves a medal. He's as loud as a yard hand. I'm just glad my beautiful, artistic friend agreed to join us. Donna's sweet, but she can be dreadfully dull.

"Lexy! Over here!" I called. I was so excited when I saw her on the pier. "Billy's getting the boat, so we can hop on in just a minute."

"I guess it's a good evening for sailing," she said frowning. Lexy hates boats. "Where we headed?"

"The boys want to inspect some land around Terry Cove. Near Hammond Island."

"Planning their future homes?"

We giggled and hugged each other. Lexy knows the guys as well as I do. Bryant isn't quite as ambitious as Billy, but he'll go with him as far as Billy's dreams will take them. I'm just happy my future's settled.

"Hey, Lex." Billy was back with his shirt unbuttoned, maneuvering the small craft for us to climb aboard.

I took his hand, and as he gently helped me across (Baby on board!), he gave me a kiss. He's terribly sexy. Next he helped Lexy across, and she pretended not to notice him. I rolled my eyes.

If only she didn't try so hard to hate him, they might actually be good friends. I know Billy's willing to give her a chance, but she's so determined I'm making a mistake getting married now.

"Bill," Lexy said, very formal. "I see you're at least willing to enjoy the beauty of our hometown even though you're bent on destroying it."

"I'm not planning to destroy the beauty of our hometown, Lex," he said patiently. "I just want to share it with others."

"And get filthy rich while you're at it."

"Yes. That is definitely in the plan," he laughed.

"You two don't start," I said.

Lexy scooted in next to me and gave me a squeeze. How I loved my dear friend. "After next week, you will never hear me argue with Bill again." She pushed a lock of my hair behind my ear. "I will have nothing but best wishes for you and your little family."

She must've felt me jump because Lexy was onto us in an instant. She's pretty clever herself. "Okay, what's going on?"

"I don't know what you're talking about." But I was blushing.

Her big dark eyes narrowed. "This sudden wedding couldn't be because you're expecting anything?"

Billy looked uncomfortable.

"You've got to swear not to tell anyone, Lexy," I pleaded, holding her arm. "It's only for a little while longer."

"You're not." But the annoyance in her voice had softened, and the light glistened on her now-misty eyes.

I smiled huge at that. "I am!"

We both screamed, and I threw my arms around her. Naturally, she had a million questions, but then

Bryant and Donna walked up. I immediately changed the subject and welcomed them onboard.

After cruising a good ways down the sound and around the peninsula into Terry Cove, Billy pulled out the surprise—a bottle of champagne he slipped out of the marina bar.

"To us and our future," he said, popping the cork.

We all shared a glass, and I don't think anyone noticed that I only took one tiny sip from mine. It was sad that Lexy was leaving, but it was going to be amazing watching Billy and Bryant conquer the coast.


*June 15, 19—*


As predicted, my wedding was the event of the season in South County. There must've been 300 people come out to Romar Beach to see us tie the knot. Both papers sent photographers to take pictures for the Tuesday edition.

We were married on the future site of Phoenician I, and coming down the aisle, I took a mental picture of the scene. Dr. Gatts in the middle with my beautiful best friend to the left, long dark hair waving in the breeze, tulle skirt swishing around her like sea foam. My gorgeous husband to the right, loose white shirt fluttering in the wind, smiling in approval. I wore my hair wrapped in a tight French twist, and I could feel my veil streaming around me like a cloud.

After the wedding, we danced and visited with our friends for hours until it was time to board Daddy's yacht and head south. The reception was all catered by the best local caterer and the flowers were all native plants, magnolias and confederate roses, calla lilies, and hydrangeas.

We'd ordered individual plates of shrimp and grits for everyone, but of course there were tables piled high with finger foods and desserts. The champagne fountain and fondue station were where most people hung out, and all our silly teenage-boy friends were busy dipping everything in the flowing chocolate.

But I loved seeing people having a good time. And I loved knowing they'd just go on and on about our wedding for at least six months. Good luck to the next local girl attempting to top my gala event.

For our honeymoon, Daddy gave us his fifty-foot yacht to cruise down to the islands. Even though Billy's an experienced mariner, Daddy threw in a captain so we didn't have to worry about navigation or making time.

The cruise was as much a part of our honeymoon as the destination, and I planned for us to spend most of it in the master suite. I may be three months pregnant, but I'll be damned if I miss out on my honeymoon nights with Billy. Everybody thinks I'm so innocent, but I've been doing my homework. I plan to knock his socks off. Literally. I've been studying some of those men's magazines Daddy hides in the garage—as if nobody knows they're there. Think again, Dad! I don't quite get how the ladies manage some of those positions, but I think I can figure out a few. Just because I can't hold Billy at home doesn't mean I can't keep his mind occupied when he's away.

So more soon, Journal. I've got a husband to occupy.

*June 28, 19 –*

Back from our honeymoon! The islands were as beautiful as I'd always heard, but we didn't leave the boat much to look at them. After that first night, Billy was so intrigued he kept wanting to get back to Daddy's yacht and see what else I'd learned.

His favorite position was something called a Reverse Cowgirl, which is basically him just lying back with me on top, sitting with my back to him. I'm sure he prefers that method because he grew up on a ranch, but I can't say it was my favorite way to go. I much prefer either facing him or in plain ole missionary style, hugged up close to his chest with him whispering and kissing my ear and cheek. But hearing his loud groans and swears, and feeling him clutching my butt was exciting enough to get me where I needed to be, so I didn't complain about repeat performances of that one.

I'm happily confident my new husband's socks were effectively knocked off. And I have to say, a nice bed and the freedom to spend as much time as you want in it is so much better than being cramped in the cab of a pickup or sneaking behind boardwalks in the dark. We'll have plenty of time to come back here and actually tour the islands in a few years once the babies are old enough to stay with Mom.

I love being married! I love imagining how it's going to be once Billy's finished with his plan, and we're the richest, most important family in South County. Of course, I'll be a great benefactress, and the best part will be all the good causes I'll be able to help. I was thinking about Miss Stella and how she dedicated her dotage to taking care of orphaned children like Lexy. I don't expect to be left alone, but I would love to be able to find gifted young people like my friend and give them a chance to become famous. Be like their old donor lady, whatever that's called.

My fondest memory of the week is how close Billy and I've become. We've been together four years, and I've shared everything with him. He was the first boy I ever slept with, but that was as high schoolers. Now we're husband and wife, and it's a different situation altogether. One night after successfully mastering a position the magazines called "grinding the corn," which is a ridiculous name and basically means missionary style only with Billy slightly higher than me (it actually might be my new favorite way), I decided it was safe to share my biggest concern with him.

He loved teasing me about our future, and tonight was no different. "When you decide you're tired of being home alone, who will you leave me for?" he asked.

"You know good and well you're the only guy for me," I said. "I guess I'll just play with the baby and go visit Mama."

"You're not going to take up with Rain Hawkins?"

"No thank you," I said, hugging his bare chest to mine. I loved feeling our skin pressed together. "I've known since I was five I wouldn't be a farmer's wife."

"What about Chuck? He's a cop now, but he could end up chief of police and then maybe even mayor."

I leaned back, curling my nose. "Have you looked in the mirror lately? Chuck has a long way to go to catch up with you." Then I leaned in and kissed my gorgeous husband. "I'm more worried about what you're going to do when I'm big and pregnant. I know you like skinny girls."

I felt him laugh as I lay my cheek against his chest again, his fingers tracing long strokes down my back. "I think you're the one who needs to check the mirror."

"I'm serious, though," I sighed. "You're so smart, and when you and Bryant start going to Atlanta, you'll be meeting a lot of sexy business women."

"I'm not interested in any sexy business women."

I sat up and looked straight into his blue eyes, serious. "Are you sorry about this? The baby? Marrying me?"

"Nope," he said with that beautiful smile. "I'm just sorry I'm not going to see you much."

"That's part of the deal. I said it didn't matter." I dropped down to the bed beside him.

He moved to lie beside me, twisting a lock of my hair around his finger. I studied his lined arm, leading up to an equally defined chest. I wasn't sure he appreciated how many women were checking him out all the time.

"Just don't lie to me, okay?" I said.

His brow creased. "Lie to you? About what?"

"Anything. Later on I mean."

"What's going to happen later on?"

"Well, nothing that's not in your plan, I hope."

He pulled me close and kissed me. "That makes two of us."

I slid my arms around his neck and his hands made their way down my body. We were off again, but I was relieved we'd at least covered the bases.

Still, I couldn't help worrying about all those long hours he'd be keeping. Billy's a good guy, but he's still a guy.

*June 30, 19 —*

We've started setting up the house.

It's not actually *our* house, it's my grandmother's old home in Fairview. Mom and Daddy gave it to us for our wedding gift, and while it's a quaint little historic place, it's nothing like the gorgeous mansion we're going to have on Hammond Island once Billy's the most famous developer in the world.

Still, it's a pretty little cottage, and we'll fit for now in its two bedrooms and one bathroom. One bathroom! Who ever heard of such a thing?

Mom said at least we'll have a guest room if we ever have overnight visitors. I can't wait to tell her about her grandson. I found out it's a boy at my last doctor's visit.

Those doctor's visits. What a pain in the ass! Sorry, that's not very genteel of me, but that doctor almost pushed me over the edge. Once he knew for sure, he practically demanded I tell my parents about the pregnancy — when I hadn't even told Billy!

I thought I was going to have to commit a felony to get that stupid doctor to listen to me. In the end, I used Daddy's heart condition as leverage. I said he wouldn't want to be responsible for causing the most important surgeon in Fairview to have a heart attack. That shut his big mouth. And after I told Billy, he came with me to all my appointments and assured the doc we were getting married once we graduated.

That stupid doctor rushed me into telling Billy before I wanted to, too. I was going to wait until our graduation party, after Billy'd had a few drinks and was feeling happy. I was afraid of how he'd take the news.

Before I told him, he'd actually suggested we wait until he finished college to get married.

"Wait!" I'd cried. "For what?"

Billy knew as well as I did that we were perfect for each other. I'm the only girl pretty enough to be the wife of a future leader like him, and I'd be damned if I let him get distracted by college and drift away from me. I was not going to lose my prince charming or my mansion on Hammond Island!

Once I told him about our little blessing, he was definitely stunned, but I convinced him we should just get married and he could carry right on with that big plan of his. Little Will and I would not slow him down one bit.

Now I'm trying to decide the perfect way to spring the news on my parents. Once we're all settled, I think we should host an intimate dinner party for just the four of us. I'll serve wine, and when everyone's all good and relaxed, we'll announce the joyous news.

I wish Lexy were here. I'm sure she's off taking Savannah by storm, but she sure would help me feel more confident. I'm looking forward to taking South County by storm, but it'll be a few years before Billy and I are established the way we want to be.

When my parents moved here from Birmingham, they didn't have anything either. Daddy was just an intern at South County General Hospital, and no one had ever heard of the Weavers. A few short years later, he was the top surgeon, and that's exactly how it's going to be with Billy and me. In few short years, we'll be ruling the coast.

*July 5, 19 –*

Our little cottage is right off the main drag between Fairview and Springdale, and it's in the perfect location for all the events and activities in town. Last night we sat out on the porch steps and watched the city fireworks display. I've been so tired lately, I haven't felt like hitting any parties. The doctor said it's because of the pregnancy. I just wish Lexy were here. With her gone, I don't have anyone to talk to about how I'm feeling. Billy can't be bothered with all this women's business, and Mom still doesn't know.

Mom and I have always been close. She's a Fairview native, which is why my parents came back here when Daddy finished medical school. It's close to the beach and such a great place to raise a family with all the small-town charm and good schools.

I plan on our family being the same way, only when we make it, we're moving to Hammond Island where all the rich people live. My parents didn't want to move once Daddy made it big. Something about the drive being too far from the hospital and them already knowing all their neighbors here.

I think that's ridiculous. Everyone knows the real sign of how rich you are is where you live, and Billy's already picked out our spot on Lost Bay. The children will all go to Sacred Heart, and I'll volunteer at only the most exclusive local charities.

Of course, I'll join the Fort Bowyer DAR, the hospital auxiliary, and the Krewe de Candy Stripers with Mom. That's her Mardi Gras krewe. I might even join the Junior League, but they'll work you to death if you let them. Mom was in the Junior League ten years, and she finally jumped off that crazy train. I prefer the Mardi

Gras krewe and the DAR anyway. They're more about parties and historical events and less about running around town like a chicken with its head cut off.

Lexy thinks all that stuff is silly. I miss her so much now that she's in Savannah. She might roll her eyes at my plans for future community involvement, but when I need someone to talk to, she's always a good listener. It's true Mom and I are close, but she doesn't always hear me when I'm talking to her. And Billy gets tired of my little problems. He's completely focused on the big picture.

I can call Lexy on a moment's notice about anything, and she'll stop and listen or giggle. Once I called her for two seconds to tell her I found a huge palmetto bug in my tub, and I didn't think I was ever going to be able to bathe in it again. We just collapsed into giggles.

It's hard to find friends like that. I had hoped we'd be having our babies together, but that's not Lexy's way. She's got to conquer the art world before she'll consider settling down with any man. I sure wish she'd hurry up and get it done. Then she can come home, and we can pick up right where we left off.

*Sept. 5, 19 —*

I've been so busy setting up our house, I haven't had time to write. But the night has come to tell my parents about the baby. I'm starting to show, and I don't have enough billowy blouses to cover it. Besides, I'm tired of hiding. I want everybody to know I'm about to have the most gorgeous little boy this town's ever seen. How could I not? Have you seen his daddy?

Still, I've been so nervous all day today, it's been hard to cook and prepare. Billy started school so he's gone all the time. Then when he gets home, he's constantly talking to Bryant. He says they're working out the details of their plan, but I can't imagine what details they can work out with college not even behind him yet. Those are the most focused guys I've ever met in my life.

I had to call Lexy to let her know what was happening and get some moral support. "Lexy, I'm freaking out," I said. "It's B-day in Fairview."

"What?" I heard her frown. "I don't understand. Are you in labor?"

"No, tonight's the night. I'm telling my parents, and I'm so scared."

She breathed a laugh. "Oh, please. Your mother's going to cry, she'll be so happy."

"But what about Daddy?" I chewed my lip as I frantically twisted my hair around my finger. "What if he has another heart attack?"

"Why should he? I mean, they already gave you guys a house." Behind her I could hear music playing softly and what sounded like pages turning in her sketchbook. "You're working at the hospital, and Bill's launching his master plan to destroy East End Beach. You're all set. They're going to be thrilled."

"But that's just it," I said, still worried. "I'll have to stop working. What will we do for money once the baby comes?"

"Gigi will not let her only child and only grandchild go without. Stop worrying. That baby will have a trust fund before the year's end."

"And I don't want Daddy saying mean things to Billy. If they don't like each other, I don't know if I can take it."

"As long as you're happy, your Daddy will be fine." Her calm voice was always so reassuring to me. "Show him how happy you are, and everything'll be okay."

"I know you're right. Oh, Lexy, you're so smart. Are you dating anybody yet?"

She snorted a laugh. "Jeez, Meg, I've only been here a few months! Give me a chance to find my way around."

"I know, but you're so pretty." I lifted the lid off a pot and gave the potatoes I was boiling a poke. "It isn't right for you not to have a man."

"Not everyone needs a man to complete her life," she breathed, and I could just see her walking through her apartment, long, brown hair twisted into a knot with a pencil stuck in it. "Besides, you had your prince delivered to you on a silver platter. We should all be so lucky."

"He is a prince."

"See? All better. Now call me when it's over. I want details."


*Sept. 6, 19 —*

They took it much better than I expected. It helped that Billy was right there laying out his master plan for our future the second after I sprang the news. I couldn't stand the tension, so I finally just blurted it out in the middle of the mashed-potato course.

Mom dropped her fork. She really did. I've never seen her lose her good manners, but as soon as I put the bowl down and said, "You'll have a grandson by Christmas," her mouth flew open, her fork hit the table, and she burst into tears.

Daddy got up beaming—thank goodness! He shook hands with Billy and pulled him into the living room to discuss the matter. Right there in the middle of dinner, they got up and left. It gave Mom and me a chance to chat.

"So that was all the talk about following your dreams." Of course, she got straight to the point. "You were expecting, young lady."

"Well, I had an idea."

Her eyes narrowed at me. "If you're due in November, you had more than an idea."

"I just didn't want you to worry, Mama. And Billy and I have known for years we'd get married."

"It's all well that ends well." She folded her napkin and put it beside her plate, her formality restored. "So have you decided what you'll do when the baby comes?"

This was the part I feared. "We're still working on that," I stammered. "Billy will be at school, so I guess I'll have to keep working. Maybe you could watch the baby a few days? Only if you want to, I mean."

"Work!" She said it like I'd just suggested third-trimester skydiving. "You'll do nothing of the sort. You think your father and I would sit back and make you slave away with our grandson at home? We'll help with the bills, and you just take it easy and enjoy your little son."

"Are you sure?" Lexy was right, and I was so relieved.

"Of course. Why do you think we gave you this house? Bill's a hard worker. Once he gets on his feet, you two will do very well. And what's the point of having money if you can't help your children when they need it?"

"Oh, Mom." I got up and went around to hug her neck. "You're the best."

"I expect to be well cared for when I'm old." She winked and we laughed. I couldn't wait to call Lexy.


*Sept. 23, 19 –*

My goodness! It's been almost a month since I've had a chance to sit down and write. Once we told Mom, she went bananas planning showers and rushing me around to get registered everywhere. I felt more than silly for worrying she'd be mad. The way she was acting, you'd think she was having the baby.

Still it's fun. I was starting to get a little sad being the only girl in town who knew about our bundle of joy. Mom's been great. She insisted on going to all my doctor's appointments, and she's really keeping me busy. I'm exhausted half the time, and now it's not just from being pregnant.

Only a few more months until little Will makes his appearance. I can't wait. For now, I'm off to my third shower this month. We're going to have to build an addition to fit all the baby gear in our tiny house. But I just love presents!

Everyone talks about getting pregnant young and how it ruins your social life and limits what you can do. Well, I've never wanted to do anything except marry Billy and be a mom. So I'm right where I want to be. I'm living my dream.

*Oct. 23, 19 –*

And here we are! His room's all ready, I've packed his little bag, I've packed my little bag. Now we're in the final stages where we just sit and wait. Any day it could happen.

I hate waiting.

Sorry I've been such a poor correspondent, but that's my life now. I don't have time to write, and when I do, I fall asleep, pen in hand. Mom's been staying with me a lot lately. Billy's finishing up his first semester at college, and soon he'll start taking exams. I definitely wasn't prepared for his exam week to fall the same time as my due date, but I don't dare complain. I'm sure Billy's thinking about it, and if I say anything, he'll only get mad. This was the very thing we had our big discussion about way back in May when I assured him nothing would change if we got married.

Besides, babies are born all the time without their daddies being there. What if Billy were in the military or worked offshore? I'm not going to make a big drama over the whole thing. He'll be seeing his son plenty after we get home. And who knows, he might be there after all. Will could come on a Sunday.


*Nov. 12, 19 –*

Will did not come on a Sunday. Nope, my sweet little boy came a few weeks early on a Tuesday afternoon. And if there was ever a time that was inconvenient for everybody, that was it. Even my daddy was tied up at the other end of the hospital and couldn't be there.

Of course, Mom was with me, and she and I flew to the birthing unit even though they say your first baby usually takes a long time to come out. If that's the case, then I'd better move into the hospital when it's time for little John, because Will was out in less than an hour. My water broke, Mom and I jumped in the car, and two hours later, there he was, screaming his little head off. We cried and clung to each other. Mom and I really are baby obsessed like Lexy always says.

I called Lexy, but she must've been in class because it went straight to voicemail. I knew Billy was in class, but I left him a message anyway. Daddy walked down as soon as he got out of surgery and declared little Willie the finest baby ever to be born at South County General.

He really is a fine baby. He's got a head full of light brown hair just like his daddy's, and it looks like he'll probably stick with the family tradition of having blue eyes. He looked at all of us wide-eyed for a little bit and then nuzzled in for food and a nap. I love him already, and I kissed his sweet little head as I fell asleep.

Next thing I knew, I was waking up to Billy slipping into the bed beside me. It was late, and he was wearing the same clothes he'd had on when he'd left that morning.

"Hi," he whispered, gently kissing my head.

I smiled. "We got a baby today."

"I see that," he smiled. "What does he think about his beautiful Mama?"

"We're getting along very well. He's eaten a few times, and the nurse changed him for me. Mostly we've just slept."

"Sounds right." We both looked at his tiny face pressed against my breast. "He's a cute little guy."

Billy petted the baby's head, and I kissed my husband's cheek. "Just like his daddy."

"You feeling okay? You look great."

"A little tired. Sore, but nothing major. He was so good about coming out, I feel like I'll be on my feet again in no time."

"Good." Billy pressed his cheek against my head.

We lay quietly watching our little son for a while. Then too soon, Billy stirred, pecked my cheek and started getting up to leave. I made a little whimper and clutched his arm.

"I can't stay," he said. "Final paper's due tomorrow. But your mom'll be here, right? You'll be okay?"

I nodded making a pouty face. I actually felt my eyes growing damp. "Do you want to hold him before you leave?" I asked.

"Nah. Let him sleep. I'll have plenty of time when he gets home." He leaned in and pressed a longer kiss to my forehead before straightening up and going to the door.

I felt like my heart was breaking as I watched Billy go, but I couldn't say anything. I'd promised. I'd convinced him not to wait to get married because I'd said I could do this. I just didn't expect to miss him so much.


*March 16, 19 —*

Time is flying since Will came. I almost forgot I was keeping a journal! I remember so well being in the hospital with him, and now here he is already four months old. Easter's coming, and he is going to be so cute in his little seersucker Jon Jon.

I love going to mass with my little family. First, we're the best looking parishioners in the whole church. Billy's a show-stopper in a suit, and I sure hope all those good church ladies don't think they're fooling anybody. I can see them checking out my gorgeous husband with impure thoughts in their heads.

Of course, I'm always dressed to kill, and then we have our little angel who is the perfect combination of us both. And such a sweet little baby. Will never cries in public unless something's very wrong.

We make it through the service and greet all the old ladies on the way out. We always go to my parents' house for Sunday dinner, and then home for a nap. Billy never naps, but I'm in heaven resting with my little baby prince. It's all perfectly perfect, and I know everyone in town is just beside themselves with envy.

Billy's soaring through classes at the university in Sterling. I really do have the most clever husband. He said he'd graduate with honors, and so far he hasn't missed an *A* yet. He also tells me he's making good contacts through the business school. People with connections in Atlanta, who he says will put him and Bryant in front of top investors to make their business pitches.

I'll just be glad when summer's here. Billy's still doing intersession and summer school, but he can't take as many classes during the summer, and I'm hoping that means I'll see him more.

Even though I miss him, I'm never alone. Mom's over here all the time holding Will and helping me with him. Then we go shopping or have our nails done, and I go with her to some of the auxiliary meetings and DAR teas.

At the last meeting, she introduced me to Winifred Hayes, Winnie for short. Winnie's a bit older than me, and she's married to one of the young doctors who's interning at the hospital. We have so much in common. She loves clothes and shoes and getting her nails done. And we're both just biding our time while our absentee husbands finish their degrees.

Winnie thinks Billy's extremely good-looking, which simply shows she isn't blind. She wants us all to get together and have dinner sometime, but I haven't mentioned it to Billy. I'm afraid he'll say he doesn't have time for things like that. He's so loaded down with classes and projects.

"You should convince him to take a break," Winnie said, tucking one of her red curls back in her ponytail as we walked along the sidewalk in town. It was a lovely spring day. Warm, but with a light breeze.

"I try, but you don't know the pressure he puts on himself. He's keeping a very strict schedule." The wind blew my long hair softly over my shoulder, and little Will was happily sleeping in his stroller.

"Well, I don't understand that boy. Here you are, pretty as you can be, and little Will. And he hardly ever comes home!"

"We've talked about that," I said, "and it's only going to be for a few more years."

"A few more years!" Her face was pure horror behind her sunglasses. "That's a long time, and you're not getting younger."

My forehead creased. "What are you saying?"

"I'm just wondering what's the rush? Billy could ease up a bit, finish in four years like every other college student, and have time to spend with you and his son."

"I can't ask him to do that." I shook my head and looked down at my little boy. "I told him I was fine with his plans and how much he was going to have to work. It was my whole argument for us going ahead and getting married."

"You're a lady. It's your prerogative to change your mind."

We kept walking, but I couldn't stop thinking about what she said. It was my prerogative to change my mind, and now that Billy was a daddy, he might have changed his mind too. I decided to talk to him about it next chance I got.

*April 3, 19 –*

Well, it happened. Not even a year of wedded bliss, and Billy and I had our first major fight. I've decided to blame Winifred Haynes. It's completely her fault, and I'll tell you why. Winnie's words were still in my head when Billy got home last night. I kept thinking about what she'd said about changing my mind, and how Billy and I'd never revisited our conversation about his plans and getting married and my needs.

I figured now that his son was here, Billy might have changed his mind about working so hard. So I put little Will to sleep and tested the waters.

"Hey." I put my hands on Billy's shoulders and kissed his cheek. "How's school going?"

"Same. Lectures, notes." He closed a notebook and pushed it across the table in front of him then pulled out a different, huge book. "I've got a lot of reading to do tonight, so don't wait up for me."

"Billy," I started, chewing my lip. "I was thinking about that. You've gone from seven classes a semester to eight. Are you planning to do intersession and summer school again?"

"That's the plan," he said without looking up. "I don't think I can do more, though. Eight's the limit."

"I wasn't suggesting you take more," I said quietly, my nerves kicking in before I could continue. "I was thinking… well, have you considered backing off some? I mean, just so maybe we could do things together, as a couple sometimes?"

His blue eyes cut to mine, and my throat went dry. "Backing off?" he repeated. "What's more important than me finishing school as fast as possible?"

"Well, I was just thinking, wouldn't it be nice if we had a dinner party once in a while and had people over?" My trembling hands were clutched behind my back.

"Dinner party?" His brow creased. "With who?"

"I don't know. Maybe Winifred and Travis Hayes? He's an intern at the hospital, and she's in the DAR with me. I think you'll like them."

"And you want to have them over for dinner?" He seemed annoyed. "I don't see what that has to do with me backing off on school."

"Well, you're just always so busy." My hands were still clutched. "I never know if it's okay to make plans with other couples. And then I was thinking we have little Willie now. Don't you miss him?"

"Of course I miss him," Billy said turning back to his massive book. "But I'm doing this for his future. And yours. We can't live off your parents forever."

"I know, but most college students take four years. There's nothing wrong with slowing down some."

"I can't slow down, Meg. I've made commitments. Bryant is counting on me to keep up my end of the bargain."

"But I never see you, and I miss you." I hated how whiney my voice sounded. I hated that I was on the verge of tears. "What about my end of the bargain?"

"Meg. Don't start."

He didn't even look at me, which made me mad. "I've never said anything about it." My tone turned sharp. "But it's very selfish to only think of your needs and not mine."

He looked at me then. "What needs are you talking about?"

"Needing a husband. Not an absentee partner who checks in every night for two hours before falling asleep." My whole body was shaking. I was going back on everything we'd agreed starting out, and I didn't care.

He studied me a few moments. "Are you trying to say you're not satisfied?"

"No," I said quietly.

"Then where's this coming from?"

"Me. It's coming from me. I'm tired of being here at this house every night by myself."

He exhaled deeply and closed the book, pushing back from the table. "I told you it was going to be like this at first. I said we should wait to get married, but you said that was a mistake. You swore you could handle it."

"Well, maybe I was wrong," I said, sticking out my chin. "Or maybe I've changed my mind."

His eyes flashed. "Well, maybe it's too late for that. I'm not changing my plans, Meg. And I'm not doing anything differently. If I wait three more years, the opportunities could change."

---

"Change is not bad."

"It's not good," he said standing up. "I'm taking a shower. This discussion is over."

"It's not over if I'm not finished talking!" I shouted.

"I said it's over." He started walking past me.

"Don't walk out on me!" I clutched his arm hard as I could, feeling my nails sink in. He jerked his arm away, throwing me off balance and causing me to trip into the coffee table.

"Ow!" I yelled, but he didn't stop.

He stormed into the bathroom and slammed the door, and I slid to the floor and cried. That had *not* gone the way I'd wanted, and now it looked like I was going to have a giant bruise on my shin. So unattractive.

A painful knot twisted in my throat as I went into our bedroom and climbed between the sheets. Billy didn't join me, and I lay there staring at the ceiling for hours. I tried to read a book, but I wasn't interested in it. Finally, I decided to go out to the couch where I figured he was sleeping and say I'd been wrong, but when I opened the door he wasn't there.

I walked over to the table and all his books were gone. It was 3 o'clock in the morning! Where could he be?

I saw his note. *Studying at the library. Home tomorrow.*

After that I was just mad.


*June 21, 19 —*


Sorry it's taken me so long to get back to writing. I read over my last entry and realized I should probably give the follow-up. The short version is Billy came home the next night ready to make amends, and I caved. He's just so damn sexy.

I had gone to bed pouting. We hadn't talked the whole day, and I wasn't even sure what his plans were. Then I awoke to his warm body sliding into the bed behind mine. My eyes weren't even open before his lips were pressed against my neck, tracing their way up behind my ear and waking every tingling good-feeling under my skin.

That was followed by his hands circling my waist, pulling me tight against him and then sliding under my tank to my breasts. A few caresses, a few nibbles to my neck, and I was quickly turning into him, caught up in a tangle of forgiveness and love-making.

I guess that makes me easy, but I did say I could handle this a year ago when we talked. I should never have said that. But what else could I do? He was suggesting we wait to get married!

At least Billy's first year of college is finally coming to a close. We're coming up on our first anniversary. So much has happened. It seems like we were just moving into our new home and having little Will, and now here he is, almost six months old.

Two important things happened after my last entry involving those troublemakers Travis and Winnie Hayes. First, I'd already planned a dinner party with them that just so happened to fall right after my big fight with Billy. It was a complete disaster.

During the course of dinner, I could tell Winnie had been repeating everything I'd said about my marital problems to Travis. Then Mr. Intern decided to interrogate my husband. It got a little heated to say the least.

Travis asked Billy a lot of nosey questions about how much he was gone, and I guess he didn't expect Billy to put him in his place. Billy's young, but he's no pushover. And Travis was out of line asking questions about our baby and demanding to know how good of a daddy Billy thought he could be working so much.

The good news is Lexy joined us for our second dinner party attempt. I know, you're probably wondering why I would have those two over again, but trust me, Journal. I don't have as many options when it comes to company these days. Sad, but true. It's also why I was so excited to have Lexy home for summer break, and I couldn't wait to impress Winnie with my beautiful artist friend.

When Lexy arrived she looked gorgeous in a black wrap-dress and her long hair hanging loose. She'd brought a bottle of wine, and I gave her the biggest hug. I'd missed her so.

"Lexy! You're so grown-up and sophisticated," I said.

"I have no idea what you're talking about," she said, her dark eyes twinkling. "You're the one having a dinner party. I thought only old married couples did that."

My nose wrinkled. "Travis and Winnie are a bit older, so you know."

We went into the kitchen and her voice dropped. "Who are these guys?"

"Travis is an intern with Daddy at the hospital, and Winnie's in the DAR with me and Mom."

I put the wine on the counter, and she leaned against the bar. "So we're putting on a show for them?"

"Not a show!" I lied. "Just a dinner party. So tell me about school. What happened with Dr. Love? Are you two still together?"

Lexy had started an affair with one of her art school professors right before Christmas, and it was simply scandalous — and fantastic! I loved sharing this delicious secret with her and giving her advice.

Professor Nick Parker taught her painting (and other things) in Savannah, and he was the first male I'd ever known Lexy to be serious about. She was always much too focused on her career for boys.

We'd chatted a few months ago about some weekend trip he'd asked her to take with him, and she was planning to sleep with him. You'd never believe it to look at her, but it was going to be Lexy's first time to have sex. Nuts to think someone as sensual and beautiful as Lexy had never done it before, but there you go. I guessed I couldn't blame her. I had snatched up our best option in high school.

Anyway, I'd assumed they were a definite thing after that, but something felt off when I brought him up. As we walked inside I found out why. It seemed Professor Parker had left for a summer trip to Paris and thought they should try a separation period.

I don't understand men and all the separation periods. Seems to me if you're in love with someone, the last thing you want to do is spend any time away from them.

Just then Billy arrived, handsome as always and unusually happy to see Lexy.

"I'm glad you're here," he said, kissing her cheek.

I did a double-take. Was it possible those two had declared a truce?

"A little bird told me these guests aren't always on their best behavior," she said smiling back at him.

"Okay, what are ya'll up to?" I asked very suspicious. "I've never seen you on such good terms."

"What?" Lexy tried to act like she had no idea what I meant. "Bill and I have always gotten along. And he's your husband now. I said I'd never argue with him again after you were married, remember?"

I was still frowning. "Yes, but this is too much of a good thing. What's going on?"

"Well, if you must know, Bill asked me to get on the guest list for tonight."

"And you let me think it was my idea!" I said to Billy.

"I just thought if Lexy were here, it would take some of the pressure off me." He smiled, putting his hand on my waist and pulling me to him. "Add another layer to the conversation. That's all."

He kissed my neck, and I laughed at him. "I've never known you to mind pressure."

"Well, I'd hate it if I had to punch that Travis guy in the face. And if he starts cross-examining me about my time and my plans again, I can't guarantee I won't."

"I'll do my best to keep the subject on art," Lexy told him, crossing her arms. "You try not to go all cave man on us."

The second dinner party went far better than our first attempt. Lexy did add a nice layer to the conversation, although Winnie seemed a bit suspicious of her presence. After we'd eaten, she approached me in the kitchen.

"So she's a friend of yours?" Winnie said.

"My oldest and dearest," I smiled, scooping out the trifle. "I've known Lexy since we were in kindergarten."

Her eyebrow arched. "And how well does she know Bill?"

"We met him about the same time," I said. "Ninth grade."

"She's very beautiful."

"I've always thought so." I smiled, admiring my best friend from afar.

"And you don't mind her being so close with Bill?"

My attention snapped back to the person at my arm. "What! Now you really are out in left field, Winifred Hayes. There is nothing going on between Lexy and Billy, I can assure you."

"How would you know?" she said, an evil tone in her soft voice. "He's gone all the time. She doesn't live here."

"That's right, she lives in Savannah. Where she's in art school."

"During the summer?"

I put the serving spoon down a little too hard and picked up two bowls. "I'm sorry, but I can't let this conversation go any further. You are just so wrong."

"Don't be an ostrich, Meg. Keep your eyes open."

"I am not an ostrich." I was aggravated now. "I'm also not completely paranoid."

Of all things. For years my two favorite people in the world had done nothing but fight, and now they were becoming friends. I was beyond happy.

And I decided I'd had enough of Winifred Hayes and her rude husband. I wouldn't invite them over again.


*Aug. 1, 19 –*


The last month of summer went by too quickly with Lexy here. We spent almost every day together, and all she talked about was painting Will's portrait. We went down to the beach and set him up with toys on a blanket while she made sketches of him from different angles. I could tell her skills had sharpened in the last year, and she seemed more confident than ever about her art.

"So tell me about school," I said. "Are you enjoying being away and on your own?"

She smiled, sliding a long lock of dark hair behind her shoulder. "Yes. It's exactly how I'd hoped it would be. New people and experiences."

"Experiences with new people like Nick Parker?" I grinned.

"Especially with new people like Nick Parker." We giggled. "He's my first real boyfriend you know," she said, cheeks pink.

"I know," I sighed, leaning back on my arms. The ocean breeze kept the heat bearable, and I was in my bikini top and a skirt. "I was thinking how odd it was you never dated anyone in high school."

She twisted her long hair up and stabbed a pencil in it. "I never met anybody I wanted to date in high school."

"The whole time? Lexy, there were plenty of cute boys at our school."

She shrugged, adjusting the spaghetti strap on her white sundress. I'd always admired how her smooth, skin turned the color of coffee-milk after only a few days in the sun.

"They were all just interested in sports or hunting or sex," she said. "I wanted to be outside and painting and free more than I wanted to worry about some boyfriend holding me down."

"You're worrying about one now," I said, studying her face.

She looked down. "Is it obvious?"

"You haven't said much about him since you've been back. Last semester you couldn't talk about anything else." I watched her fidgeting and tried to lighten the mood.

"I wondered if you were there to study art or love."

Her eyes flickered to mine and she did a little smile. "Some people think the two are inseparable."

"So what's going on? Why the separation?"

She exhaled, shoulders dropping. "All I know is he wanted to go to Paris to study with some master painter for the summer."

"A male or female master painter?"

"Oh, Meg. I didn't even get that far in my worries." Her eyes became misty.

"I'm sorry!" I quickly crossed the space between us and held her hands. "I was just trying to tease you. It was a terrible joke. Have you heard from him at all?"

"No, but I'm trying to believe it's because he's very busy and international calling is complicated and expensive." She touched the corner of her eyes. "And he doesn't have my address here. I could get back to school and find a mountain of postcards."

"Of course you could!" I said. "I'm sure of it. So, you guys got pretty close, I guess."

"Very close." She glanced over at little Will, now sleeping on the palette we'd made for him. "All the way close."

"You did it! I can't believe you slept with him and didn't tell me!" I was so excited. And surprised. Lexy was always very traditional about things like that. I blamed the nuns.

"I tried calling but I never could reach you," she said.

"So you liked it?"

"Well, no. Not at first." Her eyes met mine, and we shared an understanding smile. "But after a while things improved and then by the end I liked it a lot."

"That sounds about right." I leaned forward and hugged her. "It was that way with me."

She squeezed my arms before we both leaned back again. "Only, now I kind of wish I hadn't gotten quite so close. I think I wouldn't be missing him so much if I'd been a little more restrained."

"Now don't go second-guessing yourself," I fussed. "You'll go crazy with that kind of thinking."

"I'm going crazy as it is." I watched her rub her forehead hard. "Some nights I miss him so badly... I never understood wanting something like that before."

I sighed. "Yeah, it's a funny thing. Before it happens, you never know you have those feelings in you. Then after it happens, it's like your body thinks you're supposed to be getting it regularly or something."

"Sometimes I'm not sure if I'm missing him or if I just got used to that constant attention and affection. And you know... having that need met." She blushed dark red.

My brow creased. "But you do care about him, don't you?"

"Yes," she nodded. "I mean, I think so. He's very handsome, but he's also smart and intelligent. He's the first guy I've ever talked to that I didn't have to explain everything I meant to all the time. He just got it right away."

"Well, you're both artists! You like the same things."

"I know, and maybe that's what it is." She studied her palm. "It's made a big difference in my wanting to be around him. I really love being in a relationship with someone I can talk to."

"Well, Billy was a great high school boyfriend, and I don't think we ever had that much to talk about." I shook my hair back, giggling.

"But I didn't care. All I had to do was look at him to be completely happy."

She pulled her long leg up and rested her chin on her bent knee. "How's he doing as a college husband?"

I shrugged. "Okay, I guess."

"You guess?"

"That came out wrong." I blinked. "He's great! I just see how we're changing as time passes, and things I didn't think were so important before matter to me now."

"Like what?" Her dark eyes studied my face.

"Like time. He's gone so much, and I miss him. I can't look at him when he's never home."

"Have you talked to him about it?"

"Yeah, but we just end up fighting." I dropped my hands to my lap hard. "And he's right. We had this conversation before we got married, and I said I could handle it."

"Well, people do change. That's life. You can't help if what you wanted then is different from what you want now."

"I think it's having Will," I sighed. "Everything changes once you become a mama. I look at stuff differently from how I used to now."

Lexy's brow creased, and she paused a beat before asking. "Are you sorry you married Bill?"

"What? No!" I cried. "I can't imagine being married to anyone else. He's everything to me. That's part of the reason it's so hard." I looked down, suddenly feeling sad.

"You know, another year, and he'll almost be done. Can you throw yourself into motherhood and see if that helps the time pass? He can't work like this forever."

"Oh, Lexy, I wish you didn't have to go!" My breath caught in my throat, and I was afraid I might cry. "I need you to stay and help me keep things in perspective."

She laughed and hugged me. "But I've got to follow my own little plan."

"All you people and your plans," I pouted. "I'm sick of them."

"Then make a plan of your own!" she laughed. "What do you want to be doing in the next five years?"

"Having more babies. Building my home on Hammond Island."

She laughed more. "Then you'd better stop complaining about how hard your husband's working!"

She was right. I did want the things that Billy's ambition was going to get for us. I had to find some other way to occupy my time. I had to come up with a plan of my own.


*Sept. 5, 19 –*

Daddy died on a Tuesday.

I imagined him going to work that morning thinking it would be a day just like any other. What medical problems would he face today? Then for whatever reason, his heart stopped. He was sitting behind his desk, and out of nowhere, his heart stopped and his life was over. The nurses said they did everything they knew to do. Travis said they took him immediately to the cardiac unit and tried to revive him, but he was gone.

Gone.

I could never again go to his house and sit on the porch while he smoked his pipe and read the paper. I could never again take little Will to Pawpaw to climb on his legs and make him smile. He would never again pat my head and call me his golden girl. Not ever again.

And all I could do was cry.

But the tears didn't make any difference.

Nothing made any difference.

Billy was very sweet through it all. He talked to his professors and was able to get a few days off from class. He took charge of the situation, making funeral arrangements, contacting relatives, taking care of Daddy's life insurance and financial arrangements for Mama.

Mama went to pieces. She wouldn't even leave her room or see anybody. I tried to bring Will to see her, but she sent us away. She said she didn't want him to see Gigi in a state. Those were her exact words.

I called Lexy as soon as I could think straight. If anybody could comfort me, it was her, and she'd want to know. I didn't know if she could get out of classes since he wasn't her daddy, but I hoped she could at least make it for the funeral.

She's such a good friend. She said she'd be here right away.

I've just been wandering around the cottage holding Will and crying. He's almost a year old now, and he doesn't like being held as much. But he can tell something's going on. He's very quiet and lets me hold him anyway.

Every now and then he'll say "Pawpaw?" in his little baby voice. I think he knows we're talking about Daddy, but how can he understand his old friend is gone? That he won't be making the occasional rounds with Dr. Weaver, visiting elderly patients and making them smile. I just hug him close and tell him Pawpaw's up in heaven.

My sweet little son. I know Daddy would want us to focus on Will and the future and not get bogged down in all of this, but it's hard not to cry every time I think of him. He was so proud of his little grandson. By the time the family gets here, I'll be ready to put on a brave face, but for now I'll just hold my little boy and cry.


*Oct. 15, 19 –*


Mama really fell apart after Daddy died. She seemed to lose interest in everything, and I couldn't find a way to help her. I'd take Will over for visits, and she wouldn't even get out of bed. We'd sit with her and talk, but she would just start crying. I didn't know what to do. When Mrs. Claudine Edwards called, it was like a miracle.

Mrs. Claudine lives in Arizona, and she and Mama were friends growing up. Sort of like Lexy and me. She asked me to send Mama out for an extended visit, and as much as I hated losing my favorite company and best babysitter, I knew it was for the best.

"I can't leave you with the baby like this," Mama protested. "You don't have anyone to spend your days with."

"Well, don't talk me out of it!" I tried to joke. "I was already having a hard time deciding if I wanted to send you in the first place."

"That settles it, then. I'm not going." Her lined face looked ten years older than yesterday.

"You can't stay here," I said. "It's too painful for you, and I think if you got out of this house, you might start finding your way again."

"Meg," she breathed, her forehead relaxing slightly. "I've done my best to protect you, and listen how wise you are. But if I leave, you'll be all alone. Then what?"

"So I might be alone some," I shrugged. "I just won't focus on it. If my life gets too dreary, I'll go shopping." I smiled. "What in the world do I have to complain about?"

She nodded. "You have a good attitude, but I'm afraid it makes people think you aren't very deep."

My shoulders felt tight with irritation. "What does that even mean? Deep? I've seen more deep people ripped to shreds than I can count. I'm glad I'm not ambitious or over-achieving. Somebody's got to live their life."

"I know your daddy was always at that office working and forcing life to happen. He was an over-achiever, too."

"Like Billy. Except I don't think Daddy ever really liked Billy," I said.

"Bill is like your father in a lot of ways, but he's different from him, too." Mama held my hand. "I don't think Bill's really sorted out what he wants yet. He only seems to know what he doesn't want."

"To be a horse rancher? Or to be inconsequential?" I pushed a strand of hair behind my ear. "He'd say he just doesn't like the heat and humidity."

"What about you? I've been concerned for some time that you might be the one feeling inconsequential."

"Are you kidding? Somebody's got to provide him with moral support. Him and Lexy, too, for that matter." I squeezed her hand. "They like to act so courageous and ready to take on the world, but the truth is they second-guess everything they do."

"So if I'm in Sedona, what will you do?" She studied my face.

"Shop, get my nails done, dress up the baby. I have an image to maintain after all."

"And once you're completely perfect, then what will you do?"

My shoulders dropped with my sigh. "I don't know. I've been thinking about that for a while now, and I can't seem to come up with anything to get all fired up about. Other than my family. I really want to have another baby soon."

"I can't see that husband of yours being ready for that. He wasn't particularly ready for baby number one."

"I know, but it's not like he's had to do anything." My brow creased. "I've taken care of little Will, and Billy's been able to pursue his dreams as much as he wants."

Mama's lips tightened with concern, and I studied her white hair, smooth and beautiful. "That's what worries me," she said.

"I think you're just in a worrying sort of mood right now." I smiled, hoping to put her mind at ease. "Get out to the sunshine and dry air. It'll improve your health."

"I want to hear from you regularly, and I intend to make frequent return trips home."

"You'd better!"

"And if my only child has any needs, she'd better let me know."

"I'm not in the habit of not asking for what I want," I teased.

So Mama left for Sedona, and it only took one visit for her to realize she wanted to stay there. After a few return trips, she started talking about selling the old home and making Arizona her permanent residence, but

I convinced her to wait. I have an idea of my own for filling the old family place. At least until my house on Hammond Island is built.

*Nov. 1, 19 –*

With Mama out of town, I took the opportunity to go through her old things, boxes and pictures, to see if there was anything I could help her sort and save. She'd had such a hard time losing Daddy, I wasn't sure this part would be easy for her.

I started in the upstairs study. This old house had more rooms than a family of three ever needed, but it always felt homey to me. It was located right in downtown Fairview, surrounded by roses and a black wrought-iron fence, and it practically shouted that we were important members of the community.

Looking through the old pictures, I giggled at how old-fashioned my parents were. Since Daddy was a surgeon, they'd had me very late in life, at least by the standards of their day. If Mama hadn't been so adamant about having children, they might not've had me at all. She was past forty when I was born, pre-menopausal and considered high-risk for a pregnancy. All her other friends had children who were in middle school by the time I came along, so I didn't have a lot of childhood friends. But I was beautiful.

In some of the old photographs of me I looked like an antique doll with my white hair tied in a huge bow and my solemn little face. I wasn't a loud or active child, but I don't remember being unhappy. With older parents, I learned quickly to be seen and not heard.

Daddy in particular didn't like a lot of racket when he got home in the evenings or early mornings.

I kept finding pictures and old documents, and every time I saw my little face, I remembered how lonely I was back then. Not sad, but seriously in need of a playmate. Mama had her social obligations, and I was expected to keep quiet and look pretty for all of them. I found one picture of me, and my long blonde hair was conspicuously short. It was cute in a little pixie style that I don't think I ever wore again after it grew out.

The cut was the result of an unfortunate incident involving a piece of bubble gum. A kindly old man gave it to me at the bank, and I'd hidden it. I knew Mama would never let me have it for fear of cavities, so I sneaked it at nap time and then fell asleep with it in my mouth. It turned into the biggest rat's nest in my hair. Mama screamed and called Daddy to come home at once. He, of course, thought something more serious had happened and was angry at both of us when he arrived.

I remembered he said he would have to amputate, and I burst into tears. I had learned that word in the movies, and I didn't know what he was going to cut off. My hands for taking the gum? My head for chewing it? It was only my hair.

I thought I was the ugliest little girl after that haircut. I thought I looked like a little boy. As I examined the picture now, I saw that I was actually kind of cute. Classic Mia Farrow, and Daddy had been my very own Vidal Sassoon.

I hadn't realized I had tears in my eyes until Billy slipped in and found me.

"Hey, what are you doing up here?" he said softly. "I was looking for you everywhere."

I laughed and brushed away the tears. "I was looking at these old pictures. I thought I could help Mama by sorting through all this stuff."

"You're crying." He took the picture from my hand and looked at it. "What's this? You?"

"I think I was five in that picture," I said. "I'd fallen asleep with gum, and Daddy had to cut all my hair off. I was remembering how ugly I thought it made me look."

"I think it's cute." He studied the picture and then his blue eyes met mine with a smile.

"Me too." I smiled as he picked up another picture.

"Your parents were old when they had you," he said.

"Early forties."

"What was that like?"

"Lonely," I sighed, flipping through the box. "But they got me anything I wanted. Daddy was well-established when I came along."

"And you weren't lonely for long." He reached over and touched my hand. "I know you and Lexy met in kindergarten, right?"

"Well, that was at school. But she was all the way out on Port Hogan Road," I said. "I remember sitting in that room and looking out that window at the big kids running around and riding their bikes. Mama never let me go out alone."

Billy chuckled. "I guess that's one good thing about living in the country. There's nobody around to bother you."

"You guys were practically outsiders."

"We weren't really far enough south to qualify for that title," he sighed. "We didn't fall into any group, I guess."

"Still, it was just you and your daddy." I studied his perfect face. "I guess you know what it's like to be lonely."

"I don't remember being lonely. Dad took me everywhere he went. But I remember being scared sometimes." He rubbed his neck, causing the pale blue polo to go tight across his chest. "He'd start drinking and missing Mom."

"Was he violent?"

"Nah," Billy shook his head. "He'd just sit and listen to old country songs til he passed out. But I was so little, I didn't know if he would die or if I should try to move him or what. I'd usually just go to bed and pray."

"Billy!" I whispered. "That's so sad! You never told me this."

"Well, it wasn't much of a memory to share," he shrugged. "He didn't do it every night, and I loved him. When I got older, I'd usually take off when he'd start drinking. Take one of the horses or something."

We were quiet a while looking at the old photos. Billy never talked much about his childhood, and somehow it made me feel closer to him now, like he trusted me more.

"Don't do this," he said. "Let your Mom take care of all this stuff next time she's in town."

"Okay." I helped him collect the old documents and put them back in the cardboard box, and we walked back downstairs where Will was napping.

Even with Billy gone as much as ever, part of being married is being together when everyone leaves. That's when the events that tie you together happen. We might still be building our relationship, but I'm encouraged that we're learning more about each other. Mama's wrong. Billy and I are going to be fine.

---

59

*Jan. 15, 19 —*

Lexy's home!

Oops. I'm supposed to say Alex now.

Yes. My best friend moves back from Atlanta and announces she's going by a different name. Seems everyone at art school called her Alex, and now she thinks it sounds more professional. I told her it's a big mistake. *Lexy's* got flair, and it rhymes with *sexy*. And if there's one thing I know, sex sells.

She actually laughed when I said that. And she gave me the okay to slip up every now and then. More like all the time. I'll never get used to calling her Alex. It sounds too... masculine or something.

I don't care, I'll be glad to call her Hortense if that's what she wants. I'm just so happy she's home. It's been ages since I've written anything. Sorry, Journal.

Since Daddy died and Mama moved to Sedona, Billy's been working practically around the clock hoping to finish school by May. I tried throwing myself into motherhood, but there's only so much conversation you can have with a fourteen-month-old.

I tried volunteering at the hospital, but it was so sad being there with Daddy gone. It made me even more miserable. I tried attending a few DAR functions, but the ladies weren't so thrilled about having a toddler knocking over all their pretty table arrangements, and I guess they were more Mama's friends than mine. So I'd taken to hanging around the house or going to the little park most days.

I'd been so lonely these last few months, when Billy said ~~Lexy~~ Alex had agreed to come back and help with the design of the Phoenicians, I actually screamed. He said she was going to take over all the interior design work, and he must've promised her something major to get her to leave art school, although she'd already left Savannah to do a semester internship at some big advertising firm in Atlanta. All because of that stupid Professor Nick. I needed to get the rest of that story.

"I can't believe Billy convinced you to come back," I said when we were finally together.

"You know your husband and his big plans," she said, hugging me.

"But you had your own plans." I squeezed her arms before stepping back. "All you could talk about was getting to Savannah and then on to Atlanta."

She shrugged. "I guess I realized my plans weren't making me happy. I was just another cog in the wheel."

"That professor really did a number on you, didn't he." I chewed my lip as I studied her eyes, hoping she'd tell me more.

"Breaking up with Nick was rough. But it was more than that. Really." She smiled. "All that time in Atlanta with Suzanne, I never felt right. I was always the fish out of water."

"Suzanne your roommate? I thought you guys got along so well!"

"We do. Of course, we do! But I'm just... different." She shook her dark hair and played with a button on her charcoal blazer. "Those guys would be all talking about deals and moving in for the kill, and I'd be trying to work out how I could get down to the beach," she sighed. "When Billy showed up and made his big pitch for me to come back... It was such a relief to see someone from home."

"He is always nice to look at." I grinned.

"Oh, you." She rolled her eyes. "That's not what I meant. It was like I could finally relax and be myself again. Joking around and talking to him just put me at ease for the first time in a while, and when he offered me the job, it just felt right somehow."

My lips poked out as I considered what she meant. "I guess I understand that. He's like home, a safe place. And here I thought you and Billy would never get along."

"Funny you should say that. I was thinking the same thing," she said. "But I came back just as much for you as for your husband. Maybe more so."

"For me?" I frowned.

"You and this place and Miss Stella. I missed my home. All of it. The colors and the flowers. It's so beautiful here. This is what inspires my art. Not the cold concrete and the drone of the city."

I nodded, thinking about that. "When you left you said you hated this place and if you didn't get out of here you'd go crazy."

"I know," she said, closing her eyes. "And you said I'd learn that being around people who loved me was a good thing."

"You weren't gone very long." I wanted to be sure she was sure of her decision. "You might've found people out there who loved you. And Atlanta's not all concrete and drone. It has colors and trees."

"And cars. Oh, God." She pushed her fingers into her hair. "The traffic in Atlanta is a nightmare."

"So you came back to get out of the traffic?"

"No. I just… time passes and people change. You know that."

I nodded.

"And aren't you glad I'm back?" She asked. "I thought we were supposed to be some great team. This is a terrible reception I'm getting here. Instead of happiness, it sounds like you're trying to send me packing again."

"No!" I cried. "I'm sorry. I am glad you're back. Since Mama moved to Sedona, it's been just me and little Will, and you know how much Billy hates Winnie Hayes."

"Oh, God." Her dark eyes rolled. "Those people are the worst."

"Winnie's actually nice. Her husband I think is the bad seed in that relationship."

"She doesn't protest too loudly. In fact, it seems like she's right there giving him ideas half the time."

"Maybe you're right," I said, hooking my arm in hers. "But it doesn't matter now! You're back, and we're going to pick up right where we left off."

"Well, with one slight modification. Unlike last time, Bill is going to expect me to report to work every now and then."

"Just leave Billy to me."


*Sept. 10, 19 —*

I dug out my journal for the first time in… I can't believe it. Almost four years have passed since that last entry! There's no way I can go back and fill in all that's happened, so we'll just have to start with where we are now.

When Lexy (I'm still calling her Lexy) said she'd come back, I'd been so looking forward to spending more time with her and us getting back to the old team we'd once been. As it turned out, she was more of a team with Billy and Bryant than with me, and I was home alone as much as ever. Every night I was completely miserable when Billy came in, but he never seemed to notice.

He graduated with honors, of course, and I hoped when school ended he'd adopt a more family-friendly schedule. But with college behind him, he started working harder than ever at the office. I was usually asleep when he got home, and if I wasn't, we never seemed to have anything to talk about.

When Will was a baby, that had been fine, but the first day I dropped him off at kindergarten, I knew something had to give. I was crying hysterically when I reached the car, and I had to drive back to the house and have a mimosa so I could get control of myself. That's when I called Lexy, and of course she came running.

I couldn't believe when she suggested I stage an "accidental" pregnancy. It was like an omen, and that silly mimosa had loosened me up so much I spilled the beans about little Will.

Here you go, Journal. Moment of Truth. (Now that Lexy knows, I don't know why I shouldn't write it here.) I did not accidentally get pregnant senior year. Yep. That's right. I did it on purpose, and I can't believe I got drunk and told Lexy.

Now don't start thinking I'm so devious. It was the only way I could see to hold onto Billy back then with him and Bryant starting on their big development plans. It was like he was forgetting all about our future together, my dreams, and it was making me desperate. The fact that I'd intentionally gotten pregnant with little Will was something I planned to take to my grave, but I was safe. Lexy would never tell Billy.

Then the other day, when she suggested I "accidentally" get pregnant out of the blue like that, I felt like she was inadvertently saying what I'd done before had been okay. So I told her.

And I've thought about repeating what I did a lot. As the days passed, and I kept finding myself home alone, I decided it might work.

I was just so angry with Billy. He wouldn't return my calls during the day, and when I suggested we have another baby, he was so dismissive and cold. He didn't even seem to care that I was suffering.

I decided to give him one more chance, so last night when he got home, I planned to bring up the subject gently. But he looked so happy and satisfied after a day accomplishing his dreams, I completely lost my temper.

"Hard day at the office?" I asked sarcastically.

"You should see the way it's all coming together, Meg. It's going to be exactly the way I dreamed it would be." His blue eyes gleamed with satisfaction, and the fist of anger tightened even more in my chest. "Bryant's got the crews running like they were choreographed, and Alex keeps turning out interiors that you just wouldn't believe."

"I'm so glad the three musketeers are having such a great time self-actualizing." That was a word I'd learned in one of my magazines. It meant following your dreams, something I was never allowed to do, it seemed.

"Yeah, I guess that's what we're doing," he said, looking down. "What did you do today?"

"I brought Will to school, came home, watched TV, read a magazine. Waited for school to get out. Picked up Will, and then made your supper."

His brow lined. "Is that a good day?"

I slammed to my feet. "It's the most pointless existence I can imagine."

"Well, maybe the part about TV and the magazine, but the other parts weren't pointless." He actually had the nerve to look concerned. "Will loves having his mommy there to pick him up and play with him, and I know I'm glad you made us dinner."

"Bill!" I shouted. "I want to be more than a nanny and a personal chef. I want to have another baby!"

"Meg," he groaned. "Don't start."

"I'm not a child. You can't just dismiss me like that. You always just try to dismiss me." My silly eyes felt hot with tears.

"I'm not dismissing you," he said, rubbing his forehead. "I'm asking you to wait and be reasonable. We'll have another baby as soon as we have our new house."

"It's going to take at least a year to build that house. I can't wait a year."

"Sure you can. And then you can have as many babies as you want."

"I want to start now," I demanded. "It'll take nine months for another baby to even get here, and that's if we managed to get pregnant today, which it would have to be immaculate the way things have been."

He didn't answer, and I felt bad for attacking him that way.

"I'm sorry," I said. "But I feel like I'm going to do something desperate."

"Like what?"

"Like… I don't know. But I want another baby."

His eyes flashed at me. "I said we have to wait."

"And I said I don't want to wait."

For a moment we only glared at each other. Then his jaw clenched. "I'll be very unhappy if we get pregnant again right now."

"Well, it would be your fault if it happened," I said, pushing my hair back. "You're turning me into a desperate woman."

He nodded. "I'll try to get home more and spend more time with you. We can get through this. It's like empty nest or something."

"It's more than that."

I'd gone to bed angry with him. I didn't even want to kiss him goodnight, and I'd stayed angry for months. I hated the way I was feeling, and I was sorry that I was taking it out on him. But I couldn't help it. I was mad, and Billy didn't seem to care.


*Jan. 15, 19—*

I can't believe it. Just when I'd given up on us, Billy turned around and surprised us all with a trip to Mexico. He must be the sweetest husband ever. I was sad, and he found a way to take us all on vacation. He called it a business trip to investigate the competition, but I couldn't care less about that. I had to go shopping.

Mama was coming home to keep Will while we went, and it was going to be the six of us—Billy and me, Bryant and Donna, Lexy and Suzanne. It was so odd Lexy didn't have a man to take with her on trips like this. I'd been pretty self-absorbed, and looking back, I couldn't remember her going on any dates since she'd been home.

"You should try setting her up with one of your friends," I said to Billy that night. I was lying in bed reading a book while he undressed.

"Who?" He sounded confused as he positioned his slacks on the wooden hanger.

"Lexy."

"You mean Alex?" He glanced up at me.

"I'm sorry, but I cannot call her that."

Billy laughed. "So you're wanting me to set her up with someone?"

"It's just not right that we're all going on this great couples' weekend, and she's bringing a girlfriend."

"I think it's great," he winked. "More pretty ladies in bikinis."

"I've never seen this Suzanne," I said, dropping my book. "What if she's not pretty?"

"I couldn't care less. I only plan to look at you." He walked over and flopped on the bed facing me.

"You're very sweet," I smiled. "And a big fat liar."

He rolled onto his back, palms flat on his stomach. "You think I'm getting fat? I guess I don't get out of the office much anymore. Not like when we were kids and we spent the whole summer slinging hay bales."

"Billy!" I laughed. "It's an expression! You're perfect, and I meant the only thing you'll be looking at are high-rises and amenities."

"I'll be checkin you out, too." He rolled back on his side, facing me.

"Ugh, well, don't check too hard. We're just coming off the holidays, and this trip was a surprise. I haven't been to aerobics as much as I'd like."

"Maybe that's why you've been feeling sad." He reached out and caught my leg, sliding his hand down my calf.

"I'm feeling sad because I want to have a baby." I picked up my book again. He rolled onto his back once more.

"Meg. Please."

"I know! You don't want to talk about it."

"I was hoping this trip might be a little distraction from that. Have some fun, get your mind off things. Spend some time with your friend."

"And it's a tax write-off."

"Not only that, I'm looking forward to spending time with Marco. I plan to pump him for all the information I can get."

"The owner? I'm sure he'll tell you whatever you want to know. Everybody likes you."


*Jan. 16, 19 –*

Luxury accommodations are the only way to travel.

Marco Dominguez was one of the owners of Tango Sol, and he put us all up in individual cabins shaped like tiki huts. They were gorgeous with dark wood floors and tall four-poster beds shrouded in mosquito netting and separated from the more traditional hotel accommodations by a series of paths that ran down the side of a hill covered in little waterfalls.

The ceilings in the huts went up to points and had an open-air feel, but we never had a bug problem. I assumed there had to be some bug-proofing somewhere that I just couldn't see. It was Mexico, after all.

We also had our own porches overlooking the side of the hill and leading down to the beach, where the long expanse of sand was dotted with hammock-bound palm trees for relaxing in the cool sea breezes. It was absolutely beautiful and perfectly romantic.

If I were to make one recommendation for change, though, it would be removing some of the waterfalls. They were everywhere. One big waterfall crossed the path that separated the swimming pool on the dining level from a smaller pool below. It flowed right over the path, and while it was pretty, the only way to cross it was by getting your feet wet and either ruining your shoes on the outside or taking them off and then getting your shoes all wet on the inside. Or running around barefoot, which was ridiculous. I had a pedicure to consider. I intended to recommend Billy not copy that idea.

For breakfast I ate nothing but mango and drank their local coffee. It was all so wonderfully fresh. I'd never tasted mango straight from the tree, and instead of being tart and bitter like what we have back home, it was like eating a slice of vanilla cream pie. It was the most delicious fruit I'd ever tasted, and the natives laughed that it was all I ever ordered for breakfast. After we ate each morning, the girls would all go and lie around the pool or walk out to the beach while the guys met and talked business with Marco.

Lexy seemed to be having a good time with Suzanne, and I only got the chance to talk to her once about bringing a friend instead of a boyfriend. She laughed and said something about me being just like Miss Stella. As if I have anything in common with that old bitty. Lexy could be so stubborn sometimes. I'd decided when we get back home I was going to be more vigilant about hunting down a man for her. She could fuss all the way to the altar.

In the meantime, I also decided to pursue my other little plan. Enough time had passed that it would probably work. And the fresh breezes and relaxing atmosphere put us all at ease. There was nothing like drinks with dinner to set the tone for a romantic evening, and the last time Billy and I had taken an exotic vacation was on our honeymoon. That was a good memory for both of us.

Two weeks before the trip, I'd started quietly dropping my birth control pills down the sink while I brushed my teeth every night, and I was hoping the island fertility gods would smile on us this trip. Billy might say he didn't want to have any more kids, but I remembered how happy he was when I was expecting little Will and then how it was at the hospital. He'd be glad in the end, and I was hoping for little John next.

It wasn't hard in this setting to get my handsome husband in the mood. I'd packed the most sheer nightgowns I owned, and I planned not to wear panties or a bra with them. After showering, I brushed my long, blonde hair smooth and stepped out of the bathroom smelling like coconut and hibiscus. I could practically see the sheet rise from where I stood.

Not that I minded in the least. Billy was perfect as ever, with his cool blue eyes and his light-brown hair highlighted from the sun. Lying in that mosquito-netted bed, sunkissed and lined, in only his white boxers, he was like a movie star.

The first night, I took my time, starting out by placing his palms over my breasts, with only the filmy fabric of my gown between our skin. Our lips met, softly at first, then increasing in intensity as our bodies remembered and our desire grew. By our fourth night, we were less gentle. I didn't even bother with the buildup. I'd leave the bathroom completely nude and dive into his waiting arms. We'd roll around in the sheets, kissing and laughing, missing each other and finding each other again, surging with happiness and warmth and electricity until we both cried out in release.

It was fantastic, and I was confident we'd have our new baby in nine months.

Lying on my back, with Billy's arm hugged across my waist, I gently traced my fingers over the lines in his back as he slept beside me on the cool white bed. The mosquito netting swirled around us, and I closed my eyes to dream of my perfect little boy just waiting to join his family.

*Jan. 20, 19 —*

It was hard to return from our exotic rooms in Mexico to our little cottage in Fairview and back to the groove of normal life. Little Will was thrilled Mommy was home, which helped a lot. He was getting to be such a big boy. Mama said she couldn't stay, so she was leaving in the morning. And with the morning, everyone would return to work.

I'd be alone again.

At the same time, I was excited to be back. Billy and I'd had four nights of uninterrupted adult activities, getting re-acquainted with all our favorite sexual positions and even inventing some new ones, and I was confident all my sneaking around had paid off. I might have to name this baby Marco in honor of the location, although that could backfire if it had dark hair like Billy's daddy. I giggled. I was already planning his little room theme and colors when the phone rang.

"I want you to decide where you'd like to have dinner tonight and see if you can get a sitter," Billy announced on the other end of the line.

I blinked. "What's the occasion? Did something big happen?"

"Nope," he said, sounding as happy as he had in Mexico. "I just made a resolution that I'm not going to work late again, starting now. There's no need for it. We're right on schedule."

"Billy! That's wonderful! Did Lexy say something?"

I heard him frown. "No, why?"

"No reason." I was not about to kill his joy by saying I'd discussed him with her. "What are you in the mood for?"

"Whatever you want. I'm not picky."

I hung up the phone elated, and I immediately started going through my mental Rolodex of single guys. Lexy and I had talked in Mexico about how alone I always was, and she'd said she would try to get their team on a more family-friendly schedule. If Lexy had worked it so that she and Billy were home more, I was going to have to return the favor by setting her up on some dates.

Let's see, there was Rain and Chuck…

*March 5, 19 –*

Twins.

The doctor said I'm having twins.

I felt my heart drop to my feet, and I thought I might throw up.

Billy was going to be furious.

It had only taken a few weeks after the trip for me to notice something was different. I'd taken a home pregnancy test, and it lit up in less than a minute. At first I was sorry. Billy has been so sweet and attentive these last several weeks. He really listened when I said I was sad, and now I was going to have to tell him I was pregnant. He'd know it wasn't an accident—especially after our fight before the trip. I'd all but threatened him, and I knew he knew what I was thinking.

I kept waiting for the right moment to tell him, but after another month, I noticed I was gaining weight faster than I had with Will. I thought it was just because it was my second pregnancy. I'd heard you started showing faster with number two, but I had to be sure. So I left Will with a sitter and made my doctor's appointment. A quick physical exam, and I was sent back for an immediate ultrasound. Sure enough, two heartbeats. I needed help fast, so I grabbed the phone.

"Meg?" Lexy's voice was instantly concerned. "Is everything okay?"

"Oh, Lexy!" Suddenly I felt like I couldn't breathe. "Help!"

"What is it?" she said. "What happened? Is Will okay?"

"I just left the doctor's office. He said I'm having twins."

"What?" For a moment she was confused, then instantly happy. "But that's wonderful! Right? And wow. Twins."

"Shh!" I hissed loudly, quickly unlocking my car and climbing inside. "Are you at work?"

"Where else? Your husband is a ruthless taskmaster. And now he says no overtime. I barely get a break."

"He doesn't know yet," I said in a low voice.

"What? I thought you two had decided together—"

"No," I snapped. "I did what you said and dropped the pills down the sink."

"Wait," her voice was nervous, and I could tell she was already changing the story on me. "Meg, no. Not that."

"You told me to!"

"I also told you to volunteer or get a part-time job. This is not good."

"Oh my god, Lexy!" Panic hit me hard, and I was almost in tears. "You can't turn on me now! Billy's never going to forgive me, and now it's twins!"

"Calm down," she said softly. I could hear her walking fast. "First, he will forgive you. He'll be shocked, and he might be a little annoyed, but he will forgive you. Keep positive. Bill loves babies. Remember how happy he was when you were expecting Will?"

"But he thought that was an accident." My voice was still a high-pitched whisper. "He's going to know I did this on purpose."

"How would he know? You're being paranoid. Just act very surprised, maybe throw in a little shock, and say you have no idea how it happened. Blame Mexico and all the antibiotics you were taking."

"It's not going to work," I said, trying to focus on the road. "He knows I wasn't taking antibiotics. And we had a fight. I practically threatened him."

"What?" I heard her frown.

"After you visited that day. I kept stewing about what you'd said, and we ended up having the biggest fight later on. I said I wanted a baby, and he said he'd be disappointed if I turned up pregnant... Oh, Lexy!"

"You never told me—"

"I know!" I cried, walking fast into the cottage. "He's going to know I did it on purpose."

"Now stop. Just stop, stop, stop. We're talking about a baby here."

"Babies!" I cried, throwing my purse on the counter and dropping into a chair.

"Well, still. It's not like you got caught with another man. This is a good thing!"

"I need you to be here when I tell him."

"No." I could tell she was shaking her head. "I can't do that. This is not my business."

"It most certainly is! This was all your idea."

"Meg! Stop saying that!" she cried. "I didn't mean for you to actually do it!"

"Then why did you say it?"

"I don't know! You were sad! I wanted to make you happy! I would've dressed up like Big Bird if that would've made you smile."

"Please come over," I pleaded, holding my face in my hand. "Just come over to see Will, and I'll tell him when you're in the other room. I just need you to be here in case he loses it."

"Bill would never hurt you, especially not if you're pregnant."

"I know, but I'm scared. I need moral support, and you're so brave."

She exhaled loudly into the phone. "Okay. What time?"

It was a huge relief Lexy was coming. I decided to stop off at La Belle Monde and have a massage on the way to pick up Will. Since I'd talked to that doctor, I'd been completely clenched.

In the beginning, I'd felt a twinge of guilt for deceiving Billy with the pills and all, but I was convinced once he saw his new little son or daughter, all would be forgiven. Now that he'd been working so hard to be home and spending time with us, I wasn't so sure. And I'd never expected to hit the jackpot.

Twins.

*April 23, 19 –*

Time is supposed to be some great healer, but I think it's all a lie.

I hate time.

Time is my enemy.

It's a great, shapeless blob that expands and contracts depending on who's controlling it.

I have to figure out what to do with it every day. When I'm not looking, it's this sneaky presence that creeps in and says I'm getting older, and all my dreams are passing me by. Or it's this empty space. This big empty space filled with nothing.

No one ever has any of it to give me, but I've always had more than my share to spend. And if I had all the time I've spent alone in my life, maybe I could use it to go back and start over and do everything differently.

Billy is so mad at me. He's almost completely stopped coming home. I haven't seen him in two weeks.

I can tell he's been here to get clothes, and I can see he's showered. But he never sleeps here. It's like we're separated, but somebody forgot to send me the notice. Do you even get a notice when you're separated or is it something that just happens? I tried calling him once, but he would only answer my questions with Yes or No, and after listening to the hum of silence, I said goodbye.

How could what I've done be so bad? I can't believe he's so unhappy about having twins. I should be the one freaking out, but instead it's him. He says it's not about the babies, that he loves his children. He says it's because I lied. I deceived him.

I don't really get that, because when you're married and you sleep together, you could always get pregnant.

You're supposed to be okay with that when you sign on the dotted line.

And here it comes again. Time. It just keeps passing. I started sleeping with little Will in his big boy bed until I got too big and uncomfortable. I'm growing like a giant whale, and these days it's nonstop doctor's appointments. I never had to go so much with Will. My back is killing me, and last week I was spotting. The doctor says I've got to go on bed rest, but I'm fighting that as long as I can.

Tonight for supper, Will and I dined on delicious leftovers. I've been cooking for three, but there's only ever two to eat it. I can't believe Billy won't even come home long enough to see his son. Will doesn't even ask about Daddy anymore. He's so used to him being gone all the time.

I was so angry and sad after I'd tucked him in his little bed, I decided to take a long, hot bath. That's where I was when I heard the door. My heart jumped.

"Billy!" I called as loudly as I could without disturbing Will. After a few minutes, he walked back into the bedroom and sat on the bed. "Billy, is that you?"

"It's me," he said.

A wave of happiness hit me so hard, I almost wept. "Oh, I'm so glad you're here. Give me a second."

I pulled myself out of the tub and quickly dried off, wrapping up in his robe. It was the only one that barely fit me now.

"You're really growing," he said.

I nodded. "I know. It's kind of scary, but the doctor says I'm right on track."

His eyes traveled up my body but stopped before they reached my face. "Do you feel bad?"

"I did, but I'm feeling a lot better now."

I went over to sit beside him. He put his arm around my shoulder and kissed my forehead. My body trembled with need, and I was fighting tears. But the last thing I wanted was to start crying like a baby in front of him.

"Are you staying?" I asked quietly, afraid of his answer.

He nodded, and I reached my arms around his waist. I pressed my face on his shoulder to stop the tears. We stayed that way for a few minutes, and then he stood and started taking off his coat.

"Mama said we could move some of our stuff in the big house and live there after... after my delivery," I said, watching him.

"I'd thought about that. I'll get some of the guys to come over, and you can tell them where you want everything put."

"I was thinking we don't have to move everything. Just clothes and a few pieces of furniture. The beds. Will's stuff."

He nodded, continuing to change.

"Oh, Billy, are you ever going to forgive me?"

He stopped. "I just need some time."

Then he went into the bathroom to shower, and I crawled up on the pillows. At least he was home. I could work with Time on this one.


*Dec. 15, 19 –*


It's been two months and three days since the babies were born, and I'm just getting my feet under me again. For the record, having twins is exhausting!

I'd never been so glad little Will was in school until I brought my two golden angels home and started caring for them. Before, I'd missed my little man. He was my constant companion. Now, I never stop moving.

Looking at their adorable faces, I wished we were at a point where I could hire a nanny. Things were coming together, and we were starting to have more money in the bank, but we were still tied to a budget. I guessed I'd have to wait. I couldn't put that pressure on Billy at this stage in the game. Not now that he'd finally gotten over being so angry at me about the whole thing. I never expected that to last so long. I thought I'd lost him, and I'd been on my best behavior ever since.

John is a good little baby. We call him Jack, and he sleeps right on schedule and does exactly what he's supposed to do. Lucy is constantly in motion. She cries when I put her down, she wakes her brother if I lay her too close to him, and then he screams. Oh, what I wouldn't give for a day at the spa. Mama came back from Sedona for the first several weeks, but after she left, it was just me and the babies. If only I had an extra pair of hands to help me all the time!

Billy was still working as much as ever, but at least he was coming home now. We still hadn't slept together since the night I told him about the twins, not that I'd really felt much like that. I was just glad he wasn't sleeping at his office anymore. That was the hardest two weeks of my life.

I'd been willing to take a chance on him being mad when I'd hatched my little plan, but I'd never meant for it to be like that. I wondered if the twins part made it worse. I wondered if I'd only been expecting one if he'd still have been so angry.

It didn't matter. Things were getting back to normal, slowly but surely.

*May 15, 19 –*

I know. I'm the worst Journal writer now, and I used to be so faithful!

I'm doing my best, but with all these babies, it's hard to find time to write. Let me see, where are we now?

Spring.

It's spring, and I've decided to try and get out with the twins more while Will is still in school. Three children is really two too many for one person, so I'm attempting to get back in circulation before summer comes. I have no idea what I'll do then. Hire some teenager, I guess. Billy will just have to understand.

There's nothing I love more than driving over to Newhope to stroll the blocks between Church and Section Streets and visit the French Quarter on De La Mare Avenue. The streets all have wide sidewalks that are adorned with native spring flowers, stargazer lilies, impatiens, and fresh-faced daisies. Newhope actually plans for flowers in their city budget, and the planners know how to decorate a town. They have flowers peeping out from behind every window, hanging from the streetlights and even around the trash cans.

It's the happiest time of the year to be here, other than when they light up all the trees at Christmas, and with the babies asleep in the stroller, I can wander through the small shops and immerse myself in high fashion. Girls come from Atlanta and Charleston to open stores here catering to the tourists who vacation at the Grand Hotel in Clear Pointe, and they always have the most appealing selections.

There's one store devoted entirely to purses, and the owner is so friendly. She always tells me to park the stroller by her desk, and I can try on all her quirky bags. One is made from tennis shoes and another from old album covers. One looks like a satin pillow with the faces of Japanese geishas painted on the side. They're all works of art, and I have to struggle not to buy ten of them.

From there I make my way down to the shoe store where the owners have set up a little play area for kids. So thoughtful! I can try on heels that look like they came straight off the runway in Italy. Snake and leopard skins, feathers and Lucite, daisies and open-toes. They're all stunning. I sneaked a pair of ten-inch bright green heels in embossed crocodile. They're gorgeous and they're on sale, so that counts for something. Daddy left me a little legacy when he died, and while everything's still Mama's, she gave it to me now. It's fun to have a bit of breathing room, and I deserve a little treat after working so hard.

In the clothing store, I tried on all the latest in New York fashions. The girls there helped me decide on a pair of jeans and a bright tank top to match my new shoes. I could pair it with a scarf or jacket for cooler evenings, and they helped me choose some chunky accessories to tie everything together perfectly and even match my purse. I just had to buy them. They were practically made for me. We all agreed. And since I was getting closer to my pre-twins size, I needed to update my wardrobe. What would people think if the wife of the most important developer on the Gulf Coast were wearing last year's fashions?

At the toy store on Newhope Avenue, I picked up a few developmental toys for the babies. I wanted them to be smart, and they couldn't just play with each other all the time. They were starting to wake up when I decided we'd better make our way back to the car. The stroller was almost tipping over backwards from the weight of all the bags I'd looped on the handles. But I felt so refreshed.

I decided if my plans with Billy hadn't worked out, and I'd had to figure out a way to support myself, owning a little shop like that would've been the perfect thing. I'd always had impeccable taste, and I would have no problem finding the hottest items at market in Atlanta or Dallas.

Driving home, I imagined the possibility of things being different. I remembered the first time I saw Billy at school. Lexy and I were walking from one class to another, and there he was, leaning with his back against his locker looking in a book. I saw those blue eyes, and I think I said out loud that he was the one. He was already tall but skinny. He hadn't really filled out yet, but that would come later. Like most of the local boys, he'd end up spending every summer doing what amounted to manual labor on the farms, but I wasn't complaining. All that heavy lifting paid off for us girls.

I remembered he was so serious and focused even then. Bryant was on the football team, but not Billy. He taught himself to play golf. He taught himself to do everything. And then they got their big idea junior year. Up until that point, we'd been practically inseparable, but once he and Bryant got started on their plan, he did nothing but read, read, read. Everything he could get his hands on about development and business and economics. It was practically impossible to divert his attention, and as the end of senior year started closing in, I'd had to do something to keep my dreams on track.

I didn't regret it. Not even a little, even with things like they are now. We'd find our way back together. This was just a temporary setback, and these storeowners would have to settle for my patronage rather than my companionship. I wouldn't do anything differently. I loved my life, and I loved my babies. I just wished I wasn't so tired all the time.

I was asleep most nights when Billy got home, but that was one bright spot. I could feel him over there beside me again.

The other night, I managed to get both twins to sleep at once and decided to sit up and wait for him. By 10 o'clock, I was asleep. Still, I roused when he slid into the bed and moved toward him. I wasn't fully awake, but it only took a few kisses to let him know I was willing. His soft lips and gentle touch reminded me why we had three babies. That was a good night, and I'd drifted to sleep in his arms.


*Aug. 10, 19 —*

Well, I just got the shock of my life today! I would never have believed this one was coming, even if someone had sat me down and warned me.

It's been three months since Miss Stella's funeral, and in that time I haven't seen a hair on Lexy's head. Every time I call, she tells me she's tired or she's working on some project she simply can't leave.

It was getting to be too much. I could deal with a husband I never saw, but not a best friend. Will had just started back to school, so I decided to drive to her little cottage in Dolphin Shores and pay her a surprise visit with the twins. She hadn't seen them since the funeral, and I hoped the sight of their little sunny faces would cheer her up.

I was the one surprised when she answered the door.

"Oh my god! Lexy, you're pregnant!" I shrieked and hugged my best friend, laughing.

"Meg, what are you doing here?" She turned white as a ghost. "You brought the twins!"

I ignored her odd reaction. "Let me see you!" I said. "When did this happen? Who's the daddy?"

She literally looked like she might faint. "It's… well, it's somebody from work. You don't know him. Oh, Meg. I really wasn't expecting to see you today."

I blinked, not sure how to take that. I had always dreamed of us having babies together, and even though I was a little ahead, it wasn't by much. "I'm sorry. Are you feeling bad?"

"No." She shook her head not meeting my eyes. "I just hadn't told you about this, and… and now here you are." She stepped back. "Come in. Sit. Let me get something for the babies. Do you want some coffee?"

"Sure, thanks. But Lexy! Stop being weird," I went to the table, putting the twins down. They were crawling and pulling up on everything, which made it hard to sit for long. "So who's this guy at work? I know everybody there! Is it Rain Hawkins?"

"What? Oh, god, no." She swallowed hard, clearly worried. "It's a guy in Atlanta."

"Somebody from the advertising firm?"

She looked puzzled, but quickly shook her head. "No. He's… umm… He's one of the investors. I'm just so embarrassed about all this. I couldn't tell you. We were all out and there was alcohol, and, well…"

"Miss Passionate Romance? You always wanted to be swept away."

85

She laughed, but it seemed more desperate than happy. "This is more like being swept under and out to sea."

"So what's the deal? If he's an investor, then he's loaded! Have you told him? Are you getting married?"

"Um… well, yes and no."

"Lexy!"

She breathed. "Oh, Meg. It's so complicated. I can't marry him. I'm just… I'm just going to have the baby and take care of him myself."

She looked so stressed, I was hesitant to press her for more details.

"So it's a boy?" I asked, hoping to ease her mind.

She nodded.

"Are you okay?" I asked. "Do you have enough money?"

"I'm fine. Money's not a problem," she said. "I've got plenty of work to do, and Bryant asked me keep going as long as I can through the pregnancy."

"Billy'd better be acting right. Why, you're practically family!"

"Bill's… fine." She studied the table. "He hasn't said anything."

"Well, you tell him if you need anything." I got up to refill my coffee and tried to think of happier words. "A little boy," I said. "That's wonderful! I have so many little boy things. I can give him all of Jack's little hand-me-downs. Most of it's barely even worn."

"Oh, no," she said. "That's too much."

"What's mine is yours! And what about a baby shower? We need to get that going. Have you registered anywhere?"

"Meg." She shook her head. "That's… no. I don't want a shower. Really. It's okay. I'm taking care of this."

"Oh, Lexy," I said, sitting across from her and taking her hands. "I can understand you being embarrassed about *how* it happened, but after all, it's your first baby! And it's a sweet little boy. You have to be happy about it."

"You don't understand." She wouldn't meet my eyes.

"What? About accidents? Are you kidding?" I breathed a laugh. "Listen, just because things aren't ideal, that's no reason to lose your joy over your first baby."

"Yes, but you were at least with your husband. I'm… well, I'm alone."

"You are never alone if I'm around. And we're going to be excited about your new baby. What are you planning to name him?"

"I don't know." She pulled her hands away, and sat up straighter. "James is an old family name, but I want it to be something different. Something unique."

"Of course you do! You wouldn't be you if you didn't name the baby something original."

I watched as she ran her fingernail down the line in the tabletop. "What do you think about Comet?"

"I hear it's a great toilet cleaner."

She smiled, and I was so glad to see my friend relax ever so slightly. Lucy crawled over and started fussing for her lunch, so I picked her up and slid her under my shirt.

Lexy watched me before speaking again. "You're right." She looked down again. "That's terrible. What about Indigo?"

"He'll never be at a loss for what color pants to wear."

"Eric?"

---

87

"That's not unique."

"Well, I was thinking of the Vikings." Her dark eyes flitted to mine and then away again. She picked up a spoon to stir her coffee. "He might be an artist, but he also might be an ambitious developer-conqueror like all the other fellows around here."

"Like Billy?"

She dropped her spoon, splashing coffee on the front of her shirt. Then she quickly rose and grabbed a rag.

"You're right. Eric is too common." She seemed flustered. "Julian. What about Julian?"

"Oh, yes! I love it!" I smiled. "It's unique, but soothing. Sounds like the ocean."

Julian.

Driving back to our home in Fairview, I was beside myself. Billy had to know about this. I couldn't believe he hadn't told me! I guess he'd wanted to let Lexy do the honors. Or maybe he couldn't care less. I knew he wasn't big on pregnancies and babies these days.

I was wide awake when he arrived home that night, ready to get to the bottom of it all. After rattling around in the kitchen a while, he finally came back to the bedroom, handsome as ever, and started stripping off his suit and tie. For a few seconds, I waited and watched. I didn't want to deter his progress.

"I went to visit Lexy today," I finally said.

He stiffened, but then quickly went back to undressing. "How's she liking her little beach house?"

"She seems happy there. I didn't really get a chance to ask her. I was too surprised."

"Surprised? By what?" He actually seemed unaware.

"Have you seen her lately?"

"She's working more with Bryant these days." His voice grew quieter. "I haven't seen Lex in… probably four months."

"Since the funeral?"

"I think you're right. That was the last time."

"Well, that's odd." I sat up frowning. "How can you two work in the same office and never see each other?"

He shrugged. "She said she wanted to work evenings a while back, so she comes in after I leave. Her assignments are mostly written out now."

I nodded chewing my lip. "She must be trying to hide it from you."

"Hide what?"

"Well, I'm not sure if I should even tell you now. You clearly don't know." I changed positions, moving back down to lying in the bed.

"Meg, I'm tired. Either tell me or let me shower."

"She's pregnant."

I was very disappointed in Billy's reaction. He didn't even flinch. Just stood and went back to undressing.

"Did you hear me?" I said.

"So she's pregnant. There's no law against that."

"Billy!"

He exhaled, and I watched his shoulders drop. "What'd she tell you?"

"That's about it. She's pregnant, and she said it's some guy in Atlanta. She said she isn't even seeing him! Think she's telling the truth?"

His back was still to me. "Why wouldn't she be?"

"Well, who could it be? Do you have any ideas?"

"I don't keep tabs on her."

"Billy, this is serious."

My brow clenched as I watched him now in his boxers, putting away his tie and belt.

"Why?" he said. "She's still working as far as I can tell. Bryant hasn't complained to me about anything. As long as she's doing a good job, getting the work done…"

"I can't believe you," I cried. "I just tell you my best friend is expecting a baby with some mystery man who could be anybody, and all you can think about is work?"

Finally, he came over and sat on the bed, taking my hand. "What do you want me to say, Meg? You want me to fire her?"

"Of course not! I just thought you'd be more interested."

"I'm interested that she's well. You seem to think she is, right?" I nodded. "And she's getting her projects done. Bryant hasn't said anything, so that must be working out. I don't know what else I can do about it."

For a moment I simply studied his face. Then I released the breath I was holding. "I guess you're right. I just can't believe you're not more… concerned."

"I'm as concerned as I need to be." Then he stood and went into the bathroom.

My husband. If I live to be a hundred, I will never understand Bill Kyser. I tell him the biggest news this year, and all he can think about is hitting the showers.

Personally, I can't stand not knowing more. I wonder how I could find out. Maybe Bryant would know. What if it's Bryant! No, Lexy always thought Bryant was annoying, loud, and boisterous. It's funny she's working with him instead of Billy, though. She and Billy seemed to have gotten past their differences. Maybe she's embarrassed for him to know. She always did try to put on such an air of superiority around Billy.

I'll bide my time and be a good friend, but I'm going to find out who this baby belongs to if it's the last thing I do.

*Sept. 15, 19 —*

Time is unpredictable when you're a mama. It seems like the days will never end, and then you look up and months have gone by. It's also very monotonous. I take Jack and Lucy to the park some days, but it's almost more trouble than it's worth to get them all packed up and outside. The minute we get anywhere, I have to stop and feed one of them or one of them has a poopie diaper. I know from experience this will pass, but it's small comfort in the trenches.

We're closing in on the one-year mark, and the twins are getting so active. Will's a sweet big brother to them. He gets in from school and goes straight to play with them, which gives me a little break. He's teaching Jack to catch and Lucy to walk. I've told him it's too early, but he wants to be a good helper.

Billy is still working all the time. I summoned the nerve to tell him I wished we saw each other more, and he told me to schedule a regular date night for us. I didn't think we could afford it, but who am I to contradict him?

Our first date was dinner at Christine's, an upscale seafood restaurant in Dolphin Shores. It was awkward, but I chalked it up to being the first time we'd had an adult conversation in practically a year.

I wore a new green dress I'd picked up at one of the Newhope boutiques, and I was almost back to my former size. It had taken more work getting back in shape this go-round.

"You look pretty tonight," he said.

"Thanks." I watched as he swirled the amber liquid in his tumbler. Billy had started having a scotch every evening about six months ago. I hadn't really questioned him on it. I figured it was to ease work stress.

"Do you want to talk about the babies?" he asked.

"Not really," I said. "Tell me about work."

"Not much to tell. We're moving ahead with the next phase. Alex has agreed to stay on and finish interiors through the convention center, and units in one, two, and three are selling as expected. We should start seeing big checks coming in soon."

"That's so great, Billy. Maybe we can hire a nanny."

"You're tired, I know. I'm sorry I've been working so much." He studied his thick crystal glass. "I know I'm not much help with the kids."

"It's okay." I tried to smile. "You wanted to wait."

"Yes. I did."

His answer made me uncomfortable, and we were quiet for a few moments.

"I don't want to argue with you," I said. "But aren't you happy now that we have them?"

"They're beautiful little babies, and I'm glad they got your blonde hair."

"And your beautiful blue eyes." I smiled and reached across the table to lace our fingers.

I knew once the money started coming in things would be different. He wouldn't work so much, and we'd reconnect. Maybe we could even take the boat out some. I missed our sailing trips.

"Will's doing very well in school," I said. "His teachers say he's one of the smartest kids in the class. He's already reading. You should hear him."

"You've done a great job with him. He's a sweet little guy."

I nodded. "He misses his daddy."

Billy slanted his eyes, and immediately I wished I could take the words back.

"I can't keep having this conversation with you," he said. "I'm too tired to even have the same old arguments again. To remind you what you already know."

"I know! I'm sorry," I hastily said. "It's just that... I miss having someone around to talk to."

"You could go to Sedona and visit your mother."

"And pull Will out of school? That wouldn't work."

"She visits you a lot," he said, finishing his drink.

"I know. It's just the minutes that fill the days. They can be very lonely."

We didn't seem to have much to say after that, and we didn't have another date night. Billy blamed it on work, but I blamed it on my complaining. He'd asked me to make time for us, and I'd gone and brought up the one thing that always pushed us apart. I had to try again. I had to find a way to mend this rift that kept growing bigger between us.


*April 15, 19 –*

We're breaking ground on our new home on Hammond Island this week. Goodbye city life! The five of us are headed to the exclusivity of that coveted neighborhood of quiet lanes and vast, sprawling estates.

Our house will be the biggest, Billy said. No point in being as successful as he is if you plan to hide your light under a bushel. And Billy's raking it in these days.

I guess the sad part about your dream coming true is the fear of it stopping. The fear that one wrong move and it'll all slip away. Billy works just as much now as he ever did, although he says part of it is meeting with contractors and looking at plans for the new house.

He keeps asking me for my input, but I only want two things for sure. Heart pine floors upstairs and a flagstone driveway that wraps around the house to the patio. Oh, and I'd also like a music room. Something pristine and elegant for when Lucy's grown and wants to put on small concerts for her family. She'll be an expert pianist, of course.

I also want a nice view from the balcony and patio area. Our lot is situated so that we can see Lost Bay from all angles, and I want to be able to sit outside and watch the water and the boats going by. Billy's a fan of travertine, and he wants that cool stone installed throughout the first floor. I wasn't completely onboard with that, but I didn't argue.

He also wants the exterior to be stucco, which I think is a bad idea for this climate, but he assures me the builders have a new, special type of stucco that's more durable. I just can't wait to be the king and queen of South County. I guess in a way we already are, but we need a palace to go with it.

The babies are growing so fast. Both twins are walking now. John started off first at fourteen months, but Lucy took her time. I think the little princess just liked being carried by her daddy, but she finally took her first steps around the eighteen-month mark. Now I'm wondering why I was so eager to get her going. She's into everything! I look up and she's pulled her cereal off the table onto her head, and I have to call the maid to come a day early and clean it up.

Will's doing great as always in second grade. Billy says we'll have to move him to Sacred Heart once the house is finished. Sacred Heart is the exclusive private school on Terry Cove where all Hammond Island residents send their children, and it's much closer to our house than Magnolia School. Billy says he'll get a top-notch education, but I hate it. I know. Originally I wanted him there, but I just hate my little man leaving my alma mater. Magnolia is the sweetest place, and all the teachers love him so much. I'm afraid private school will turn him into a spoiled little rich boy, and I want him to be like his daddy.

Lexy had Julian a few months ago. I remember that night so well. It made me realize how close we've all become. Lexy doesn't have any family left here, so we're it for her. I was holding her hand when she pushed his little head out, and the two of us laughed through our tears at his first baby cries. There was no sign of his daddy, but I didn't want to bring up that subject. Besides, Billy was right outside her door when Julian came, pacing the hall like any worried daddy. It was endearing.

Julian has Lexy's beautiful brown hair, but bright blue eyes. I don't know where he got them, but he's just the dearest little thing. It's made me start wishing for little Megan, but I have to wait at least three more years for that. I can't handle a newborn until the twins are in school. We have the terrible twos coming up soon, and I can only imagine what Lucy will be like.

Jack is so much like my daddy, I wish he were still around to see his grandson. He was aptly named because their temperaments couldn't be more alike. I wouldn't be surprised if he even grew up and wanted to be a doctor, although Billy is already talking about how the boys will both go to Ivy League schools and take over the business once they're done. That's fine with me, I'm ready for him to retire.

For now I'm busy picking out fixtures and deciding on colors and furniture schemes. Building a new house is so much fun, and it keeps me occupied. I'm no longer the sad little housewife covered in tiny babies. Things are changing for us.

When he's at home, Billy is so sweet to me and so involved with the babies. He reads to Will and carries Lucy everywhere. Jack's his little shadow, following Daddy wherever he goes.

We talked one night and agreed that letting so much time pass being angry and distant was a dangerous thing. It made our relationship so strained and difficult, and we missed each other so much. Now things are as natural as they ever were, and no matter how busy or tired either of us are, we do our best to stay in touch.

Now with our beautiful house, we're becoming the perfect family I'd always envisioned us being.

*Dec. 20, 19 —*

Dear Journal,

My best friend is sleeping with my husband.

Lexy is sleeping with Billy

No. What are we calling her now? Alex?

*Alexandra Marie LaSalle is sleeping with the father of my children.*

...

I don't remember much before I got to this point, Journal, sitting here writing this to you. My hands are shaking so badly I can barely hold the pen, but the scotch is helping with that.

How did I get here, you ask?

I remember racing through the streets toward my home without even noticing the street signals, the passing cars, or how fast I was driving. I wasn't crying, but my body kept lurching as if I were going to throw up.

Where had I been?

Let's see... We were at the annual Kyser-Brennan Christmas party in the penthouse of Phoenician I. We'd been mixing with the staff a while, and then I looked up and saw Billy walking down the hall to where the offices were located.

I went to get a drink, thinking I'd meet him back there. We'd never christened his new office, after all. That's when I found them. The two of them. Together. In *her* office.

Alex leaning against her table with my husband in her arms.

Him kissing her face, her neck. His hands touching her body...

Next thing I remember, I quickly pulled the car off the road and opened the door to vomit on the ground. A loud horn passed on the other side, and I sat up crying, then shaking.

Alex had tried to stop me, but if she knows what's best, she'll stay away from me. I'll happily kill her tonight.

When I arrived here, at our house, and slammed through the front door, the first thing I came to was the life-sized family portrait hanging in the entryway signed *Alex*.

I tore it off the wall and carried it out the front door. The canvass ripped straight down the middle as it caught the edge of a bronze planter. That seemed right. I threw it through the doorway onto the flagstone pavement. The wooden frame made a nice, heavy splitting noise when it broke into pieces.

Back inside, I made the rounds of the house gathering every piece of evidence that she existed. I found a picture of us on the sailboat hugging and smiling. I put my heel through her face. On the mantle was a shot of the three of us, my husband in the middle with his arms around us both. I almost laughed out loud at that as I slammed it against the mantle over and over.

Glass shards flew everywhere.

The babies will have to stay at Mama's house until the maid comes and cleans up this mess.

I walked over to the desk and took the top off my husband's decanter of scotch. I've never been much of a drinker, so I poured a tall glass to the brim. My first big gulp burned all the way down, past my shredded heart to my trembling stomach. I coughed and continued looking for evidence of the traitor in my life.

On the table at the foot of the stairs was a shot of the two of us wearing sombreros in Tango Sol. I threw that one as hard as I could, smashing the plate-glass mirror. Upstairs I dug through my husband's bedside table. I was looking for a letter, a picture, any evidence of how long this had been going on right under my nose.

The one person I trusted most in the world.

The world's biggest liar.

I found his journal and tore it open. A scrap of paper fell to the floor.

I'm pregnant. —A.

I picked it up and read it. Then I blinked and read it again. All at once the truth slammed into me like a medicine ball straight to the gut.

Julian's father… Julian's mystery father… Those bright blue eyes…

The scream was out of my mouth before I even heard it, pulling my muscles so hard, my whole body bent in half. My heart exploded as I realized how long, how blind, how stupid I'd been. All those nights of working late… How many times had they humiliated me? Laughed at me behind my back?

The pain ripping through my chest felt exactly like a hook had been inserted, twisted around, and jerked out fast. Never in my life have I hurt like this, not when Daddy died, not when Mama left, not even when I thought I'd lost Billy after the twins.

I dropped to my knees as a low moan forced its way from deep inside me, as tears flooded my eyes, as I slowly curled all the way to the floor.

She stole everything I had.

My only dream.

I will never forgive her as long as I live.

# *Anna* – December

For a long time, all I could do was sit and stare at Meg Kyser's final written words. Then, after many silent minutes, the book slid from my hands to the floor.

It was quiet in my room. The only sound was the ticking of the second hand on my little clock. Time. She hated time.

I lay my head down on the pillow listening, my stomach in knots, and tried to sort through all the thoughts swirling in my brain. I'd asked over and over what was wrong with Jack's family? How could they be so broken, so messed up? Now I knew.

I thought of Lucy after her overdose last fall, how hopeless she'd been. If only her mom had been here. If only she'd had a mom growing up. I wondered what kind of advice Meg Kyser would've given her only daughter about loneliness. I thought about Lucy and how similar she was to her mom. How much she looked like her. And how her dad did everything he could to avoid her. It all made sense now.

I rolled over on my bed and stared at the wall for a minute. Then I reached into my nightstand drawer and pulled out the picture Lucy had taken of Jack and me at that first dance. My heart still caught when I saw his gorgeous smile and bright blue eyes, but tonight my feelings were different. Sorry.

I remembered the old picture I'd found at the newspaper office of his mom, Mr. Kyser, Ms. LaSalle, and a bunch of their friends at Scoops when they were in high school. Jack was the perfect mixture of his parents—light blonde hair, clear blue eyes, athletic build.

He was so handsome. I ran my finger down the side of his face as I gazed at the image of us together, happy.

A hot tear slid down my nose, and I pushed the frame back in the drawer a little too hard. I was sorry, but I wouldn't cry for him. I hated this thing had happened to his family, but I wouldn't go down that road again. I couldn't. I wasn't sure how any of this changed anything, but it wouldn't make me forget what our relationship had been like.

I lay on my bed several minutes longer. The other two journals sat on the bed beside me, and I expected they contained very different versions of what I'd read. But I didn't want to go there just yet. I wanted to talk to a friend.

I lifted my phone, sliding my finger across the different contacts. A glimpse of golden hair and a goofy grin made me stop. Lucy had snapped a silly self-portrait and saved it on my phone with her number last fall, and every time I saw it, I couldn't stop a smile, even now.

Things *were* slowly changing between her and her dad. She'd convinced him to let her stay here spring semester instead of moving to New Orleans with Jack and Will. And since she'd found B.J., she'd been happier than I'd ever seen her. I touched her number.

"Anna? What's up!" Her cheerful voice made me feel a little brighter.

"Hey," I started but my voice was thick. I cleared my throat. "Merry late Christmas!"

"Same to you! So? What did you do? Get any special surprises?"

If she only knew. "Oh, nothing much and not really," I said. "I'd already told my parents what I wanted, and they usually just stick to the list. You know."

"Hmm." Her tone sounded puzzled, like she'd expected a different answer. "I thought... Never mind. I'm glad you called — I need your help."

"With what?" I sat up quickly. It was silly, but I was eager to do something for her, to make up for what I now knew.

"I need you to go Christmas shopping with me," she said. "I know, it's past Christmas, but I need something for B.J. when he gets back from Birmingham, and he made me promise not to get him anything over twenty dollars. Can you believe that?"

"Well, sort of." I imagined how it must feel to date the daughter of the richest man in town. From what I remembered, all B.J. did outside of school was lifeguard. And it wasn't lifeguard season anymore.

"I've told him we're not in a competition, but he just insists," she sighed. "Where can I find him something special at that price?"

"We could hit the farmer's market in Fairview," I said.

"Anna. I'm not getting him a fruit basket."

I actually laughed then. "No! Mom said several of the artists have booths there. They bring their leftover stock from Christmas on the Coast and sell it at a discount."

"You are brilliant!" she cried. "I knew you'd help me. I'll pick you up in the morning at ten."

* * *

The farmer's market filled a four-block square in the streets of downtown Fairview, and while most of the western spaces were filled with produce, coffee, and local honey, the eastern rows were stocked with an assortment of unique, artistic creations, from shovels converted into torches to pottery to handmade baby clothes to pewter serving platters.

The humidity had blown away overnight, and the first hints of a chilly New Year's Eve were floating in on the breeze under clear blue skies. I'd grabbed a light, black cardigan to wear over my t-shirt and jeans, and my spiral locks were tied back in a low, side ponytail. Lucy, by contrast, looked liked she'd stepped off the fashion pages. She was dressed in black footless tights and a red tunic dress. Her light-tan leather blazer matched her ballet flats perfectly, and her smooth blonde hair was swept down her back and over one shoulder. I tried not to think about how much she probably looked just like Meg. It was too heartbreaking.

"It sounds like you and B.J. are pretty serious now," I said as we slowly inspected the wares in each booth. "Are you still having trouble remembering your assignments at Month's Bay?"

She smiled at my teasing. "My retention skills have suddenly improved," she said, waving a pewter salad tong. "Once I realized I needed to keep up with him or we wouldn't see each other as much."

I laughed, still amazed at her wanting to work at the coastal reserve protecting sea grasses and labeling sea turtle nests.

But her tone grew serious. "And yes. We are getting serious. He takes me to mass every Saturday."

My eyebrows rose. "Saturday mass?"

She nodded, lowering the large spoon and lifting a silk scarf.

"We usually go out to eat or to a movie after. It's all very corny and proper, and I love it."

"That must be a nice change for you," I said, picking up a leather wallet that had Aztec designs embossed on the cover.

"What do you mean?" Her voice was offended, and I dropped the wallet, my eyes flying to meet hers.

"Oh my god, that came out totally wrong. I'm so sorry. I just meant, well, there was that thing with Julian, and then..." Jack had told me about her past, her pregnancy that had ended in adoption and the older man who was responsible for it. But I wasn't sure she knew I knew.

"You mean the jerk?" She knew. "Yeah, he's a nice change from that guy."

She paused, still holding the scarf. "I told him about that, you know."

"About what? The accident with Julian?"

"About the baby. I told him I'd had one."

I was stunned. "How'd he take it?"

"Very well, actually," she said, lowering the scarf and looking ahead. "We were talking about me going to school at Sacred Heart. That's when he suggested we go to mass together. His family's all back in Birmingham, so he's here alone. I thought it was sweet that he wanted to take me to church, and at one of our dinners after, I just told him. I felt like he should know."

I nodded. "That's good." Then I stopped. "I'm sorry. It's more than good, it's really great. You've been through a lot, and B.J. sounds amazing."

She grinned. "He is a good change. We're getting to know each other, taking our time. And now there's no pressure. No big secret waiting to come out."

I bit my lip at the irony of that statement. My stomach was suddenly heavy with guilt over what I knew as we stopped at a table of handmade jewelry. I briefly thought of Julian and my ring when my eyes landed on a tiny silver sailboat. I reached out and touched it lightly with my fingertip.

"Oh!" Lucy picked up the dime-sized charm and turned it in her hand. "It's perfect for Jack—he'll love it! You've got to get it for him!"

My eyebrows pulled together as I watched her. "Wait—don't you know?"

Her frown matched mine. "Know what?"

"Oh, Lucy." My shoulders dropped as my eyes closed. "That's why you gave me that picture of us together. You didn't know we broke up."

Her jaw dropped, but just as fast she closed it. "Wait... That was for real? But I thought you were just taking a little break while he settled in at school."

"No," I shook my head. "It's no break. It's over. We're done."

Her forehead was still lined. "But I don't understand," she said softly then she shook it away. "So that's why you didn't see him at Christmas."

Her words caused that stupid pain in my chest, but I clenched my teeth. I wasn't going backwards. I didn't want to see him at Christmas, and I couldn't help it if Lucy had been out of the loop. Mine and Jack's non-couple status was his decision, and I was done riding his merry-go-round. It was over.

"Don't look so disappointed," I said, forcing a smile, making my voice be calm and not angry. "It was mutual, and I'm totally over it."

"Okay," she shrugged, and I watched as she picked the sailboat off the padded mat. "I think I'll get this for him anyway. You know how my brother is about his boat."

I didn't want to discuss it. "We still haven't found anything for B.J.," I said, continuing down the row.

She looked around puzzled. "I know, and I'm about ready to give up. I'll never find anything that suits him at that price."

Just then she froze. I looked back, and a little grin crossed her lips. My eyes followed hers to a life-sized clay sea turtle sitting in one of the yard-ornament booths.

"No." I grabbed her arm.

"Yes!" she laughed. "It's perfect!"

"It's not romantic at all."

"Shh!" She rushed forward and squatted, putting her hands on each side of the turtle's head. "You'll hurt Henry's feelings."

"Oh no." We were both giggling now, and I was glad. All the Jack tension was released.

"And it's twenty dollars!" She cried, flipping the price card over. "It was meant to be. It's how we found each other again... sea turtles. Henry is perfect."

"Well, you've given him a name. Now you have to buy him."

I followed her to the cashier and watched as she settled up. Then we walked back to her car, Henry tucked under her arm with a huge red bow around his neck. "I know life gets hectic once school's back in, but don't be such a stranger," she said, giving me a squeeze.

I nodded and gave her a quick hug back. "I won't. And I hope B.J. loves his new friend."

She smiled and wiggled Henry under her arm. "Me, too."

\* \* \*

Back home, I threw together a turkey club for lunch and then jogged back up to my room. Mom and Dad would be gone one more day, so reaching under my bed, I pulled out the dark, fabric-covered journal.

My heart ticked up a little faster at the sight of it. I had no idea what version of the story this book would hold or how it would change things, what I might find out about Julian or his mom.

My fingers trembled as I opened the cover. I took a deep breath and read the first lines.

# Book 2 – Lexy

*May 31, 19 –*

Salt. Fresh fish. Warm, moist humidity, moldering wood.

The air is filled with bright oranges and deep reds, white-hot yellows and brown.

Low buzzing of construction down to my right, strong rush of wind, pushing my hair back.

Crash... sizzle. Crash... sizzle.

The ocean is rough and happy today, beckoning me to run down and join in its dance.

So my best friend Meg gave me a journal as a graduation present, and here I am writing in it. It's funny. I had actually considered following her example and keeping a record of all my thoughts and feelings, and then she surprised me with this gift.

She gave one to each of us — Bill and me — and said since we were embarking on our big life plans, we should record the journey. She loves doing things like that, turning each moment into something memorable.

Let's see… what to write about this beginning?

It's a crazy time for all of us. So much is changing. This morning I decided to run to my usual escape down by the shore to relax and find my center. I was meditating when I remembered being a little girl and stripping off all my clothes so I could run and jump naked into the surf. It was always so warm and swirly, and I would pretend I could turn into a mermaid and

109

swim down deep to rule some magical kingdom. The memory made me smile, and I peeped through one eye at my surroundings.

Nope, too many early vacationers to attempt a repeat performance. Even here on Port Hogan Road, the beach condos are taking over. Damn Bill Kyser. His big plan is only going to make things worse.

In those days, I could come down here almost any time and be alone. That's when I'd started my habit of skinny-dipping. Now I have to be content to sit on the shoreline, eyes closed, legs crossed simply breathing in the air and listening to the sounds of my home. My inspiration.

I giggled at the thought of me skinny-dipping now. I could just see the headline, "Local Girl Caught Naked in the Gulf!" Miss Stella would get a big laugh out of that.

My benefactress has a wicked sense of humor despite her reputation as one of the most straight-laced members of society. I know her better, though. I had a wonderful time growing up here. She says I'm her favorite little orphan, and she's encouraged me in everything I've done.

Orphan.

Technically, I'm not an orphan. I wouldn't even be here if my slacker dad hadn't dumped me with the nuns after my mother had her nervous breakdown. He cut and ran right back to New Orleans, leaving me with the good sisters at the Little Flower Convent.

Loser.

A man who deserts his family isn't worth the time of day, if you ask me.

When my mother died a few years later, he never even came back for the funeral. Miss Stella told me not to hold it against him, and I've decided to take her advice.

I'd actually like to thank him. Miss Stella's given me a better life than any I could've had with him. A beautiful life full of color and art and living by the sea.

In two weeks, I'll be in the biggest wedding in town, which still makes me laugh sometimes. Who would've ever believed a waif like me could be inseparable friends with someone like Meg Weaver? I guess chalk it up to small towns and childhood memories.

But it's more than that. Meg's like my sister, even if we're like night and day. It's funny, we *are* sort of like night and day—her glowing sunshine, and me quiet night.

She's determined to marry her Billy, and nothing I can say will change her mind. He'll be the ruin of our hometown, and she'll be right there on every community board and snooty rich-wives club supporting him.

But I love her.

I've never met anyone as sweet or as loyal as Meg, and I'll gladly stand up for her to marry whomever she pleases. Even if it's someone I wouldn't touch with a ten-foot pole.

Today I went to her house to try on the maid of honor dress she picked out for me. I imagined it would be some terrible Pepto-Bismol pink number with lots of frills and lace. Meg is very girlie, and she loves all the trappings of the princess set.

When I arrived, her mom, who we all call Gigi, was in the sitting room entertaining one of her DAR friends. She motioned me upstairs, and I wondered again why she was letting Meg get married so young. Especially to Bill. He's so focused on his big dream. There's no way he can love Meg as much as he loves himself and his plan. But these old hens only see one thing: grandbabies. They see beautiful Margaret Weaver marrying (okay, I'll admit it) gorgeous Bill Kyser, and they go all *Gone with the Wind*. If he's ambitious, well that just makes it all the more romantic.

I think it's a total mistake. Meg's so tender, he's sure to end up hurting her.

Up in her room, she was giddy with excitement about her big day. "Oh, Lexy, I never thought you'd get here. I can't stand it! You're gonna die when you see the dress."

"Well, you don't want me to die," I laughed, flopping on her bed. "Who'd be your maid of honor? Pamela Browning?"

"Pamela Browning!" she shrieked. "Oh, Lex. You're hilarious! Wouldn't that just toast her buns?"

We both laughed at that. Pamela had shamelessly flirted with Bill since she moved to Fairview junior year, and we all expected her to do something desperate the night of the wedding.

"OK, toasty buns," I said, sitting up. "Go ahead. Let me see it."

She opened the armoire, and my eyes flew wide. I gasped when I saw the dress she'd picked out for me. Meg might act like a dumb blonde, but she's got my number. It was beautiful. Dark maroon with an airy tulle skirt. She laughed at the look on my face, and I carefully touched the delicate, clearly expensive fabric.

Then I put my arms around her and kissed her cheek. "I love it," I whispered.

"You are going to be so beautiful in this dress, Lexy, I'll be lucky if anyone even looks at me." She rested her temple against mine.

"I'll blend into the wallpaper next to you," I said.

Meg could be a model. She's the all-American girl with long shimmering blonde hair, blue eyes, and a perfect figure. When they cast the Barbie dolls, she's clearly what they're going for.

Once, a while back, I'd considered using her to practice my portrait work, but then I decided no one would buy it. It would be impossible to believe someone like her exists in the real world. As I watched her pacing, discussing her wedding plans, it struck me she was actually glowing. I couldn't figure out how she did it.

"And you have to wear makeup to my wedding, Lexy, now don't roll your eyes." She pulled out her tools. "You're lucky to have such an even skin tone and those lashes or you'd never get away with it."

I did roll my eyes, but she ignored me. "Here, let me just put a little shadow on your lids and some lip gloss. Now look. Perfect."

We looked in the mirror, faces together, and I exhaled a laugh. Like I said, night and day.

"Oh, Lexy, we're the perfect team," she said.

"Team for what?" I tugged her golden lock and crossed my legs under me.

"Anything! You have to stay here."

"Not this again," I groaned. "No way. You can bury yourself in this place if you want, but I'm getting out."

"You make it sound like prison," she pouted. "You know, you might realize the older you get, that it's not so bad to be around people who know you and love you."

"I understand it being right for you. But I can't stay here, Meg. It's too small and claustrophobic. I'll go crazy if I don't get out of this place."

She sighed, tossing her makeup brush on the counter. "So Billy wants us all to go out on his boat next weekend. You in?"

"I don't know," I picked up one of her gigantic wedding magazines and started turning pages.

"I've got a lot of packing to do, and you know I don't like boats."

"Please, Lexy," she begged. "You'll be leaving soon, and I'm afraid it'll be one of the last times we're all together."

"Who else is going?" I glanced up at her.

"Bryant and one of his girls. I don't know. Maybe Donna?"

I didn't mind Donna Albriton. "Okay," I agreed.

Being with Billy tends to bring out the hostile side of me, but I love Meg so much. I don't want her to think I don't approve of her future husband, even if she is _way_ too young to be getting married.


*June 11, 19 —*

I can't believe I hadn't figured out Meg was pregnant!

Of *course* that's why they're getting married way too young. Bill would never have strayed from his carefully laid plans without something major happening.

Now I know, and now I'm sworn to secrecy. And I also know there's no changing her mind — not that there was ever a chance of that. Even at five years old, all Meg wanted to do was grow up to be a wife and a mommy. She saw Bill in ninth grade, and the first thing she said was, "It's him."

I felt a pain in the pit of my stomach. She hadn't even spoken to the guy, and there she was staking her entire future on him. But Bill's always been kind to Meg. It's funny, he seems as in awe of her as everyone else is. She's so sweet, it's hard to believe. And she's so innocent, you wonder how she manages to make it through a day without getting lost or injured. She's in the perfect location to live her life happy, secure, and protected straight through to the end, surrounded by her grandchildren and great-grandchildren.

I, on the other hand, am getting out of here as fast as possible. Not that I don't love my hometown. It's a beautiful place that I will always carry in my heart as my inspiration. I just need to meet different people. I need new experiences and more stimulation. Seeing the same old faces and the same roads and store fronts day after day has become so monotonous, I'll turn into my crazy mother if I don't leave.

And yes, I confess, I'm hoping for a better selection of guys. Ones who aren't so focused on the big game or drinking beer or shooting guns.

Savannah is going to be the answer to my prayers. It's bigger, but not too big. And it's on the water, so I can go down and commune with the ocean as much as I need to. I'll miss Miss Stella and her great house on Port Hogan Road, but I can come back and visit anytime.

So I agreed and last night we all went out on Bill's boat. I can't relax on a boat, but I couldn't say no to Meg. She's right. In a month I'll be gone, and I don't know how long it'll be before I see my dear friend again.

It's unclear how her being Mrs. Bill Kyser is going to change our friendship. I hope not at all, but of course, I have no idea how my going to SCAD will change things. I confess, I'm as sad-nervous-excited-melancholy as my dear friend facing my future.

I watched Bill a little more closely last night. I was sure he was shaking in his boots at what all was coming with fatherhood on top, but you'd never know it to look at him. He's so focused. I don't know where he gets it.

His dad is as laid-back and easygoing as the next good ole boy rancher.

Maybe it was too many hot summers driving the combine, but Bill's been harping on this plan of his for two years now. He and Bryant, the tycoons of South County.

We had one short exchange on our outing last night. He had just set the boat on course when he sat down beside me.

"Congratulations, Daddy." I smiled at him.

He frowned.

"What's the matter?" I said. "Nervous?"

He laughed once. "You don't think I should be?"

"I think you should be scared to death."

*June 16, 19 —*

Meg's wedding certainly had style—just like her. It was the fairytale event she'd always planned, complete with the cruise into the sunset. Watching her and Bill leave, I imagined the end of all the stories where the fairytale princess lives happily ever after, and I wished them the best. I really did.

And with that behind me, my sights moved to art school and chasing down my dreams.

I've got two weeks to get ready, and Miss Stella is helping me pack all of my art supplies and clothes. Last night she came and sat on my bed to talk a few minutes.

"I remember the day you came here," she smiled taking my hand in hers. "You were such a tiny little thing with those big black eyes. I loved you the minute I saw you."

I crawled across the bed to put my head in her lap. "I remember I was so scared in this house all alone," I said, hugging her thick waist. "When I was at Little Flower, I'd shared a room with seven other girls. This was the biggest place I'd ever seen."

She combed my long hair with her fingers. "You perked right up after you started helping me in the garden, and then after you started school."

"After I met Meg. I remember the first time I saw her, she was like one of those little Christmas angels. Perfect in every way."

Miss Stella chuckled. "I wasn't surprised at all by your friendship. Margaret Weaver might seem like she has everything, but I recall her having trouble relating to other children."

"That's funny. I never noticed." I traced the eyelet hem of her gown with my finger, thinking. "She always seemed to know everyone and have lots of friends."

"Knowing people and having friends are two different things. But the two of you were right for each other. You're an old soul, and she gravitated to that."

"To hear her tell it, she gravitated to my looks," I laughed. "Something about us being exact opposites."

"Children are funny." I could feel Mrs. Stella braiding my hair. "They're fascinated by the strangest things. But Meg's attraction to pretty things affects her judgment."

I lifted my chin, catching her hazel eyes. "What do you mean?"

"Two people can marry young, and it can work out. But Bill Kyser doesn't even know who he is yet, and he's very distracted by his ambition."

I put my head back down and closed my eyes. "Meg's pregnant."

Miss Stella didn't answer.

"I don't think she's told her parents yet," I said. "Will you not tell them? Please?"

I felt her sigh then. "I don't make it into Fairview much. I don't see why I'd have any reason to cross paths with Georgiana Weaver."

"Thanks."

"That situation will work out however it's meant to be." She went back to combing my hair with her fingers. "So you're leaving for art school. I remember when you came running in this house saying you wanted to be a famous artist. You were so little, I just laughed."

I sat up to face her then. "You laughed and then went out and bought me an easel and a palette and a canvass and all the art supplies you could find."

"Well," she looked down, "You've always brought me such joy. I can't wait to see what you do."

"Thank you, Miss Stella. Thank you so much for everything."

She wrapped her arms around me and held me tightly. "Now don't let some young man come along and distract you. You go straight through art school and worry about boys later."

"Yes, ma'am!"

We giggled, and I turned out the light. In a few days, I'd be on my way.


*July 20, 19 –*


It's almost been a month now, and I love Savannah!

The college is spread out over six blocks in the northern part of the city right in the middle of the historic district. It's not far from Forsythe Park and that famous fountain, and I can walk down Drayton Street and be there in less than ten minutes. I plan to set up an easel one day and do some different views of it.

Forsythe Park is a busy place. It's a mile long, and there are always people jogging around it and events in the grassy center. I came to Savannah early so I could move in and have time to explore before classes started.

Landing a scholarship that included room and board was a miracle, and I was thrilled my only worries would be figuring out gas and entertainment expenses. My college apartment is right on Jones Lane, and I've spent the first few weeks wandering around and getting to know the city.

Savannah's a big tourist town, but I'm used to that. The streets around campus are filled with little shops that carry student art, and I visited several and met the owners. Hopefully I can get some of my paintings in a few of them.

I'm also just a few blocks from where the ghost tours start. I've never tried my hand at folk art or spiritual stuff, but maybe I'll do a few and see how they sell. Everyone is so nice and encouraging here. I can't wait for classes to start.

My roommate hasn't arrived yet. I decided to let the school just assign me a roommate, and now I'm hoping that wasn't a mistake. Some art students are very quirky and competitive, but I'm trying to stay optimistic. At least we're both artists. That'll give us something in common.

I drove to Tybee Island today to check out the beach and my options for meditation. It's just a short ways down Highway 80 to the water, and I want to find the perfect spot to close my eyes, relax and let the creativity flow.

The shoreline here is different than in South County. Back home we have short, sandy-white beaches met by turquoise blue waters. Savannah has rocky, high-tide areas where the water comes in and then goes out for miles of wet, brown sand. It's beautiful in a strange, desert-island kind of way. It also fills the bill on my desire to add new sights and landscapes to my collection of mental pictures.

I sit down on a large rock and look out at the flat expanse of sand. The ocean's out there even if I can't see it, and it's just waiting to charge back in when the tide changes.

Butterflies migrate through here in the fall, and I heard there's a pirate festival, complete with parades and floats. All of this is perfect for the experiences I want to have. I miss my best friend, and I still worry about her sometimes. But I'm so happy here.

This is where my life begins.


*Sept. 1, 19 —*


Classes have started, and I am loving SCAD! I'm only taking one painting class. The rest of my time I wanted to focus on things I've never tried, either because I never had the equipment or because I didn't have anyone to teach me.

That's the greatest thing about being here. The sculpture studio has all the tools I need to chisel and shape, my pottery class is equipped with wheels and kilns, and there's even a glass-blowing studio and a metal-arts building. I could learn to weld if I wanted. That would be a neat trick to show the boys.

A few weeks ago Meg called to say she's happily settled in their new home. It was her grandmother's little cottage between Fairview and Springdale, and if I know Meg, it's decked out with all the latest interiors and looks like a tiny version of her future mansion.

She's nervous about telling her parents about the baby, but I tried to assure her that they're going to be thrilled. Meg gets her baby-love honest. Gigi is the most baby-obsessed person I've ever met next to her daughter. The way they go on, you would think those tiny humans were the greatest thing since the invention of the spa.

We were both so excited to finally chat again.

"What's happening?" Meg cried. "How's Savannah? I've never gone more than a day without talking to you."

"I know! It's totally weird. Have you changed? Is your hair still blonde?"

"Good god, yes," she laughed. "I'd look like a rat if I wasn't a blonde."

"You would not."

"Stop changing the subject. Have you decided to come back yet?"

"No way, I love it here!" I lay back on my twin bed. "Everything is so creative. There are whole shops devoted to selling art, and the historic buildings and fountains are just begging me to paint them. I went down to Tybee Island, and it's totally different from our beaches at home. I can't wait to set up an easel down there."

She sighed in my ear. "I wish I could visit you."

"You should!" I jumped up inspired. "There's time before the baby comes."

"I don't know. I would, but the thought of a seven-hour drive right now makes me feel exhausted."

"I can believe that." My shoulders dropped. "So how are you? Happy? Is Bill being sweet to you?"

"Billy is a doll, and our honeymoon was for the record books."

A grin crossed my lips. "Did you do what you were planning?"

"Mm-hm. You should've seen the look on his face."

"Sounds X-rated," I laughed. "I hope you didn't scare the baby."

"Never heard a peep out of the little guy. Of course, he probably enjoyed all the rocking."

We both laughed then, and I was glad to hear her sounding so happily married. It was difficult for me to let Meg go. She was my first friend from the day she came bouncing up to me at the Magnolia School like it was written in the stars that we would be inseparable. We were like sisters, and I wanted her dreams to come true, too.

But now that it seemed she'd gotten her wish, I was safe to let her go and focus on my own dreams.

*Oct. 15, 19 –*

The most exciting thing I'm trying this semester is Raku pottery. It's like combining clay pottery with glass-blowing, and the finished pieces are so beautiful. They have a shimmering metal exterior. But it's tricky to master. First, you're working with extremely high heat, and the pieces can shatter so easily. I haven't pulled one out of the fire whole yet. But I love it!

Evan Gray is in my pottery class. He's from Montgomery, and he's very attentive. Says we have a home-state connection. Evan wants to be an illustrator, and he keeps asking me to have lunch with him. I like Evan, but I'm not really interested in getting sidetracked by romance right off the bat. And while he's sweet, he's not exactly my type. For one thing, he looks like he could still be in high school, all skinny and baby-faced. I came to college to have new experiences, not to spend all my time with the same kind of boys I left at Fairview High School.

Despite all my new artistic endeavors, my favorite class remains painting. I can't get away from the satisfaction of taking a blank canvass and coaxing it to life with my brush. I have to admit, I have an enormous crush on my professor, Nick Parker. I know, no dating the professors, but he looks so young, and he's intensely handsome. Tall, with longish dark hair and piercing green eyes.

When he comes around to critique my work, he always places his hand on my lower back. It's very exciting. I look down so my hair falls to hide my face. I hope he can't tell I'm blushing.

Oh, and I've changed my name. Well, not really, but once we got going in classes, all the professors kept calling me Alexandra. That would just never do, so Evan shortened it to Alex, and it stuck. I like it! Alex. It sounds very smart and confident. Alex. Meg will never go for it, and imagining her frown makes me laugh.

Suzanne Bailey wound up being my roommate, and she is not quirky or competitive. She's great. Suzanne's interested in graphic design, and she's focusing on computer-generated art and advertising. It's a smart way to go if you really want to make money in art. I mean, unless you're Andy Warhol or George Rodrigue. I expect she'll end up working for some big firm in New York or California, and don't think she doesn't expect the same thing! She and I are getting to be great friends. She's originally from Charlotte, and I told her I think North Carolina sounds like the most beautiful place. I've never been to the mountains. Miss Stella didn't take us on vacations.

I don't have any classes with Suzanne, but we try to go out and hit the Buccaneer pub, the local college hangout, at least once a week and catch up on what's happening in our lives. By the middle of the first semester we were Thursday night regulars. It was always Suzanne and me, but often we'd be joined by whoever she was dating at the time, other art school friends. Sometimes Evan would join us. We'd meet up in one of the wood-paneled booths, someone would sneak a pitcher using a fake ID, and we'd rehash the week and update each other on what was in store for the weekend.

"I'm completely hopeless at Raku pottery!" I wailed that particular Thursday.

"Impossible," Suzanne said, pouring drinks for everyone.

"No, she's really hopeless," Evan laughed.

"That's just mean," I pouted, causing him to laugh more.

"What's the problem? You're so good at everything else," Suzanne said.

"I don't know! It's like I've got a mental block or something. I can get the pieces all the way to the end, and then when I have to apply the metal finish, they always shatter. Evan! How come it never happens to you?"

He winked and pushed his light-brown hair back. "Because I'm an artistic genius."

"Seriously," I frowned. "I've never seen you break a piece. Not once."

"I took Raku in high school. There was a studio near my house, and the owner was a friend of my mom's."

"See? That's totally not fair!" I wailed. "What am I going to do? I really love the class, but I'm going to fail."

"You're not going to fail," Suzanne said. "Half of the grade is effort. I mean, you can't help it if you're a bull in the china class."

"Some friend," I said, taking a sip of the draft beer Evan had just poured us.

"So, what are you doing tomorrow?" Evan said to me.

He'd been asking me out for weeks, but I'd managed to avoid him. I was hoping to stay on the market in case Mr. Parker made a move. He'd been giving me a lot of extra attention in class lately, and maybe I was just setting myself up for disappointment. But a girl could dream.

"Oh, well," I tried to think fast. "I've made a study date with a girl in my painting class. We're supposed to be working on this project…"

"Uh huh. I get it. Bug off, Evan?" He was teasing, but I caught the edge in his voice.

"I'm sorry. Maybe we can do lunch after the break?"

"Maybe." He turned back to his beer.

We went on visiting and catching up on the week. Suzanne was learning to use some new design software, and her current project was to create a marketing campaign for a line of men's deodorant. We had fun coming up with different catch phrases until it was time to call it a night. Evan walked us back to our apartment and said good-night.

"You're going to put him off if you keep saying no," Suzanne said as we walked up the stairs.

"I know, but I don't want to date Evan right now." I dug around in my small bag for our key.

"So just go out with him once," she said, leaning against the wall. "Get him off your back."

"It won't be like that. He's asked too many times." I found the key and fumbled with the lock.

"Well, I haven't noticed you checking anyone else out. What's the deal? Who are you waiting for?"

"Nobody," I said, but I had to press my lips together to keep from smiling.

"Really?" Suzanne leaned in close, eyes narrowed. "Then what's that all about?"

"I don't know what you're talking about," I said.

"The smile?"

"I'm not smiling." I got the door unlocked and we both pushed into the living room.

"And blushing!" she cried. "Who is it?"

"Shut up! I am not blushing. It's nobody." I threw my keys on the counter and hung my coat on a peg.

"You can be cagey if you want, but we live together. I'm going to find out."

"Then you'll find out when there's something to know."

Suzanne shook her head and went to her room. I was already imagining what I would wear tomorrow to painting class.

So much happens in college so fast! I love being independent and meeting new people, and I love being immersed in art. Savannah is my favorite place in the world. It's all going exactly as I planned.

*Oct. 20, 19 –*

I'm a bad girl, and I love it!

My first (real) college date, and it's with my professor. Yes! It all happened this week. I was working on my painting of the large anchor down on Butler Street, and Mr. Parker came by to critique my work.

"I like your use of color, Miss LaSalle," he said, and he placed his hand on my lower back again. *Zing!*

"Thanks," I managed to whisper.

"You've got real talent," he said in that low voice of his. My arches literally tingled. "Can you stay after class to discuss a few options I think you might find interesting?"

"Yes, sir," I said, unsure if it could mean anything more but definitely hoping.

His office was in the very back of the room behind glass windows, and when I went in and sat down, I noticed several nudes stacked against the back wall. He saw me looking at them, and I felt my cheeks warm.

"I share my office with Ms. Finch, the figures instructor," he said, waving at them.

"Oh, yes. I'll take that next year." I pushed my hair behind my ear.

"I think your work shows distinction," he said, leaning in front of me against his desk. "You have a unique approach that's fresh and vibrant. Have you considered apprenticeships?"

I glanced quickly up at him. "No, sir. I mean, I'm just a freshman. I was thinking I'd get through this year and then see what's next."

"You shouldn't wait. Strike while the iron's hot." Then he looked up. "My next class is coming in. What are you doing Friday?"

"Friday? I have class—"

"Friday evening? Are you dating anyone?"

My heart literally stopped. "No." I tried not to let my voice tremble.

"Good, then I'll pick you up around seven. We can have dinner and discuss it. And call me Nick. Mr. Parker's my dad."

"Okay… Nick."

He got up and swiftly left his office to start his next class. I followed slowly, my head in a cloud. Nick Parker was so hot. I couldn't believe he was taking me to dinner Friday. I wouldn't be able to eat a thing.

Suzanne thinks it's a mistake. She thinks I'll get in trouble since I'm enrolled in his class and he's grading my work and all. I don't care. I'll gladly transfer classes or even take this one over if I have to. I am *so* doing Friday and hopefully more.


*Oct. 21, 19—*

I am going out with my professor.

Look—I just put it in writing. It's official!

I am officially breaking some rule. I guess. Is dating a professor a written rule or is it just frowned upon? Who cares, I'm doing it, and it's going to be fantastic!

The hardest part is figuring out what to wear. Naturally, I called in the most fashion-forward person I know. Meg.

"I'm so happy to hear your voice," she sighed after answering.

"You must be about to bust," I said. "What do you have? A month to go?"

"Yep. And I am. It's amazing how big I'm getting. I have no idea what my feet look like, but Mom and I are going for pedicures next week. Apparently once you get in the three-week window, labor can start at any time, and I'll be damned if I have my baby with chipped polish and scaly feet up in the air."

"You really are too much," I laughed. "But that's exactly why I'm calling!"

I could hear her frown. "You always had such nice feet. I chalked it up to all that walking in the sand."

"I am strangely not surprised that you've checked out my feet. But no! I've got a date!"

"Mmm!" she made a noise. I could only assume she was drinking something. "With who?"

"Well..." I closed my eyes and just said it. "My professor. Nick Parker."

"Your professor?" she shrieked. "Isn't that illegal?"

I snorted, dropping my head on the bed. "It's not illegal. But it is frowned upon. And I'm having the hardest time figuring out what to wear. I really like him. He's older and more mature. And I don't want to look like a kid."

"You always look beautiful," she said crunching on what sounded like popcorn. "Just wear what you would any time."

"That won't work." I sat up and stared at my open closet. "You know what I wear any time."

"And so does he, and he asked you out. So he must like it!"

"Your logic is sound, but we're not going to class." I stood and walked over to the hanging garments. "We're going to a restaurant in the Victorian District."

"Sounds very proper indeed," she said in a fake British accent.

"Good God, I hope not!" We both giggled again. "Oh, Meg, I'm so excited. Help me!"

She sighed. "What did you take with you? What are you looking at?"

I pulled two hangers apart. "I've got my maroon velvet top, and I was thinking about a long, flowy brown and maroon patterned skirt."

"That sounds very elegant!"

"It's something I'd wear to mass."

"Nope." She crunched again in my ear. "What's next?"

I kept flipping hangers aside. "I have a black shirt and jeans?"

"Too movie night. What about that blue sweater and your brown short skirt?"

I quickly swiped hangers to find it. "My blue sweater's a cardigan."

"So button it up! It'll give him something to think about unbuttoning later."

"You are *so* pregnant!" I laughed. "Are you just one big hormone now?"

"Practically. And the heartburn's killing me." She breathed deeply again, and it sounded like an effort. "You don't have to let him undo your cardigan, but it never hurts to have him thinking about it."

I shook my head. "Who ever knew you were so conniving?"

"How do you think I kept Billy Kyser on the hook for so long?"

"Clearly by being a total tease!"

She crunched again. "As my current condition proves, I was not teasing. So you're going to dinner and then what?"

"Then I don't know." I walked back to sit on my bed again, my knees crossed under me. "That's all he said."

"How old is he?" I could hear her frown.

"Not sure, but he looks young. He can't be over thirty."

"That sounds *tres risqué*. And he's handsome?"

I stretched out on my side across the bed. "Very. Dark hair, green eyes, killer smile."

"Um-hm," I heard her smile. "I expect all the details."

I sighed after we hung up. Meg was great at boosting my confidence, and I'd been meaning to check in with her anyway. I'd lost track of time since school started, and she'd be giving birth before long.

I'd hoped to visit her again before then, but it seemed our lives were diverging. I shook my head. No time for that.


*Oct. 23, 19 –*


It happened... and it was even better than I imagined it would be!

I was swept off my feet the moment Nick arrived to pick me up with one long-stemmed red rose in his hand. We chatted all through dinner about art and getting established in the field. It was a dream come true dating a man who's also an artist like me.

Being a professor, he's very in the know, and he told me all about new techniques and trends he sees coming. And we discussed colors and textures and ways of looking at the world. Even Suzanne isn't that tuned into the medium. She's all lines and pixels.

After dinner we took a carriage ride through Forsythe Park, and he put his arm around my shoulders. My heart was flying, and I could barely breathe wondering if he might kiss me. He didn't in the carriage, but he did ask if I would keep it quiet that we were seeing each other. That way, he said, I won't have to worry about anyone questioning my grade.

Not that he thinks I need assistance, of course. He said I've got a lot of potential to go far in the art world. I could've told him that.

Outside my apartment, he gave me the most innocent kiss on the cheek. I was almost disappointed until he said something about next time and even hinted at us spending a weekend together on Tybee Island. I didn't want to seem immature and unsophisticated, so I was very *blasé* about the whole thing. I pretended it was all very old hat to me, but the truth was I was wigging out inside.

I've never spent a weekend alone with a guy, and I'm a little embarrassed to say I've never even done *that* with a guy.

Give me a break, Journal! It's not like there were so many options back home. I always figured it would happen when it happened, which until now hasn't happened.

I will definitely have to call Meg again before I see him.

Of course, Suzanne was waiting up to hear the whole thing start to finish. I had to make her swear not to tell anyone. Not that I mind if she does, but after he asked me to keep it quiet, I couldn't tell him I'd already blabbed to my roommate. That would definitely be unsophisticated. She still says I'm making a big mistake, but I'm ignoring her. What's college if you don't try new things? We're just getting started, and I want to see where this adventure leads.


*Jan. 10, 19 —*


Christmas break's over, and I'm back at school. It couldn't get here fast enough! Sorry I left you here in Savannah, Journal, but I can quickly fill in what you missed.

Of course, I had to go home to see Meg and her precious little Will. What a doll he is. I never realized how small new babies are! I spent almost every day at her house holding him and talking to her about being a new mommy and about Nick.

Before I left for the break, he again mentioned us spending a weekend on Tybee Island together, and I'm so nervous. At least Meg has some experience in that department.

"How do I know if I'm doing it right?" I whispered, looking around to be sure no one overheard me.

"Lexy, you're almost twenty years old," she scolded. "If you have to ask that, he is *not* massaging the right button. It should come naturally."

"But what if it doesn't?" I looked down at little Will lying asleep in my arms. "I'm scared, Meg. I don't know what I'm doing, and... Ugh!" I shook my head. "The sisters at Little Flower would have a cow if they knew I was even thinking of this."

"If the sisters at Little Flower have a cow, I'd be more concerned about what they're doing than what you're doing."

We both burst into giggles.

I played with Will's baby foot while Meg leaned back on the couch. "He's so handsome," I sighed. "He's the first guy I've ever cared for who gets it when I talk about sensory experience and how it influences the way you create images."

Meg lifted a long strand of her hair and started braiding it. "Sounds right up your alley."

"I've been dying for him to touch me since our first date, but you know..."

"I know." She said the words through her breath. "You've never done it before, and you're scared."

"And he doesn't know I've never done it before. It might freak him out."

"I certainly don't know why." She rolled to her side to look at me. "At least he'll know you're clean."

"Oh, god. Don't even bring that up! I've already been guessing all the terrible things that are going to happen to me if I do it."

"Stop psyching yourself out," she fussed. "Use protection, and it should be a lovely experience for you."

"Should be?" My brow creased, and tension filled my shoulders again.

"Well, I've never met the guy. I trust you that he's dreamy and romantic, but it helps if I've seen him and talked to him myself. Then I could give you a more confident assessment."

She was right. It wasn't fair to put her on the spot and expect her to know anything about him. Instead, I opted for Suzanne once we were back, having our reunion night at the Buccaneer. Naturally, she went all broken record on me.

"No!" she cried. "No, no, no. You should not by any means have sex with your professor!"

"You're so blunt." I groaned, taking a big sip of my beer.

"Why are we sugar-coating it? Do you know how much trouble you could get in?"

"I'm of age. It's not like we're doing anything illegal."

"Still. What will you say when your entire academic career is called into question over one weekend of passion?"

"Mmm," I smiled, running my finger up and down the side of my frosty mug. "When you put it like that, I say who cares!"

Suzanne rolled her eyes, but that settled it. A weekend on Tybee Island it was.


*Feb. 1, 19 —*


So my weekend on Tybee Island was... informative. And not at all what I was expecting.

We arrived late in the afternoon, so we strolled on the beach a bit, talked about art and ideas for paintings, then when it got darker, we went back to the house Nick had rented.

He opened a bottle of champagne, and I joined him on the large pillows he'd placed on the floor in front of the fireplace. A few sips, and he was sliding toward me, kissing my neck, my shoulder, sliding my hair away from my face and tracing a line with his tongue behind my ear. That part was very good. My body was humming, and my breath came quickly. I tried to put my glass down when his hands fumbled their way under my shirt and quickly to my breasts. A little noise slipped from my throat as he caressed and pinched lightly. I'd never been touched that way by anyone.

It was hot, and everywhere his hands went caught fire beneath my skin. But I couldn't seem to catch up with him or find his rhythm. I finally got my glass to the table without spilling too much wine down my arm. I wanted to find his skin, to slide my hands over his chest and really invest in the moment. We were *making love*.

But he was already under my skirt when I turned back, pushing it up over my hips and tugging my panties down. I barely registered the sound of the foil wrapper in his hands when he laid me back against the pillows, and I felt his eager first thrust. No hesitation, no question, just in.

Pain killed my mood. Pain and an uncomfortable feeling of fullness. I tried to adjust my position, but Nick didn't seem to notice any of my discomfort. He gasped a few times. His voice was strangled as he ground out something like *so tight* and continued thrusting. I held my breath and bit my lip, trying not to cry out, and after a few more minutes, it was over.

Seriously.

Over.

He rose above me, swirled his tongue around in my mouth a few times, and then stretched back on the pillows with a satisfied sigh. He reached for me, pulling my head onto his chest then he stroked my cheek and back. Before long his hand stilled and his breathing turned heavy. I was stunned. That was it?

A few minutes went by, and he didn't move. He was definitely out for the night. I rolled over onto my side, out of his arms, staring at the wall as a single tear slid down my nose. That was not what I expected from Mr. Sensory Experience. Especially not for our first time.

Then I felt it coming.

I jumped up and dashed to the restroom just in time to catch the first drop. I sat on the toilet for at least ten minutes wiping and trying to apply pressure. Was this normal? Did everyone bleed this much? I put my head against the sink and silently prayed that I wouldn't die. I knew something bad was going to happen to me for this, but please, please, please don't let it be something bad *and* humiliating, like hemorrhaging to death in his bathroom.

Then I really started to cry.

If my mother were around, we would probably have talked about this when I was in high school. If it weren't midnight, I could call Meg. As it was, I didn't have anybody to talk to. I was on my own.

I sniffed a few times and straightened up. Taking a deep breath, I grabbed the reins and acted like the college woman I was. I got myself together, grabbed a pantiliner and crept back to the bed to sleep alone.

The next day, Nick apologized for "dozing off," he called it. He explained it was the late nights grading midterm projects and promised to make up for it. I decided to give him the benefit of the doubt, and the next night we tried again—this time in the bed. He started again, kissing my neck, his hands sliding under my shirt to my breasts. I was able to join in the experience a bit more, opening his shirt and kissing his chest. Sadly, he wasn't as defined as I'd hoped, but he was a bit older than me.

When he pulled me onto his lap this time, it didn't hurt as much. I tried to rock into him more, remembering Meg's explanations of her honeymoon techniques. He liked what I was doing, I could tell by his groans and gasps of how good I felt. And then, just as it was getting good for me, it was over. My lips tightened. Clearly, he hadn't really been talking about how good *I* felt, as his firework went off just as mine was getting lit. And then like before, instead of trying for more, he simply slid me off his lap, put my cheek on his chest, and went to sleep.

I lay in the darkness with my brow creased. I didn't get it. I had to be doing something wrong. Was my body going too slow? Did some women finish faster? Was I missing a step? I so wanted to call Meg and ask her, but it would have to wait until I got back.

*Feb. 2, 19 —*

Suzanne thought my weekend of bad sex and narcolepsy was beyond hilarious. She rolled on her bed laughing at my confusion and disappointment.

"I told you not to date a professor," she said, shaking her head. "He can't help it if he's old and can't keep his eyes open."

"He's not that old!" I argued. "I'm thinking I must've been doing something wrong."

"In my experience, a guy would never poop out with someone like you in his bed. Unless he was doing some seriously heavy drinking."

"He wasn't! We had a few glasses of champagne. You know, enough to take the edge off, and that was it." I tugged my feet onto the bed. "And he didn't poop out before. Just immediately after. I don't know what to think."

"I think you need to find a hot young stud your own age and get treated right. This guy's a dud. Throw him back."

My lips pressed into a frown. "I can't. I like him, and well, he's my first. I want it to be special."

Suzanne shook her head. "You're very sweet, but few of us get that magical first experience. Actually, I'm trying to think if I've ever heard of anyone having that."

I wondered about Meg. I really did need to get her take on the whole thing. But I didn't have a chance to talk to her before Nick was calling me again for another date.

This time it was a completely different ballgame. Dinner led to drinks and then back to his apartment. We were barely inside the door before he dropped to his knees and was lifting my skirt, removing my panties. My back was to the wall, and I could barely catch my breath or the back of his head as he kissed me, exploring with his tongue in a way that shot me over the edge at lightning speed. Then just as quickly he stood back up, lifting me higher and finishing the experience. I was confused, but boy was I satisfied. And at least I understood now what everybody was talking about. I wondered why *this* Professor Parker hadn't shown up for our dirty weekend.

"Maybe he really was tired from exams and grading." I argued to Suzanne when I got home and told her how it went this time.

"Maybe," she frowned. "That just seems weird to me. You sure he wasn't sneaking anything on Tybee Island when you weren't looking?"

"I never smelled or saw anything."

She made a face.

"Well, I don't care," I said. "Tonight was fantastic. Oh my god. And I'm glad we're over the hump."

"Sounds to me like you just found it."

I rolled my eyes and laughed. Suzanne was the perfect roommate.

*May 8, 19 —*

This semester just flew by, Journal!

I spent practically every weekend with Nick. I even started sleeping over at his apartment some nights during the week. It all started when he suggested I come back to his place after class on a Wednesday afternoon, so he could show me a new technique. I thought he'd been talking about art until I walked in the door and he caught me by the waist, sliding my stomach onto the dining room table.

I wasn't sure what to do, but I soon understood as his hand slid my panties to the side. He massaged the front as he entered from behind, and it didn't take long for the fireworks to go off. I couldn't breathe as his lips made their way from my hair to behind my ear and down my neck. His hand never stopping below my waist, and I decided this was a technique we should add to our private curriculum for further exploration.

The year was like a dream being with him, and it wasn't all just physical. We talked about my plans to be a fine artist, and he said I was doing it at the perfect time. Big corporations were hiring artists to create looks for entire buildings, and he thought with my distinctive style, I could attract the attention of companies in Atlanta and Nashville. Possibly even beyond. He thought Houston and places in Texas would be interested in using my vibrant, beachy style. I spent the entire spring semester loving being in love, believing it was forever.

Finals week sneaked up on me, and I was happily finishing my class projects when I realized it was almost time for summer. Sadly, Raku pottery never emerged as my alternate medium, and I decided to let it go after I shattered almost every vessel I made. My instructor was very understanding, and I still ended up with an *A*. I suppose it was for effort, or maybe it was just a pity grade. It was abundantly clear how hard I was trying to get it right. I just did not have the knack.

By contrast, I felt pretty confident about my grade in painting class, and I was just finishing up my final piece when Nick asked me stay after on our last day of exams.

"Yes, Mr. Parker," I said with a sly grin as I entered his office.

"Alexandra. I've been meaning to talk to you about the summer break. Are you planning to go back to Alabama?"

"I haven't decided. I mean, I don't have to go back. I'm sure I could take some summer classes if you liked."

"You should only do that if you want to. I was recently offered the chance to study with a master painter in Paris."

I almost couldn't breathe. "Paris! How wonderful!" I couldn't believe he was asking me to go to Paris with him! Could I afford it? How would this even work?

"Yes, it's a rare opportunity," he said. "I'm very excited about it, but it means I'm going to be very busy. I wanted to let you know in case you had some summer courses you needed to take…"

"No. I'm free! And I would love to go to Paris with you."

"Oh," he paused. Then he shifted uncomfortably. "And I would certainly love to escort you. But I don't think I'll have any time for fun, and Paris is a long way away."

The room grew quiet as I realized he was not inviting me to go with him. I could feel the bright red slowly creeping into my cheeks. "I'm so sorry!" My breathy laugh sounded too high. "I feel so stupid. I completely misunderstood—"

"I didn't mean to imply," he paused, then his tone changed. He almost sounded fatherly. "Alexandra. You know I love the time when we're together." He walked over and put his arm across my shoulders. "But sometimes there are periods of separation."

"Of course." My silly eyes went blurry, and I fought crying with every ounce of my strength. "I'm sorry I jumped ahead of you. I've got lots of things to do here. Please go and have a wonderful time."

He patted my arm. "That's my girl. You'll be alright then?"

I nodded too vigorously. "I'll be fine! I'll head home, do some painting, catch up with friends."

"My pretty little painter," he sighed, touching my chin. "You have the most exquisite face. I'm leaving Friday, so I probably won't have time to see you again before I go."

He kissed me on the cheek and then exited his office. I couldn't move. That was it? He was leaving Friday? Would he even call? I rose on trembling legs and walked back to my apartment.

Suzanne was there. She was packing to go home for the summer, and I imagined I'd be doing the same pretty soon. When I walked in, she did a double-take before walking over to hold my hand.

"What's the matter, Lex? You look like you failed a class."

I felt like I'd been hit with a bat right in the stomach. "He's leaving for Paris on Friday," I managed to say.

My roommate frowned. "Who's leaving for Paris?"

"Nick." I dropped slowly to the bed. "He asked me to stay after class so he could tell me he's leaving for Paris on Friday and won't be back 'til the fall."

She stopped packing and came to sit beside me on the bed. "Oh, honey. Are you okay?"

I couldn't look at her. I was having trouble focusing on anything. "I don't know. I mean, he didn't say we were breaking up. He just said he'd be very busy and he wouldn't have time to entertain me."

"You weren't thinking you'd go to Paris with him alone?" she said. "For one, you don't even speak French."

I shook my head, still numb. "It doesn't matter because I wasn't invited."

She sat on the bed and looked at me. "What are you thinking?"

"I'm just... I don't know what to think." I looked down at my hands in my lap as flickers of pain began radiating out from the center of my chest. I felt the muscles in my cheeks start to pull as tears flooded my eyes.

When she spoke this time, Suzanne's voice was soft. "I think he's a total dirt bag, and now he's broken your heart."

"Has he?" I looked up at her blinking fast, tears dropping onto my cheeks, which I hastily wiped away. "I mean, he said we were having a period of separation. I mean, I guess that means I should just wait and see what happens when he gets back."

"I wouldn't wait for him," she said hugging me close. "Not for one second."

*June 20, 19 —*

Suzanne was right. I shouldn't have waited for him. But I've spent half the summer doing just that, thinking about Nick and counting the days until fall classes will begin again. He's just so encouraging to me in my art, and he's so sexy to be with.

I can't complain that he mistreated me somehow by going to Paris alone. I'm probably just too young and immature. I don't understand this is how adult relationships sometimes go — periods of separation like he said. And it's only for the summer!

Being back at Miss Stella's house is wonderful. I love being in my old room and waking up in the mornings to the smell of her rich coffee. Miss Stella is a classic old Southern lady. Her big Victorian home is stuffed with antiques and lace and old Edwardian chairs and armoires, and her yard is a garden of flowering plants and trees.

I remember arriving at her home when I was only five years old. I thought I'd moved into a castle. She took me in and bought me a whole new wardrobe and enrolled me at the Magnolia School with Meg. She opened a new world to me full of refined tastes and experiences. Since I've gotten back for the summer, I've pretty much just hung around the house with her.

Occasionally, I'll walk down to the shore, but mostly I wait. Wait for the days to pass and fall to come.

I was at the beach reading a book when Bill stopped by for an unexpected visit. The last time I'd seen him was when I'd visited Meg and Will at Christmas.

"What brings you to Port Hogan?" I said. "I thought you were taking classes nonstop."

"Heard you were back," he said, that serious expression on his face as always. "Miss Stella said you were down here."

Bill never visited me, and I had to confess, the suspense was killing me. "So what's up?"

He flopped down on the sand beside me. "How's art school going?"

"Really?" I creased my brow. "You're here to talk about art school?"

He looked down at his hands and shook his head. "No, I was just wondering if you were happy there or if you thought you might move back home."

I exhaled a laugh. "I didn't expect you to miss me so much."

"I have reasons for asking."

I took a deep breath before answering. "Truthfully? I don't expect to be moving home for a while, if ever. Why?"

"I just know Meg misses you." He looked up at me with those bright blue eyes of his. "She's been hanging out with Winifred Hayes, and that woman is a damned nuisance."

I laughed. "That's the first time I've ever heard you say a word about Meg's friends. She must be pretty bad."

He looked back down, and I watched him slide a finger through the sand. "Will you be home all summer?"

I nodded. "At least another month or so."

"Maybe you and Meg could get together. Get her away from her new friend."

I sat up fast and dusted my palms together. "Why don't you talk to Meg about this yourself? I mean, she is your wife now. This is the kind of thing husbands and wives talk about with each other."

"I'm not interested in arguing with her over her friends."

"You don't have to argue."

He sat up and assessed my little beach camp. "What are you doing out here? Reading?"

"Trying to, but there's so much talking."

He frowned, but I laughed. "You want me to call Meg and invite her out?" I asked.

"How about you come over for dinner Friday? She's inviting those two, and you can see what I'm talking about."

"Are you inviting me to dinner Friday?" I teased. "We really have grown closer."

He stood all the way up then, dusting off his pants. "I'm sure Meg'll say something about it when you call her. Our house at seven."

"I'll see you then."

I watched him walk back to his truck waiting at Mrs. Stella's house. I'd never really understood Bill Kyser, but he was turning out to be okay. When we were in school, I'd given him a hard time about his big plan, but mostly it was just something I did.

I don't want to see high-rises taking over our hometown, but I don't really think stopping Bill is going to keep them from coming. Those developers have been marching their way from Panama City westward for years, snatching up undeveloped tracts of sand and stabbing in towering concrete masses everywhere you look.

I just started riding Bill about his plan one day and never seemed to quit. Maybe I could change that. I guess

I'm more sensitive to people's feelings since mine have taken it on the chin.

I gave Meg a call and got on the guest list for that dinner.

*Aug. 1, 19 –*

August at last! I'm back in Savannah.

Sorry you got neglected, Journal. What did I not write down?

Oh! That dinner with Meg and Bill was actually fun. I totally got what Bill was saying about Winnie and Travis Hayes. And what kind of name is Winifred anyway? Those people were too much, and I was sorry Meg was left with only that type of superficial "friend" to spend her time.

Saying goodbye to her had been hard. Even little Will cried when I left, which naturally made me cry. We had been together nonstop after that dinner. I'd painted Will's portrait, and Meg had said she was going to have it framed and put in his room in their little cottage. I told her I'd paint her another, bigger one of him when they finished their house on the island.

Now, finally, I'm back at school. Suzanne's back as well, but she only brought a small suitcase and isn't moving in. When she told me why, my heart broke. She landed an internship at a big advertising agency in Atlanta, and I have to find a new roommate after the first week of classes.

"I can't believe you're abandoning me like this," I said. "Who will I go to for advice on my love life?"

"You say that as if you've ever listened to anything I told you," she smirked, tossing an arm over my shoulders.

"I listened. It's just, sometimes I have to do some trial and error work, that's all."

"You should look up Evan," she said, placing her head against mine. "He's back, and the summer months were very good to him."

I sighed. "Evan's nice, but he wasn't too thrilled when I cut things off abruptly last fall."

She smiled and gave me a squeeze before releasing me. "As pretty as you are, I think you could change his mind if you wanted."

"Besides, I'm still with Nick," I said, trying to be positive. "I can't go chasing after somebody else when I'm still seeing him."

She gave me a skeptical look. "And have you seen the narcoleptic professor yet?"

I pushed her arm. "Stop calling him that. No, I haven't made it to his office yet, but I'm planning to give him a call in a few days."

"A few days? If you guys are so together, what are you waiting for?"

I looked down. "I was hoping he might call me first."

"Oh, Alex. You're hopeless."

I didn't need her to tell me that.


*Aug. 25, 19 –*

Several days did go by, and I never heard from Nick. I called and left a few messages, but he never returned my calls. I decided to chalk it up to the craziness of getting back in town from a trip abroad and preparing for the start of classes, but I was getting a sick feeling in my gut.

School was in session, and this year I'd signed up for figure drawing. I knew the instructor Ms. Finch shared Nick's room, and that had been part of my motivation for taking the class. Now I was dreading getting there, but I had to face this sooner or later. I decided to make it sooner and arrived early.

My heart stopped when I saw him. There he was, his shaggy dark hair swept back, his long elegant hands spanning a finished piece as he made a point about color or composition on the canvass. I could hear the vibration of his voice, and I leaned my head against the door frame watching him through the glass. He was dressed in his usual blazer and jeans, and I imagined sliding my hands up his body underneath them. I wished we could blow off classes and spend the afternoon catching up.

It was very selfish of me to begrudge him a trip to study with a master painter. Now he could show me all he'd learned, and it would be like I'd gone and studied with a master too.

I tore my eyes off him to survey the new class of students. Freshmen. They were so bright-eyed and chubby-cheeked. The excitement and nervousness of not knowing what to expect and not wanting to fail was plain on their faces, and in some of the eyes I recognized my own first-year infatuation with this handsome instructor who stood there holding the keys to all things art.

Nick stepped down from the platform to make his way around the room. I remembered his way of checking each canvass and offering constructive criticism. His tips were usually helpful and not petty or small the way some art instructors' were. I saw him pat a male student on the back, and then he stopped at the canvass of a pretty blonde female. He pointed to the top of the canvass and then turned to look at her. He smiled. He turned back to stand beside her and look at her work. His hand went down and lightly rested on her lower back…

"Alex, you're here!"

I almost jumped out of my skin at the sound of Evan's voice. I turned quickly, putting my back against the wall outside the classroom, and noticed Suzanne was right, he had changed. He'd filled out or something. His shoulders seemed broader, but I couldn't care. I couldn't see anything except Nick caressing that pretty blonde student.

"Are you feeling okay?" Evan's brow creased. "You look like you're going to puke."

"I'm sorry." I shook my head and looked down. "I was just early for my next class. How was your summer?"

"No complaints here," he said. Then he leaned past me to look through the window. "Looks like Professor Slimeball's found his newest Freshmeat. Can you believe that guy?"

I blinked. "Who? Professor Parker?"

"He's infamous. It's the same game every year," Evan groaned. "Finds some unsuspecting freshman to hook up with then ditches her just in time for summer break. Asshole. Didn't he try that shit with you last year?"

My stomach felt like it was lurching. "Yeah," I said. "We went out a few times."

"Well, good thing you're smarter than that." Evan placed his arm across my shoulder, but he was right. I did feel like I was going to puke. "So I was thinking, we never seemed to make a connection last year. Maybe we could try again? You up for grabbing some lunch with me sometime?"

I had to get away from Evan and this building and the stench of old walls and molding paint before I lost my breakfast. "I gotta go, Evan. I'll see ya around."

I turned and fled back to my room as the tears started streaming down my face. I couldn't believe I'd been so stupid. I'd waited all summer to get back and throw my arms around him and tell him how much I'd missed him. I'd laid awake nights sweating in the heat and humidity of Miss Stella's poorly insulated old home thinking of him and wondering if he missed the touch of my hands and the feel of my lips as much as I missed his.

I was such a fool.

My apartment was empty, and I threw myself on the bed to cry until I had no more tears left. Hours later, Suzanne came home. She only had a few days before she moved to Atlanta, and I didn't know what I'd do without her.

"Alex? You here?" I was curled in a ball in the center of my bed listening to her bang through the door. "What's up?" she called.

I rolled over to look at her, not even sure if I wanted to talk yet. I shook my head.

"Oh my God!" She crossed the room to me quickly. "You're a wreck! What happened?"

My voice sounded almost feral as I wept out the answer. "I saw Nick."

"And?" she urged.

"And nothing. I didn't even speak to him. He was teaching a class and then he went and started touching this blonde girl."

---

151

"Touching? What do you mean? Like he was feeling her up?"

"No, he put his hand on her back."

Suzanne shook her head. "I'm lost. Have you been back here crying all day because you saw Mr. Parker put his hand on another girl's back? Don't you think that's overreacting a bit?"

I sniffed, wiping my nose with the back of my hand. "It's the way he put his hand on her back. Down low like he used to do mine."

She slumped back. "Well, did you talk to him about it? Did you at least stop in and ask about Paris?"

I rolled over and put my face in the pillow. "No. I saw Evan first."

"And yeah, right? Evan wins 'most improved male student' this year."

I shook my head, face still in the pillow. "I don't know. He looked different I guess, but it was more what he said."

"Which was?"

"That Nick does this every year. He picks up with some new 'fresh-meat' and then dates her until summer break. Just like he did with me."

Suzanne pressed her lips together. "You have to confront him."

"I don't want to confront him. I want to die."

But my roommate was getting mad. She stood and started pacing our small apartment. "You have to go in and act like nothing happened and give him the chance to either say it was nothing or break up with you. You can't just throw in the towel over a potential misunderstanding."

"You think it was a misunderstanding?" My voice rose a bit.

"I think you need to find out."

Suzanne was right, although I knew in the pit of my stomach this was going to go badly. "He hasn't returned any of my calls," I said. "Don't you think that means something?"

"It might, or it might not. What if his phone's not working?"

"I never took you as an optimist."

"And I never took you as a quitter."

*Aug. 30, 19 –*

So here's how it all went down, Journal. Today I left early again for class, and while he wrapped up his lecture, I slipped into Nick's office before he saw me. As the students were leaving, I saw him talking to the blonde freshman again, but I decided to stay put and focus on Suzanne's words. I was no quitter.

Before long he walked through the door. When he saw me, he seemed to tense. "Alexandra! What a pleasant surprise."

"I didn't mean to surprise you," I said. "I tried to call a few times, but I guess you didn't get my messages."

"Oh, I got them," he smiled, stepping forward to kiss my head. "It's just been so busy with classes starting and getting back into the swing of fall semester."

"How was Paris?" I asked.

"What? Oh, Paris. Very French." He laughed.

"Is that good?"

"That depends on how you feel about the French."

I wasn't letting him off that easily. "And how do you feel about the French?"

"It varies from day to day, but enough about me. How was your summer?"

"Short, but long at the same time." I studied his face. "I missed you."

He smiled, making his eyes go warm. "My sweet little painter. That's kind of you to say."

I waited, and when it became clear he was finished speaking, I curled my toes and jumped in. "So when are we getting together again? I was hoping we could catch up."

He shook his head and walked around his desk, back to me. "I'm afraid my schedule is going to be so full this semester. I'm sure you understand. You're probably just as busy, no?"

I crossed my arms, determined to make him say it. "I can make time for you. I always have."

"Yes, well," he turned to face me then, a sad little smile on his lips. "I guess what I'm saying is maybe it's time for us to stop making time."

My jaw clenched. "What do you mean?"

"I mean..." he dropped into his chair. "Oh, what do I mean? It was fun while it lasted? Let's don't make this hard, Alexandra. Just shake hands, and we'll walk away."

I nodded. "So you're breaking up with me."

He sighed, placing his hands behind his head. "That's such an unkind way to put it. I prefer we're bidding *adieu*."

"What if I don't want to bid *adieu*," I said. "What if I want us to be together?"

He lowered his hands, breathing deeply. Then he leaned forward on his desk. "I was afraid of that. I knew this would happen after Christmas when I realized I was your first." He chuckled, "and here I thought all you country girls were so experienced. Didn't you have a boyfriend in high school with a Chevy?"

My face grew hot. "You knew?"

"Not initially, of course, but as it was happening, I could tell what was going on. I tried to be gentle, and I hope I gave you enough space after… to take care of yourself."

I felt ill. "You mean, you went to sleep on purpose?"

He shrugged, "I really was telling the truth when I said grading midterms just wiped me out. I was tired! Besides, what could I have done? Those things are best handled on one's own."

My body was vibrating with shame and anger and wanting to kill him. "I can't believe this. Both nights?"

He shrugged. "I figured that's how long it would take. And I was right, wasn't I? By our next meeting, you were all fixed up."

I stood quickly, turning to the door. "I've got to go."

"What? Have I offended you?" He dared to sound concerned. "Don't be that way, Alexandra. We had a lot of good times after that."

"I think you're right," I said. "It's time we said goodbye."

I grabbed my portfolio and dashed out of his office. Pushing my way through the bodies in the hall, all I could think of was how frightened I'd felt that night and how alone I'd been. And in his mind I was simply taking care of an annoying distraction.

Tears were filling my eyes, and my breath was coming in short hiccups. I thought I loved him. I devoted myself to him all last year. Whenever he called, I dropped everything to run to his side, and now he was telling me I was just another dalliance. Another face in a long line of forgettable rejects.

I didn't want to cry for that scumbag as Evan had appropriately labeled him, but tears were streaking my cheeks as I climbed the stairs to our apartment. I had to leave Savannah. There was no way I could enter that classroom again. I couldn't see his face or run into him in the halls without the shame burning a hole through my body. I would have to figure out another way to take the art world by storm. It wasn't going to happen for me here.

Just then the phone rang. For half a second, I thought it might be Nick. I thought maybe he'd remembered what we'd had and was calling to beg me to come back. He would tell me he was sorry, and he was changing his ways. I'd be the last freshman art student he'd introduce to the ways of the world and then unceremoniously dump.

I hesitated for a moment before pressing the button to take the call. It was Meg, and she was crying, too. "Lexy! Oh, Lexy, I need you to come back right away."

"Meg?" I could feel myself pulling together. Involuntarily, my pain was surrendering to my concern for my friend. "What's wrong? Has something happened to Will?"

"No, it's Daddy. He was at his office, and the nurse said she hadn't seen him for a while. They were worried, and when they went to check on him, he was passed out. Nobody knew what was wrong, but they think he had a heart attack." She sobbed hard into the phone. "Oh, Lexy. He's dead."

"I'll be right there."

*Sept. 7, 19 –*

Dr. Weaver's sudden death surprised the entire community. There wasn't a dry eye at the funeral. I was glad to have the excuse to cry. I was broken-hearted for Meg losing her dad so unexpectedly, but I was also reeling from my own loss.

Losing a jerk like Nick Parker was admittedly insignificant compared to the loss of a doting parent, but it was still devastating to me. I'd trusted him. I'd told him all my dreams and my goals for the future and my art. I'd slept with him, given him my virginity. But he was just playing around, waiting for the next bright-eyed dreamer to enroll in his art class. I'd never felt so stupid in my life. God, I was so humiliated.

I sat behind the family at the funeral, and I could feel Meg glance at me every few minutes. Being in the middle of all that raw emotion really brought it out in me, and the tears wouldn't stop coming. After the service was over and we were back at her house, she took me aside to talk.

"What's going on?" she whispered. "You haven't stopped crying all day, and I mean, I know you really liked Daddy, but you guys weren't that close."

"Oh, Meg," I sniffed. "I'm just so sorry for you, and for little Will... not getting to know his grandfather. It seems so unfair. And your mom looks like she's really taking it hard. They were so close."

"Um-hm," she blinked her red eyes. "What's happened to you?"

I couldn't hide it anymore. I burst into tears. "I feel so ashamed and stupid. Nick completely humiliated me, and I don't think I can go back to SCAD. It was so awful."

I could see my friend's personal pain surrendering to her concern for me, just like mine had for her, and I wanted to curl into her arms and never leave.

"What happened?" she said, smoothing my hair back from my face.

I sniffed and quickly told her everything that happened, from the unreturned phone calls to the pretty blonde in class to what Evan had said.

"Did you give him a chance to explain?" she asked, unable to believe it.

I nodded. "That's the best part. I did, and he said last year was fun, but I was getting too attached. He said he was afraid that would happen, his being my first and all."

Everything in her face stilled. "He said that?"

"Yes." And the humiliation washed over me afresh.

"Okay, I take it all back. That guy's a complete jackass. I hate him." I watched her jaw clench. "There's got to be something we can do to get him back."

"Just forget it." I shook my head. "But I'm seriously considering dropping out. The school is so small, and I'll have to see him all the time."

She reached out and held both my hands. "I'm so sorry, Lex."

"No, I'm sorry," I said. "Here I am at your dad's funeral, and all I can think about is myself. I'm the most selfish person."

"You're not!" She threw her arms around me, and we hugged each other. "You had a horrible experience. That guy's a monster. Of course you're miserable."

We leaned back, still holding each other's arms. "But you can't quit school," she said. "Then he wins! What if you… I don't know, took a semester off or something? What do you think? Is there someone you could talk to about it?"

I shrugged. "Maybe a counselor, but I couldn't say why."

Meg rose and crossed the room, beautiful even in all-black. "Use Daddy as your excuse. Pretend he was like a father to you, and say you're taking it so hard. I'll back you up."

"Oh, Meg." She came and hugged me again, and all I could think of were her old words. How it was so wonderful to be home with people who loved me.


*Sept. 10, 19 —*

Wow. Reading back over that last entry, so much has changed! Everything, it seems. Let's see… I'm living in Atlanta now. Yes — Atlanta! I know, that was fast.

After the funeral, I *did* return to SCAD. Sure, I was humiliated and my heart was destroyed, but Meg was right. And I knew it. I wouldn't let a loser like Nick Parker take away my dream. I was stronger than that, and I wasn't quitting or running home.

And then Suzanne came up with an even better idea for taking my mind off the problem.

"Come work with me in Atlanta," she said.

"What?" I almost dropped everything.

She hopped on the bed in front of me, excited. "I've taken a job at Stellar Advertising in Roswell, and they're looking for fine arts people to create new concepts for some of their other clients. Very prestigious, ritzy-looking stuff. You'll be perfect."

"But I don't know anything about graphic design. I don't know how to use the software —"

"I'll teach you," she said. "It won't matter at first. You can sketch out your ideas and present them on storyboard. Then when they love them, which they will, I'll help you get them on the computer."

"Suzanne!" I grasped her arms. "You're the best friend ever! But what about school?"

"I've worked it out with my advisor so it can be like an internship and count for credit. Of course we'll get paid, but we also won't lose our place at school. I know they'll do the same for you."

And that's how I ended up here, living with Suzanne in a suite apartment on Piedmont, in an old historic part of town undergoing gentrification.

The two of us walk to Marta each day to catch the red line to Roswell where our offices are located, and it's the perfect solution. I'm working in the big city on projects that move fast and end up everywhere.

Suzanne is right, marketing is a fabulous field, and Professor Nick Parker is fast becoming a distant memory.


*Jan. 19, 19 –*

Not a single entry in four months, sorry Journal. So much for this historic record.

Let's see… So much has happened. How much time do I have?

For starters, I'm home. For good.

It's been a week, and I'm back in Miss Stella's big old house, feeling almost like I never left. But it's a good thing. No, it's a *great* thing.

I know. Two years ago, I'd never have believed I'd say something like that. And the last time I was here was right after Nick had dumped me. Dr. Weaver had just died, and I was considering quitting altogether, running back and hiding in a world where I knew everyone and where everyone loved and appreciated me.

Instead, I went back to face Nick and school, and wouldn't you know, it turned out to be the best semester of my life. Suzanne and I ruled Stellar Advertising, and I still can't believe I agreed to leave it all and come back here to work with Bill.

He says I'm working with Bryant also, but I know who's guiding this ship. If it weren't for Bill's dream, none of this would be happening.

And he's right. There's a lot to be said for working with friends and being back home. I didn't want to get lost in the corporate world, and Atlanta was so fast. In only six months, I was equipped with all the latest gadgets, and I didn't sleep unless every one of them was buzzing with messages and updates. I lost weight from keeping up with all the deadlines, and I also lost touch with my painting.

Suzanne taught me all about graphic design and computer-generated art, but seeing Bill again reminded me of home and how much I loved painting and being near the water. Life just flies past in the city. I didn't want to wake up an old lady with all the paintings I still had in my head faded and grey. I wanted to get them out and share them with the world.

Bill was in Atlanta meeting with investors when he called and asked me to dinner. Bryant was with him, and I expected a night of reminiscing, catching up, maybe a little bragging on how successful we all were. What I did not expect was to run into Nick Parker. Or to have Bill show him up the way he did. I was actually a little proud of my former frenemy. He knew how to play the white knight *very* well, and he made it look like I was something worth having. That Nick was a loser for not seeing it. It was an unexpected comfort, from an unexpected source that I very much appreciated.

When it was all over, he told me why he and Bryant really asked me to dinner. They wanted me to come home and work with them. They wanted to make me the Director of Marketing and Design for Kyser-Brennan Equities—creating the image for their entire corporate brand.

I have to confess, it was an offer I couldn't refuse.

So I didn't. I said yes. And here I am.

Wrapping up my work in Atlanta took longer than I expected. I was involved in several campaigns, and the partners tried to get me to stay. I almost changed my mind more than once. Why would I go back to south Alabama to work in development? It was a fickle field and very risky, and Bill didn't even have his company off the ground yet. For that matter, he wasn't even finished with college.

But I knew he would make it happen. And I don't know. I guess in Atlanta I saw something in him I hadn't seen before. He wasn't a kid anymore. None of us were. He was commanding when he needed to be, and it made me feel like I could trust him.

He'd done right by Meg, and I hadn't given their marriage a chance. But he'd proven me wrong. They were coming up on two years together now, and as far as I could tell, they were very happy. So I packed my bags and left the big city.

My last day walking to the Marta station cinched it. It was cold and windy, and I looked at the gray clouds thinking it might snow. Then I looked at the faces passing me on the street. They were all frowning and lined. To a person they had their heads down and were pushing forward, forward, forward. I thought of worker bees, and then I remembered that old expression about the Rat Race. I didn't want to be a rat. I wanted to be an artist.

I wanted to have color and fill this black, white, and gray world with beauty. I arrived at my office in Roswell a half hour later and cleaned out my desk.

The night I got home, Miss Stella was already in bed asleep, and I didn't want to wake her. I'd told her I was coming back, but I'd arrived a day early. I couldn't wait to be back home. The next morning I opened my eyes and breathed in the smells of coffee and hot, buttery toast. I was lying in bed looking at the sun streaming across the ceiling when she came into my room and sat beside me.

"My little bird is back in the nest," she said.

"And what a wonderful nest it is." I slid my head onto her lap and wrapped my arms around her broad middle. "Oh, Miss Stella. It's so good to be back here with you."

She combed her fingers through my hair. "I thought you'd stay in Atlanta. What in the world could Bill Kyser have said to make you come back?"

"Mmm. It wasn't anything he said so much as just a combination of how I was feeling and then him showing up and offering me a chance to come back. I wasn't happy there."

"Didn't you meet any young men in Atlanta?"

I shrugged in her arms. "A few. Suzanne and I would go out, and occasionally we'd meet some guys. But I never really connected with any of them. They were all so preoccupied with work and name-dropping and the importance of their clients. Always looking over my shoulder to see who was more important in the room." I sighed. "It was exhausting, always a competition."

"Don't tell me you were expecting to meet a nice young man in a bar?"

"Well, I certainly wasn't planning to date anyone from work."

"What about church?" she rubbed my arm. "Didn't you attend church anywhere? You can always find a nice man at church."

I chuckled into her waist. "I love you. And I'm afraid I didn't have much time for church." I gave her another squeeze and then sat up, leaning back against my pillows.

"That's not what I like to hear. And I don't like you being alone still. You're too pretty a girl."

"I'm sorry," I breathed. "I just can't seem to find anyone I like."

"More like you never give anyone a chance." We both looked down, and she continued quietly. "Not every man is like your father, Alexandra. They don't all abandon their families."

I shook my head. "It's not that. I just never seem to find anyone I'm comfortable with, and the one time I tried... I was burned. Badly."

"You can't let one bad apple spoil the bunch," she said, patting my hand. "You'll start coming to church with me, and we'll find someone for you to settle down with."

"Miss Stella," I grinned. "You're hopelessly old-fashioned. Don't you know young ladies these days don't need a man to settle down?"

"I'm sure I'm *very* old-fashioned, but I'll feel better knowing you have someone taking care of you."

"More like me taking care of him."

"The one who gives the care gets as much joy as the one receiving it," she said in her knowing way. "Sometimes more."

I bent my knees and wrapped my arms around them. "I think I'll just be like you. Take in some little orphan and care for it."

Her lips pursed. "That's not the same as having an adult relationship with a man. You need that, dear. It's the way God made us."

My eyebrows pulled together. "But you've been alone since your husband died."

"It hasn't been easy, and I was much older than you are now when I lost him." She patted my arm. "It would give me peace to know you were settled before I die."

I dove forward, hugging her waist again. "Well, if that's the reason, then forget the whole thing. I'd much rather have you."

She chuckled. "I'm not going to live forever, you know."

"I know," I sighed. "But can I at least get my feet under me first? I need to figure out what I'm doing here before I get distracted by one of your nice young men."

I climbed out of bed and prepared to shower. She stood and gave my shoulders a squeeze. "Don't take too long. I'd like to give you away at your wedding."

"That only makes me want to go slower."

She shook her head and left the room as I went to freshen up. I couldn't wait to hit the beach. It had been too long since I'd been on my own stretch of sand.

*Feb. 1, 19 –*

I think Bill expected me to check in when I arrived, but between classes and his family, I decided he could give me a few days to decompress and get back in the South County frame of mind.

I ended up taking a week.

Time moved astonishingly slower here, and I was finally starting to feel like my brain had stopped ticking at ninety miles per second. That morning I walked down to sit by the water and listen to the sounds of home.

My eyes were closed when I heard someone approaching, but I wasn't disturbed by the squeak of footsteps in the sand. When I opened my eyes and saw Bill dropping down beside me, I jumped. I was expecting Miss Stella coming to get me for breakfast.

"Hi, boss," I smiled.

"What're you doing down here?" he said, sitting so he could face me.

"Finding my inspiration." I closed my eyes again and breathed deeply.

"Does your inspiration say anything about checking in at work?"

"Hmm?" I slanted an eye open. "Nope. It's saying I should take a few more days to acclimate to a new environment."

"The new environment where you grew up?" I felt him lean back, but the warmth of his bent knees was still close to my arm.

"It's very different here from Atlanta," I said. "I need to find my rhythm again, my creativity."

"And how are you planning to do that?"

I opened both eyes then. "It's easier to show you if you're really interested."

"How bout you just tell me," he said.

"No, sit up." I pulled his arm until he was sitting straight beside me. "Now, here, cross your legs and face out at the water. Close your eyes and breathe. In and out. Listen to your breathing. The waves crashing, the gulls. See what other sounds you can hear."

"You talking…"

My shoulders fell. "Do you want to do this or not?"

"It seems like I said I didn't." I exhaled, and he relented. "Okay, what next."

"Close your eyes. Now, as you breathe, see what smells you notice."

His nose wrinkled. "Are you about to skunk me?"

"How old do you think I am?"

He peeked through one eye. "Same age as me."

"Well, I'm more mature. Just try it. I usually smell the salt water, sometimes fish, sometimes wood." I sat back on the sand beside him and put my chin on my knees looking out at the ocean. "It's about really concentrating on your surroundings and relaxing. Listening to your breathing and feeling your heart rate slow. They say the more relaxed you are, the more creative you are, and smell is the strongest mnemonic device."

"Mnemonic device," he repeated.

"Memory trigger."

"I thought mnemonics were like acronyms."

"Would you be quiet and cooperate?"

He sat there for a few seconds following my instructions. I turned my head to look at his face. I'd never really looked at Bill for any length of time. He was handsome, sure, but looking at him now, I decided he might make a good subject for a portrait. He wasn't perfect like Meg, and he had some interesting features…

167

His eyes opened suddenly, and I jumped. Then I laughed, pressing my forehead to my knees and blushing.

"What?" He smiled. "What were you thinking?"

"I'm sorry." I exhaled. "You caught me thinking I should paint your portrait sometime. That's all."

"Hey, that would be cool. I could put it in the lobby or something. Maybe you could do one of me and Bryant together in our suits. Conquerors of the coast."

I made a face. "See if you can grab the reins on that ego. I wouldn't do it until you're much older. Maybe as a retirement gift."

His brow creased. "Retirement?"

"Well, maybe I won't wait that long."

"So how does it work?" he said. "Would you take a picture or would I have to sit for hours without moving?"

"I could probably do it from memory," I said, holding my hands up to frame his face. "I'm more of an impressionist than a realist. I mean, my paintings look realistic, but the colors and shapes are exaggerated. So I could just do it on my own sometime. If you wanted it in my style, I mean. I could use another style. I could take a picture and try for strict realism if you prefer that."

He shook his head. "No, I like your style. But now I'm wondering what all you can do. For work I mean."

"Well, I took an art history course at SCAD, and they taught us about different Renaissance techniques and classical styles. It was really cool and interesting. You know DaVinci practically invented anatomical drawings. He even dabbled in phrenology."

Bill was lifting sand in his fist and letting it stream out as he listened. "What's phrenology?"

I studied my palm. "Oh, it's completely silly, using the shape of your skull to determine what type of person you are and your natural inclinations."

His blue eyes flickered with interest. "Can you do it?"

I shrugged. "I read about it, and of course I had to experiment on myself. But it's total garbage."

Then he scooted closer. "Try it on me."

I laughed. "You're curious what the bumps on your head say about your character?"

"Sure. It sounds like fun." He leaned his head toward me. "Like getting your palm read or something."

"That's exactly what it's like. I think the term *quackery* was invented just for phrenology."

"So it's not real. Tell me anyway."

"Well, the actual practitioners used tape measures and calipers. I don't have any of that. But let me see." I leaned over him, carefully touching his light brown hair, placing my hands behind his ears and around the sides of his head. My hair slid down my shoulder into his face, and he held it back.

"So you have a strong forehead, which means you're benevolent, and the top of your head is rounded, meaning you're decisive and persistent."

He nodded, and I was very aware of his head close to my sternum. "That sounds right," he said.

I moved back. "I guess that's why it had followers. It's like astrology. Sometimes it can match how your personality really is."

"What else?"

Carefully, I put my palms on the sides of his face, looking straight into his eyes. For some reason, it caused a feeling in my stomach...

That I immediately dismissed as hunger. Low blood sugar.

"The width of your temples is supposed to determine your love of beauty," I continued, refocusing my thoughts. "And that combined with the prominence of your brow shows your level of creativity. Like the shape of my face indicates I should be a creative artist."

"Ahh," he nodded then smiled. "Now I see how it's quackery."

I looked down. "It really is. It says people with oval heads are not creative, and there are tons of oval-shaped faces in the creative field. It's completely ridiculous."

"It's fun, though. Like handwriting analysis."

"I guess." I sat back, and he released my hair.

"You smell nice. What's that?"

"Soap. You should try it sometime."

He started to get up. "And on that insult, I'm leaving."

I grinned at that. "You never said why you came down here in the first place."

"I need to know if you're ever planning to come to the office," he said. "I wanted to show you around, introduce you to folks. I tried calling, but you must've turned off your phone."

"It wouldn't stop ringing. Some Kyser-Brennan number I didn't recognize."

"Tomorrow?"

I stood and dusted off my skirt. "I'll stop in this afternoon if you want."

"I'm on my way to class. Tomorrow'll be fine. And call Meg. She's been talking about how she hasn't seen you since you got back."

He walked away, and I watched him, thinking how funny it was the way people changed as they grew up. A person could start out being a real pain in the ass, and then without warning, he could turn into a really nice guy.

And I needed to get some breakfast.


*May 1, 19 –*

Is it already May? Working on Bill's Phoenician developments has taken over all the extra time I'd expected to have when I agreed to return home. Instead of pursuing fine art and indulging my muse whenever I liked, I'm always at the office taking meetings with the boys or sketching out the results of our decisions from those meetings. Bill and Bryant are determined to get their high-rises in the sky yesterday, it seems, and they take my plans and get them in the lineup as soon as I have them finished and approved.

I'd hoped to have more time to spend with Meg, catching up, playing with the baby, but as it turns out, time is flying and already we're looking down the barrel of a year. The ground for Phoenician I is broken, and across East End Beach, extending down to Hidden Pass, the skeletons of new giants are waiting to straighten their backs into the sky.

Each complex will have a different theme, depending on what vacationers are interested in, and Bill is doing extensive market research to find the hottest trends and vacation destinations to guide our decisions.

My challenge is finding design concepts that won't look dated in ten years. It's possible a few years could pass before some of my concepts will be ready for unveiling, so I have to keep it to images that won't need updating right away. It isn't an easy task, and I'm new to this type of work. But I love flexing my creative muscles and discovering new ways to approach the job.

I found that if I distill the themes down to their basic elements and focus on those throughout, I'm happier with the results.

The hardest was Phoenician V, the calypso theme.

I thought it was a terrible idea, but Bill was right. Island vacations were off the charts in terms of popularity. Why should Americans leave the States for a vacation when our beaches were just as beautiful as anything in the Caribbean? We also had the best sanitation, and vacationers wouldn't have to worry about things like antibiotics or immunizations or projectile vomiting if a stray lettuce leaf that wasn't washed in filtered water ended up on their plates.

I love the work, and Bill and I are becoming closer friends than I expected. We start most days with coffee and a chat in his office and then I spend the rest of the time envisioning interiors and running the results past him for approval. It's a great set-up, and although I demand control over my schedule, I find myself wanting to spend most of my hours at work.

When we toured the interiors of the buildings, and I saw my ideas becoming reality, it only motivated me to work more. And to think how hard a time I gave him when we were in high school. I'm turning into a regular developer myself.


*Sept. 11, 19 –*


I can't believe the year I just wrote up there. Has it really been *four years* since I picked up this pen?

*Four* years of birthdays?

The time has just come and gone, and except for the occasional holiday, we've been consumed in the rush of creation and getting our high-rises off the ground. Bill finished college, Phoenician II is almost finished, and we're looking to the future. That's how it was when Meg called yesterday.

I was at the office staring out the window and thinking about Phoenician VIII, for which we were playfully tossing around an outer space theme. It was the riskiest concept, and I was strongly opposed. Any type of futuristic design was bound to be out of date by the time the building even broke ground.

Still, I was having fun putting together silver-foil themed furniture and cosmic fixtures. I was imagining interiors in all white with stainless-steel accents. Perhaps even a telescopic viewing area in the penthouse or a small planetarium on the main floor. Very Guggenheim. I was even wondering if we could arrange an educational partnership with the schools for tax purposes. Maybe kids could come here to study...

The phone rang, and it was Meg. She sounded hysterical, and I was instantly alarmed. "What's wrong?" I cried. "Is it Will?"

"I'm sorry. I shouldn't be calling you at work," she sniffled. "I tried calling Billy, but I just got voicemail."

I glanced up from my worktable through the glass wall to see Bill in Bryant's office gesturing at some plans on Bryant's desk.

My eyes narrowed. "What's going on?"

"I just feel so miserable, Lexy. Can you come over for a few minutes? Are you too busy?"

"No, honey. I'll be right there."

I slid my phone into my purse and strode over to Bryant's office frowning. The two looked up when I barged in. "Hey, good timing," Bill said. "Come see what we're working on."

"So you're letting Meg's calls go to voicemail now?" My voice was sharp.

Bryant jumped in to diffuse the situation. "What's up, Lex?"

"I was going to call her back," Bill said, not meeting my eyes. "What's wrong?"

"I don't know, but I'm heading to your house for as long as it takes." I turned and strode to the door. "Not cool, Bill," I called over my shoulder.

"Let me know if it's anything important," he called after me.

I was fuming as I left the building. It only took fifteen minutes to get from our offices in Dolphin Shores to the Kyser house in Fairview, and by the time I got there, I'd cooled off enough to console my friend.

"I'm such a goose, I know," she laughed through her tears. "But I'm just going crazy without Mom or Will around. I'm only twenty three, and I have no purpose."

"What are you talking about?" I soothed, smoothing back her beautiful hair. "Will just started kindergarten. He still needs Mommy for a good ten years or so. Heck, if his daddy's any indication, he'll need you a lot longer."

"Did you see Billy?" she blinked up at me. "I didn't leave a message. He's been so frustrated with the way I've been acting since school started."

"He's not being very understanding, if you ask me."

She looked down again. "Don't. I've been enjoying you two as friends."

"We still have our moments," I said. "So what's wrong? Are you feeling a little empty nest?

She shrugged. "I guess. I just really want to have another baby."

"You do? Well..." I looked around their empty house. "Have you talked to Bill about it? A baby would probably make you feel better."

"He says we have to wait," she said. "He doesn't think we're ready."

"Wait for what? The money's coming in regularly now, and with Will at school, you wouldn't be overwhelmed."

"I know," she sighed. "I told him that. He just wants to wait."

I looked at my friend's miserable face and frowned. I was just mad enough at Bill to say it. "Have you considered a surprise?"

"What?" Her blue eyes blinked to mine.

"I'm just saying. Will was a surprise and that worked out fine. Why not have another one?"

"Oh, Lexy, we're still the perfect team!" Meg threw her arms around my neck, but I was confused.

"What do you mean?"

"I mean, you're right. It did work out just fine the first time, so why wouldn't it work again?"

"Wait." I held her arms and moved her back. "Are you saying the first time—"

She bit her lip and looked down. "Wasn't technically an accident."

"Oh, Meg." I closed my mouth, but my head was shaking. "You meant to get pregnant senior year?"

"Don't look so disapproving. It wasn't like Billy and I hadn't already decided we wanted to get married."

"But you were so young!" I rubbed my forehead. "And, that wasn't really fair. I mean, you knew what he

175

was planning. What if he'd given up on college? His dream?"

"Are you kidding? He'd never give that up." She rolled her eyes and fell back against the couch. "He did talk about us waiting to get married. But I know how to handle Billy."

My hands dropped to my lap, and I looked down. "Don't ever tell him what you did," I said softly, regretting I'd even suggested it earlier.

"You really think I'm dumb, don't you? I would never tell him that."

"You took a big risk," I said. "What if he'd walked away?"

Meg stood and straightened her navy polo dress. I watched as she pulled her blonde hair into a side ponytail. "Billy would never walk away from his family. And we'dve been fine even if he had decided to give up his master plan. You know his daddy offered to give him the horse ranch when he found out?"

"No, I didn't know that," I said quietly. I didn't like knowing this about Meg. I didn't like knowing she could be so manipulative to get what she wanted. I only wanted to think of her as innocent and sweet.

"Well, Billy'd rather die than run a farm. Of course, he turned that right down." I watched her studying the end of her ponytail as she spoke. "And I convinced him to wait and tell my parents after we were married. They'd have probably tried to stop us."

"What if everybody was right, Meg? What if you should've waited?"

Her eyes went huge. "And not gotten married? Give me a break! I've known we were going to be together since the first time I laid eyes on him."

My brows pulled together. "But you felt like you had to trick him?"

She pressed her fists into her waist, blue eyes blazing. "Not trick him. *Remind* him. He and Bryant were so caught up in their big plan, he'd forgotten about us. I was just keeping *my* plan on track."

I stood and put my arm around her shoulders, and we stared at the flowered carpet a few minutes. She was still my best friend, even if I wasn't sure what to do with this new information.

"So you want another baby, and Bill wants to wait because…"

"He wants to build our house first or something. I don't know."

I nodded. "That's actually not a bad idea. You'd have more room then."

"But that'll take years, and I want a baby now!"

I squeezed her shoulders and then released her. "What about volunteering at the hospital? I bet you could work in the nursery and be around little babies all the time."

"Billy suggested that. Or get a part-time job at one of the boutique stores."

"That's a great idea. Why don't you do that?"

She sighed and flopped on the couch. "I tried helping at the hospital, but being around all those people talking about Daddy… I started thinking about how he's missing little Will growing up, and he'll never see little John. It just made me more depressed."

I dropped onto the couch beside her. "Sweetie, you're really sad. I had no idea!"

"You have so much work to do, and… I just miss Mama."

"Have you thought about going to Sedona for a visit?"

"I'd have to pull Will out of school, and I'm not sure we have the money yet for that. It's not a cheap flight."

"Listen, I'll do my best to make it over here more for visits, okay? And you think about other places that need help. You know everyone around here. I'll bet you could find something you like to do. All you need is to fill a few hours."

She nodded. "Thanks for coming, Lexy."

"Any time you need me." I hugged my sweet friend. "You going to be okay now?"

"I think so. I was thinking about repainting Will's room, so maybe I'll do that."

I stood and pulled her hands. "What color? Need me to help?"

"Would you? Come see what I've picked out."

We spent the rest of the morning looking at paint swatches and fabric colors, and by lunch, Meg was smiling again. I returned to the office in time to catch the elevator with my two bosses.

"Just getting back?" Bill was smiling in a way that irritated me.

"Yes, and I had an interesting chat with your wife."

"I'm headed up." Bryant stepped into the elevator without us. "You two keep it civil."

The doors closed leaving Bill and me facing each other. My arms were crossed. "Meg says you won't let her have another baby."

"It's not as sinister as that," he smiled, leaning against a concrete pillar. "I just think we need to wait. And this isn't your business, Lex."

"It's my business that she's my best friend, and she's totally miserable. You leave her alone all the time, her

---

178

mom's in Sedona, and now Will's at school. What are you waiting for?"

His eyes flashed, and he straightened. "I'd like to see my children, too, okay? You think I don't know how much I work? I barely see Will as it is. I'd also like to build a bigger house so we actually have somewhere to put another baby. I will not have this argument with you!"

We were quiet for a moment, and I looked down, my chest burning with guilt.

"You're right. I really should mind my own business," I said softly. "I'm sorry I didn't... give you the benefit of the doubt."

"Thanks." He breathed, turning away. "You never do."

I nodded. "I'll try to work on that."

He glanced back, then he grinned. "Well, don't work on it too hard. I don't want you losing your creative edge."

My eyes flickered to his. "What?"

"I think hating me might be the key to your power. Don't mess with the works."

"I don't hate you," I said, my voice still quiet.

"And I don't hate you, too. Now get some work done today, will ya?"

I rolled my eyes and pressed the elevator button.


*Jan. 8, 19 –*


Mexican vacation! The money might not be rolling in yet, but I'm not complaining if the perks are going to be like this.

Bill told me I could bring a guest if I wanted, and I immediately thought of Suzanne. She'd practically saved my life with that Atlanta gig years ago, and I was using so much of what I'd learned from her in this job. It was the perfect way to thank her.

"Well, hello, stranger," my friend said. "I haven't heard from you in months. So what problem are you having now?"

I laughed. "I've missed you, and I know! I'm sorry I've been such a slacker friend. I'm calling to make it up to you. How does a weekend in Mexico sound?"

"What?"

"Working for developers has perks," I said. "We're getting this free vacation in Mexico at this high-end resort Bill wants to check out. Can you come up with airfare and meet us there? Everything else is covered."

"Ugh!" she groaned, and I heard what sounded like a notebook slap closed. "When? I'm going to have to see if I can arrange things here."

"Next weekend? Oh, c'mon. I know the guys'll let you off to come see me."

"I don't know," she sighed. "They're still bitter about your abrupt departure."

"Oh my god, that was four years ago! And it was the right decision for me." I said. "I'm having more fun than I expected, and the buildings are really coming together."

"I know. And I can probably swing it. Let me see."


*Jan. 16, 19 —*


We arrived in Tango Sol on a Thursday with plans to leave out Sunday morning. It was a short trip, but it was so beautiful. I brought a camera to capture the flowers and scenery, thinking I'd start painting again.

Suzanne and I had a cabin suite that was separated by a bathroom in the middle. Each room had a large queen bed that was all mahogany wood and white linens draped in mosquito netting. It definitely conveyed the feeling of an exotic locale. I was totally making mental notes on this place.

The first night we all had dinner together in the open-air restaurant. Meg looked beautiful and not at all like she'd been the last time we were together. Bryant brought Donna Albriton, and I figured those guys would be announcing their engagement soon. I didn't know what he was waiting for. It was so obvious they were a match made in heaven. Donna was the only girl I'd ever met who was both quiet enough and patient enough to balance Bryant's boisterous personality.

Suzanne fit right in with the group, and we enjoyed a lively dinner with lots of joking and playful insults. Marco, the owner, joined us for a few minutes during desserts and coffee, and he was extremely gracious and welcoming. When we got back to the room, Suzanne and I were ready to crash following the long flight out and the drive to the resort overlooking the Pacific Ocean.

"So how is it I've never met the model couple?" Suzanne asked, studying me.

"Who?" I frowned.

"Meg and Bill. Those guys are hard to believe."

"Oh," I snorted. "Yeah. Meg's always been like that. Just beautiful."

"He's no slouch." Suzanne's eyebrows went up, and a look that said *yum* crossed her face.

"Back off, Atlanta." I climbed onto my bed, ready to sleep. "He's totally taken."

---

181

"And how are you handling the close proximity?"

"What?" I stretched into my pillow, forehead lined.

"I'm just saying. He's very attentive to you, and you've been on ice since that slime-ball professor. Four years now."

"That's insane. I'm not on ice. I just haven't met anybody who interested me."

"And why should you?" Suzanne leaned on the bedpost facing me, her arms crossed.

I sat up at that. "I'm not following you."

"When you've got a hottie like that taking up all your time, why should you meet anybody else?"

"Bill's my boss," I frowned. "Period. Now stop trying to mess up my good deal." I lay back on the bed again. "And I don't know. There weren't any guys I liked back home when I left. Not much has changed."

"So now you just work around the clock. That's no way to be, my friend."

I sighed. "I know. But how am I going to meet anybody? I don't even want to."

"They say that's when it happens, so keep your eyes open."

"I'm closing them now."


*Jan. 17, 19 —*

Everything about this trip is perfect for my art! Today I explored the grounds with my camera and climbed high on the hillside to look out over the ocean. The water here is far more active than it is back home, and I imagine locals can surf every day — not just when a hurricane or tropical storm is bearing down on us.

The foliage is basically the same, though, bromeliads and palmettos surrounded by huge ferns that give way to towering palm trees. Hibiscus plants bloom all around, and the only alarming thing is the iguanas. I'm not a fan of the large lizards that camp out by the pools and eat the brilliant flowers. Marco assures us they're harmless, but they're the size of small dogs. I keep my distance.

My favorite part of the trip has been getting to see Meg so much. I thought about suggesting Bill find her a job at the office but reconsidered. Sometimes spouses didn't work well together, and I'd decided to keep out of their marital affairs since that whole day in September.

I was happy having time with her. I remembered how close we were as little girls as I walked to her cabin. We were going on a souvenir shopping trip, and when I arrived, she was opening and closing drawers.

"What are you planning to wear today?" she asked.

"I don't know. Shorts? A dress?"

"You should wear that red dress you got last spring."

"OK," I said.

"Would you braid my hair?" she asked.

I sat down and started brushing her shiny blonde hair. When we were kids, I'd gone through a macramé phase, and I was constantly experimenting with different plaits and designs on Meg's hair. I felt like we were in middle school again.

"It's so great here," she sighed. "It's like being in a tropical paradise. Don't you think?"

"You bet. I've taken lots of pictures, and I think I'm going to try and work some of these ideas into one of the buildings. I'm sure Bill's thinking the same thing."

"He's been meeting with Bryant and Marco every day, but Donna says they're learning tons. I think they're golfing this afternoon."

"That sounds very educational."

We laughed.

"Lexy?" Meg had that same curious tone from when we were kids. "Do you ever get lonely?"

"What?" I smiled, tugging her braid tight.

"Well, you're here with Suzanne, and don't get me wrong. She's lots of fun, but it's not like a date. And this is such a romantic setting."

"Some people think where we live is a romantic setting."

"Don't avoid the question."

"I'm sorry." I kissed the top of her head where I was making her braid. "I'm not trying to avoid your question. I have thought about that. And Suzanne was nice enough to bring it up the first night. I don't know," I shrugged, "I just... I can't make myself feel something that isn't there."

"I'm going to help you." Her voice had that scheming, matchmaker tone.

"Oh, please don't," I begged.

"Why not? Who knows you better than me?"

"You're just like Miss Stella. She wants to drag me to mass every Sunday and hook me up with some good Catholic boy."

"What's wrong with that?"

I shook my head as I tied off her braid. "It just shuts down any interest I might otherwise have. I can't fall in love when I'm being watched under a microscope."

She sat up and faced me then, her eyes bright with her new project. "What if there's no pressure? You just try a blind date, and if it's a dud, we'll move on to the next one."

"The next one?" I rubbed my forehead. "Oh, Meg. Let's just let it happen, okay? They say when you're not looking, that's when you find someone.'

"Well, you haven't been looking for a while."

"And I've been working nonstop. Maybe Bill and I can give it a rest and start having a little more personal time."

She looked at her hands in her lap. "I'm all for that. But you'll have to suggest it. If I say anything, he'll think I'm nagging."

"Done. And so is your hair. What do you think?" I held up a mirror.

Her eyes lit up. "Perfect! As always."


*Jan. 18, 19 —*

I know this is supposed to be a work trip, but I've been working on relaxing and having fun. I only saw Bill one other time after that first night's dinner, and believe it or not, I've actually found myself missing my ole work buddy.

We bumped into each other at the pool one morning when he was on his way to memorize how the kitchen operated or whatever. I was lying out on a lounge chair in my bikini. He was distracted, but we had a nice chat. Suzanne came out and misread the situation as always. Then she suggested we go into town for dinner. It was a great idea. We both dressed up in short party dresses and caught the scary bus that took tourists down the hill into the tiny village that was a haven for Tango Sol tourists.

Inside the cantina, which was lined with rainbow-colored Christmas lights, Suzanne ran to the bar and ordered two shots.

"Tequila? No way," I said, shaking my head. "I am *not* shooting tequila."

"Stop being a party pooper!" she cried, eyes closed. "We're in Mexico! We have to act like Mexicans!"

I squinted at her. "What does that involve?"

"Shooting tequila!" She slammed the thick little glass down in front of me and then lined up a salt shaker and a lime. "Lick your hand."

"I don't think I've seen a Mexican shoot tequila the whole trip!" I said, licking the side of my hand right beside my thumb. "And it's very possible you're being a racist."

"Then we'll act like American tourists in Mexico! Now, salt!"

It was a mistake, but I did the shot. Then we danced to the salsa band. Some fellows at the bar were checking us out, and Suzanne started flirting. Before long they were sending us drinks, and after a few hours, they had joined us by the bar. I was feeling dizzy, so I motioned to the waiter to get us a table.

"I need to eat something," I told Suzanne. She stayed with the guys a few minutes longer while I grabbed a menu and ordered food.

I glanced up to see her speaking briefly to them and then heading in my direction wearing a frown. "See? That's what you do," she scolded, sitting beside me. "You've got to stop it."

"What? Eating?"

"No. That guy was totally into you, and you just walked away."

I took a chip and stabbed it in the salsa. "I'm about to fall over. I need food."

"You need sex."

"Oh my god! Shut up!" I nearly choked on the chip in my mouth. "I'm not hooking up with some guy I just met at a bar on our last night here. That's just gross... and dangerous."

"You don't have to hook up," she whisper-shouted. "You can just have fun. Make out with him down on the beach. In the moonlight..."

"That's how women go missing, you know."

"I've got my eye on you." Then she did a little zig-zag wave.

"You're not inspiring confidence," I laughed. "And I'm sorry I didn't notice Pablo's advances."

"It's that Bill Kyser."

"Would you stop with that?" I pushed her arm. "You're wrong, and it's irritating."

"It's irritating because I'm right. You've invested all your emotional energy in someone who's unavailable. It's safe. He's your cocoon."

I rubbed my eyes, placing my elbows on the table and trying very hard not to get mad at her drunk self. "I don't even know what that means. But if you're suggesting I'm after my best friend's husband, then you don't know me at all."

"I'm suggesting you've got to stop spending so much time at work and open the door to other possibilities. How else do you expect to find someone? Remember how you were in Savannah? You were open then."

"And I got ripped to shreds."

187

"Look, I told you that guy was a mistake. And Evan was right there just waiting to help you pick up the pieces. You fled the scene."

"It was your idea!" I cried. Then I looked down. "Anyway, I think I made the right decision going to Atlanta with you. And now that we've eaten, how about one more shot!" I figured that would shut her up.

"You're on!" She leaned heavily on my arm as we walked back to the bar.

"Here's to being open," I said, lifting the little glass.

By the time I reached the door of our cabin that night, the world was rocking like a sailboat, and I felt like I was going to lose my dinner. Then I looked down and saw I had lost something. *Where was my shoe?*

I walked back down the wobbly path, but half-way there I realized my mistake. It was too dark, and I couldn't see a thing. Luckily, I ran into Bill. He was surprised to see me roaming around in the dark, and he convinced me to go back to my room. Everything was fuzzy, and I rested my head on his shoulder, holding his waist to keep from falling as we walked back. Holding onto him was unexpectedly warm and comfortable. He didn't speak, and as we made our way up the path, I thought about what Suzanne had said.

For a long time, I hadn't liked Bill very much. I didn't think he was right for Meg, and I didn't like that all he cared about was money and those developments of his. He had a sweet dad and good friends, but he was completely consumed with conquering the coast. Then I'd gotten to know him a little better, and I actually liked him. As a friend, of course.

But tonight, just for a moment, and strictly for comparison purposes--*nothing more*—I wondered how my life would be different if I had met Bill first...

---

188

I tilted my heavy head back on his shoulder and studied his profile as we walked to my cabin. He was funny and thoughtful, and while he was completely focused on his goals, he did care about his family. And this trip was proof he liked to pamper the ones he loved. How might things have changed if we'd wound up together?

It didn't matter. I shook my head down. We were friends, and I wasn't going to let my tequila-soaked brain or Suzanne's imagination spoil that.

At my door, we shook hands, and I said something to him. I can't remember what it was, but it made him grin. Then I went inside and fell asleep thinking about everything that had happened as the room slowly turned. One thing was for sure, I was never acting like an American tourist in Mexico again.

This morning I'm paying for our girls' night. The sun is so bright, I had to put on my sunglasses to pack, and when the valet came for our luggage, I had to put on a hat to keep from crawling back inside the dark hut. One of my shoes was on the doorstep with a note.

*Found it. Your friend, Bill.*

I still can't remember what I said to him last night. And I don't know why Bill would have my shoe. I picked it up and stuffed it in my bag.

March 15, 19 –

Me and my big mouth. I knew the minute I said it back in September that I should never have advised Meg to fake an "accidental" pregnancy. I was angry at Bill for not taking her calls, and it was more an offhand comment than a serious suggestion.

Meg had just been sad for so long. Then after the Mexico trip, things had gotten better. Bill was being really great about spending time with her. He would cut us off at 5 o'clock every day so he could go home and be with his little family. Meg had stopped complaining, and I was actually getting to paint more.

Now things had gone south at an incredible rate of speed, and I felt horribly responsible.

Meg was having twins, and Bill was furious. I thought if she just went with it, pretended it truly was an accident, she might get away with it. I didn't know they'd had a fight and she'd practically threatened him. This time he knew he'd been tricked, and he was madder than I'd ever seen him. I was almost a little afraid of him.

Weeks have passed since she told him, and the situation has only gotten worse. Bill never goes home, and I feel like I have to do something to make this right. Meg turned to me, and I advised her to do the one thing that could potentially end their marriage—or at least drive a permanent wedge between them.

Our no-overtime policy has ended, and we're back to working as long and as hard as we want. Bill leaves for dinner, I guess he's eating out these days, and then he comes back after we all leave and sleeps in his office. I don't know how many nights he's been doing it.

One morning I stopped off at the coffee shop on the way in and grabbed him a cup. I thought maybe if I focused on the bright side and helped him put things in perspective that would help. Maybe if I reminded him how much he loved her, he wouldn't feel so betrayed.

Maybe there was some way to absolve myself of this guilt.

He seemed less angry after our coffee chat, but he still won't go home. Tonight after working late, I decided it was time to own up. Pain gripped my insides thinking of what I was going to tell him, but I stuck my head in his office anyway. He was sitting on the couch looking at a book.

"Staying late again?" I asked, the smallest tremble in my voice.

He didn't look up. "There's always plenty to do around here."

"Can't it wait til tomorrow? You should call it a night and go home."

"After while." He continued reading, and I studied his light brown hair, messy and still a little highlighted from our trip. His skin tanned.

I took a deep breath and went over to sit beside him on the couch. Then he looked at me. "What's on your mind?"

I wouldn't meet his eyes, instead I focused on my nervous hands. "I have to tell you something, and it's going to make you mad. But I'm hoping it'll help you forgive Meg."

"What is it?" His tone was sharp, and my stomach dropped.

"I told her to do it," I said quietly, closing my eyes.

"What?"

My chest clenched, but I kept going. "The whole fake accident, the pregnancy. It was my idea. I told her to do it."

For several long seconds the room was completely silent. I couldn't breathe. My heart felt like it had stopped beating.

Then he stood and walked across the room. "Are all women selfish liars or is it just the ones I know?"

Tears sprang to my eyes, but I blinked them quickly away. He had to hear what I was saying. He had to forgive her. "I'm so sorry, Bill. I should never have interfered."

"No," he snapped. "You shouldn't have."

"You have every reason to be as mad as you are, but can you at least forgive her now?"

He was quiet. For several long moments I waited, studying his back.

"You know my mom left my dad when I was a little kid," he finally said. "She wanted to chase her dream of being a singer. It didn't matter who she hurt, she was going to do it."

I didn't see the connection, but I didn't say anything.

"You told Meg to lie to me, but she didn't have to do it," he continued. "She could have thought of someone else for a change."

"I'm sure I influenced her decision," I argued. "She always listens to me."

He shrugged. "Well, thanks for telling me. I already knew you weren't on my side."

Tears flooded my eyes now. "Oh, Bill. That's not fair."

"No?" He turned and the smile on his face was no longer friendly. It was cold, and I wanted to die from how badly it hurt. All the progress we'd made as friends was gone.

"Meg and I had that conversation months ago. That day you didn't take her call," I said, touching my eyes. "So much has changed since then. I understand more, and I *am* on your side. I'm so, so sorry."

He turned back to the window, and my gaze dropped. Tears fell onto my cheeks. But I wasn't sure why I was crying now. If it was because Bill still wasn't going home or if it was because he didn't seem likely to forgive Meg.

Or if it was because now I'd hurt him, too.

"She's not a child, Lex," he said, still looking out the window at the dark waters of the canal. "At some point she's got to be responsible for her actions. And I can't be worried about what you two are talking about all the time."

"I promise you," I said, looking up at him. "I will never open my big mouth again. It won't happen."

I watched him inhale deeply, then he turned back to me. "Go home. You're tired."

"So are you." I tried one last time. "Please go home to Meg."

"Why do you care so much?"

"Because it hurts me to see you like this." I stood, wanting to approach him, but I didn't. "I think of you as my friend now, too."

"Right." His brow relaxed. "The shoe."

I blinked a few times, then I shook my head. "I meant to ask you what that was about."

"Some other time." He walked back to the couch and sat, picking up the book again. "You were being very sweet."

I sat on the couch facing him. "So you'll forgive me, but you won't forgive her?"

"You had that conversation with Meg the day you left the office and came back so mad at me. Right?"

I nodded, also remembering what he'd said at the elevator. The day I realized he did care — as much about

193

his family as about being manipulated. I'd sworn that day to butt out.

"That was ages ago, Lex," he continued. "How many more times did you tell her to lie to me?"

My voice was quiet. "Just that once."

"Well, Meg and I were having that conversation for the hundredth time in Mexico. I told her I'd change my schedule. I told her I'd be home more. The Mexico trip itself was part of me trying to make things better for her, but none of it mattered. She did what she wanted to do anyway."

"But it did matter!" I said it, but my argument felt weak. "Maybe by then it was too late for her to change things."

"Maybe."

"So you're not going back?"

"Back to what? To being another one of her pretty playthings?" His jaw clenched and he looked at the book. "My only purpose is to give her what she wants. But I have no feelings, and what I say doesn't matter."

My chest felt heavy, and I was only making him angrier. "I'd better go," I said. "I just wanted tell you what happened. And say I'm sorry."

He nodded, not looking up. "Thanks."


*March 7, 19 –*

Sitting here writing this, I remember the day it happened as if each moment were written in a book in my head, and I could go back and flip through it and pinpoint every place I went wrong, each time I could've made a different choice, a choice that would've changed the end of the story.

But now it's too late. Now everything is spoiled.

A year had passed since my conversation with Bill that night in his office. Meg had the twins, and I thought those guys were making it through their long separation. The babies were gorgeous, and Gigi said they were the exact image of Meg as an infant. They both had her golden hair and blue eyes. Just perfect.

Bill was at the hospital, and he seemed glad. He was very sweet with them, but I could remember a time when he was more affectionate to Meg. It hurt me to see them still so distant.

Gigi was in heaven. She had come back from Sedona to help get them over the early days at home, and I couldn't help but wonder if Meg was glad Will was in school. I smiled thinking of how frantic she'd been his first day of kindergarten. That fateful day I'd opened my big mouth. She probably counted the minutes until the bus arrived to take him away in the mornings now.

As for work, we were charging through the last few buildings. That particular Sunday finished off a week-long push to complete Phase VIII. We'd barely left the office except to eat, shower, and sleep. Everyone was exhausted.

It was a fun project, though. We'd gone with a Mexican theme for Phase VIII that was based heavily on Tango Sol, and I'd pulled out all the pictures I'd taken on the trip for ideas. Remembering how much fun we'd had made it a labor of love, and I found a funny shot of Meg and me in sombreros from the day we went souvenir shopping. I had it framed to give to her.

I was finishing up the lobby sketches when Bill breezed into my office and started shutting the blinds and turning off the computers. He was dressed in a short-sleeve button up shirt and khaki shorts with

Sperrys, and he was happier than I'd seen him in a while.

"You're very perky for how hard we've been working." I looked up from the table where I was adding the color to my sketches. "And why are you shutting down my office?"

"Everyone's taking a break," he said. "We all need some fresh air and relaxation, and I was thinking it would be a perfect day to take the boat out for a few hours."

"Are Meg and the babies coming?" I smiled, thinking I'd like to see them.

He shook his head. "She took them into Newhope. It's just you and me, Skipper."

I wrinkled my nose. "You know I hate boats."

"We need to work on that."

"Eh… come see what you think about this first," I said. "I'm a little concerned it might be too colorful. I mean, it was colorful there. I have the pictures to prove it. But I don't want it to be tacky here."

He walked over and leaned beside my table. I glanced up at him as he studied my drawings, thinking how foolish I always was to hang on his approval. Every time, my stomach was in nervous knots until he declared my work brilliant. It had been the same since that very first day in high school, when I'd sketched out his very first high-rise development dream. He'd taken one look, and I thought he was going to kiss me. My cheeks tingled remembering how it felt to make him that happy. I'd only wanted to keep provoking that same reaction every time.

He slowly lifted the heavy paper, studying every part of the design. "Brilliant. As always," he said, and I silently released the breath I was holding. "Our guests will feel like they're in Mexico. And with our scenery, they'll have it all."

"All but the iguanas." I scooped up my pastels and started arranging them in their tray. "Those things were gross."

"Chicken. Hey, I like this," he pointed to my idea for the trim work. "The Aztec details are a nice touch. Also, the waterfall. It's like you read my mind."

"Those waterfalls were the best part."

"Now come on. You haven't left this spot in two days." He caught my hand, and I put the pencil down, smiling.

"That's technically not true. I went home and showered and got something to eat."

"Doesn't count."

"Okay, but just a few hours. I have some things to finish today."

I hadn't been sailing since that last trip we'd made years ago before the wedding. Driving over, I remembered when all of us would spend every day of every summer on the water either in somebody's boat or just swimming and lounging by the Gulf. I still had a bikini stuffed in the glove box of my car, remnants of a youth spent growing up near the coast.

When we were parked at the marina, I heard a popping noise as I grabbed my suit.

"Champagne?" I asked.

"Cheers," he said, holding out a small solo cup.

"What's the celebration?"

"We're almost finished, it's a gorgeous day, it's spring. Who needs a reason?"

"Well, I'm glad to see you so happy," I smiled, taking it from him. "Cheers. But only one for me. I meant it when I said I wanted to work tonight."

We tapped plastic cups and tossed back the wine. I grabbed my suit and went to change in the restroom before we left, using Bill's discarded shirt for a cover-up. It was one of the first warm days of spring, and already it was getting into the mid-80s. But the breeze kept it cool. It was a perfect day to be on the water.

When we got out on the sound, the first thing I noticed was how few others were out with us. We were either too early or too late to get caught in the usual boat traffic. The second thing I noticed was my reaction to seeing Bill tying the ropes and maneuvering the sails. It had been a while since we'd been swimming together, but he hadn't changed a bit.

When we were kids, I'd seen Bill half-dressed so much, I'd taken it for granted. We were all like that growing up down here, running around town in shorts, bikini tops and flip flops nine months out of the year. My heartbeat picked up when I saw his tanned muscles flex and the lines in his stomach.

I'd drunk my second glass of champagne too quickly, and it was making my head fuzzy. But not so fuzzy I couldn't tell this was dangerous.

All those things Miss Stella and Suzanne had been saying flooded my mind—it had been too long since I'd been with a man. Five years now. And I didn't know if it was the power of suggestion, but I was having thoughts about Bill I'd never allowed in my brain before. Thoughts of how sexy he was, of how it might feel to have his skin against mine. My cheeks grew hot.

"You'll never get a tan with that on," he laughed and pulled my shirt front toward him.

What was in my head must've been plain on my face because when our eyes met, there wasn't much time to react. His expression turned serious, and he stepped toward me, holding my arm as he loosened the mainsail, allowing it to go slack. We were a breath apart, and the wind carried the warm scent of his body right into my face. I could barely breathe. He stepped back and hit the switch to lower the anchor before taking my hand and guiding me down.

I felt like I had somehow left my body. As if caught in a spell, I followed him, and the moment our feet touched the floor of the apartment below, we were in each others arms. He held my cheeks as his lips found mine then his hands moved to my shoulders, quickly sliding his shirt off my body. His mouth traveled to my neck and then to the line of my bikini top. I shivered, clinging to him, desperate and feverish.

He straightened up again, covering my mouth with his. I felt him fumbling with the strings of my bikini, but I pulled back.

"Wait." I could barely gasp out the words for his kisses and my heart flying in my chest.

He lifted his head to look at me with those beautiful blue eyes. That was my chance. The moment I could've changed it. One simple choice, the other side of the coin.

Just then a breeze rocked the boat, and I leaned forward into his arms. My will dissolved as his mouth sealed over mine again, and I helped him find my laces, untying the strings of my bikini top. Two swift pulls, and we were naked, skin against skin. He lifted me with a groan, and I couldn't help myself, I wrapped my arms around his neck, my legs around his waist.

We fell back onto the bed, me on top, and as our bodies slid together, I inhaled deeply his warm scent. Our mouths rocked together with our movements, and all I could do was hold him as waves of desire overwhelmed me and I gave in completely.

I kissed his neck, it was salty like the ocean. I kissed his cheek, it was scratchy from his stubble. He rolled us over, and his lips moved from my shoulder to my jaw then my temple. He kissed my closed eyes and whispered soft words I almost couldn't bear to hear.

*We shouldn't be here. We shouldn't be doing this.* The stern voice in my head was no match for the tide of emotion pulling me under, drowning me. He lifted his chin with a groan, and I kissed his neck as aching pleasure flooded my torso, both of us clinging to each other in release.

Before long, we were lying still in each other's arms, breathing heavily. We stayed that way for several minutes, allowing our bodies to return to calm. Neither of us spoke. I didn't know what to say, where to even begin.

I rolled away, my back to him, but his arm went around my waist, drawing me tight against his chest. His warm lips pressed against the top of my shoulder, and my arms tightened over his in response.

Oh, god, what had happened to me? I was reeling, stunned by the realization—I loved him. I loved him so much. Yet at the same time, how long had this been growing inside me? Growing between us? Years, it seemed.

We only lay that way a few moments before he softly ran his fingers up the line of my stomach. I arched against him, and he rose up, leaning over to find my mouth once more, my arms wrapping around his neck. If the first time could be called an accident or a mistake or could be blamed on too much wine, I couldn't rationalize away the second.

He pulled me above him, my hair spilling all around us, and I kissed him eagerly, hungrily. His hands cupped my breasts, moved to my waist, and gripped my butt. We slid together, rolling over again until he was on top once more, looking into my eyes as we moved. I traced my fingers over his face, memorizing the colors of him—beige, sparkling blue like the ocean, honey brown with golden highlights. Gorgeous.

Heat flushed beneath my skin with his touch, his mouth branding a trail of fiery kisses all over my body, exploring every curve and fold until the tightness in my belly grew so strong, I cried out when it finally burst through me. His mouth covered mine again as our bodies joined once more, and we finished together. I held him as tightly as I could, the words whispering silently, over and over in my brain, *I love you.*

Tears filled my eyes. I could never say it out loud. I had no right.

But it was wonderful and amazing.

And horrible and tragic.

And wrong.

I knew what was out there waiting, the pain that would crush us both. But in this small room, in this secret place beneath the waves, I had something beautiful. I could pretend no one would ever know or be hurt by what we'd done. It was a precious lie I wanted to believe so badly.

I must've fallen asleep because when I opened my eyes again, it was dark, and Bill was sleeping beside me. We hadn't gone far from the marina, which was helpful. I slipped away without waking him, putting on my bathing suit and swimming to the pier. I changed into my clothes and drove home.

Tomorrow I'd turn in my resignation. I'd leave East End Beach and never come back. Meg would never know what I'd done to her.

---

201

That I'd betrayed my closest friend.

*March 8, 19 –*

But I didn't do it.

Sitting here writing this, I know it was a mistake, but somehow I couldn't leave.

The phone rang, startling me from my sleep, but I didn't answer it immediately. I watched it buzzing and vibrating, flashing his number, but I couldn't pick it up. It stopped ringing and chimed out there was a message waiting. I pressed the button and listened to his voice. It sent a shock of longing through me that confirmed what I'd decided. I had to go. I couldn't be trusted with him again.

"Lexy, we've got to talk," he said. "Please call me when you get this."

I pressed the button to return his call.

He answered immediately. "Where are you?"

"Home, but I'm going back to Atlanta. I can't stay here now."

"Please don't leave. Just wait. I need to see you again." His pleading tone tore through my chest painfully.

"No. I can't see you. Ever again."

"I don't know what to say." I could hear the frustration in his voice. "I'm sorry? It was all my fault? I should've known better?"

"We *both* should've known better." My voice was sharp.

"We aren't kids anymore. She trusted you. She trusted me."

"Don't bring her into it."

"Why not? She's the one you should be thinking about. She's all I can think about."

"Just..." he sighed deeply. "You can't go back to Atlanta. What about the project? Everyone's worked so hard, and it's almost finished. No one else can come in and pick up your work. It's too distinctive. It's exactly what I want. You're exactly what I want."

My chest clenched, and I closed my eyes, pressing my forehead into my arm. "Maybe I can finish it from Atlanta. I'll finish Phoenician VIII, and then I'm off the team."

"Finish it here. Please don't leave." He hesitated, and his voice cracked. "I promise. I won't let it happen again."

"*I* won't let it happen again," I said. "And I don't want to see you. I'll come in after everyone leaves and finish up. Don't call me either. Leave a note if you need anything."

My only answer was silence. I took a breath, not sure what he would say next. Then he spoke.

"If that's what it takes. Just don't leave."

And that was all it took for me to make my second mistake.


*April 5, 19 —*

Our arrangement was working. I only went to the office at night, and I only communicated with Bryant. I avoided every opportunity of seeing my best friend's husband after that day on the water.

Weeks passed. It took longer to complete Phoenician VIII because I was only able to work two or three hours a night after everyone left, and I was so tired all the time.

As promised, Bill stayed away, but something was changing.

I tried to blame the late hours and the trouble I was having sleeping, worrying about Meg. If she knew what I'd done, it would kill her. Her entire life was wrapped up in him and her little family. I knew that. I always knew that. It made me sick every time I thought about what I'd done to her. I was lower than the lowest insect that crawled under the cow piles out on Highway 42.

After the third week of exhaustion, it hit me. I surveyed my calendar to be sure I wasn't mistaken, and a quick trip to the drugstore confirmed what I already knew. My stomach sank to my toes, and I really was sick then. I cleaned up, splashing water on my face, then I leaned against the wall in my small, office bathroom blinking at myself in the mirror. I felt completely numb. I didn't know what to do or where to go. There was no one I could tell.

Almost no one.

I jotted a note and put it facedown in the seat of Bill's chair before I left the office last night. He would know what to do.

*May 18, 19 —*

It was late spring, the most beautiful time of the year here. Everywhere you looked flowers were blooming and butterflies were drifting past on the breeze that was constantly blowing. The start of spring might fill some with dread at the oppressive heat on the way, but it was impossible to escape its glory.

Wisteria was the first flower to appear. It only bloomed once in the very early months, its purple clusters of flowers hung from the vines like large bunches of lavender grapes. The scent was strange and woody, and I almost felt like I could taste it in the back of my throat. Giant bumblebees loved the wisteria blooms, and they were always out in teams crawling up the blossoms and collecting pollen.

Azaleas arrived close on wisteria's heels, and though I'd heard gardeners and extension workers argue against planting too many azaleas, since the flowers only lasted a few weeks, it was hard to agree with them when confronted with a mass of hot magenta faces pulsing their colors in my direction.

Some people opted for white azaleas, and it was stunning to see a fist of white blossoms so pure and glowing against the dark green backdrop. I preferred the pinks. If only because who would believe such a bold color could come from an otherwise plain-looking bush.

Azaleas didn't have a scent, but I held them to my cheek thinking there must be something more I was missing. The dark, intense center of the blossom extended out to a lighter shade of the same color, and the soft petals were freckled like a child's nose. I tried to find some way to impart this wisdom to my art. To follow the natural flow of dark intensity out to light in my use of color and my understanding of it. If my vision was blurred, and all I could see was the continuation of color, I would still know where the heart lay and where the arms extended outward.

Hydrangeas came next, and I had to admit, they were my favorite flower. The giant clusters of pink, purple, and blue blooms grew in bunches as large as my face, and Miss Stella's garden was stocked with layers of the jagged-leafed plant. They were her favorite, too, because she liked experimenting with the composition of the soil to see what colors she could create from year to year.

One year she managed to get a creamy pink bloom, and we were both overjoyed. It was the most delicate color I'd ever seen—pure off-white at the base that gradually grew out to faint pink tips at the ends of the petals. Again, I was amazed at the ability of nature to produce something so gorgeous. It was a miracle.

The sisters at Little Flower would say nature was the perpetual evidence of God's power and his love for us. I could hear them say it demonstrated the breadth of his range, that he could create something as complex and destructive as a human being, yet also something as life-giving and beautiful as a flower. Walking through the garden on that day, I decided I agreed with their philosophy.

The blooming trees Miss Stella kept were red buds, dogwoods, and Japanese magnolias, and the scent of magnolia was like nothing you could ever forget. Heavy and sweet like antique perfume. I leaned against an arbor braided with wisteria vines and dripping with purple clusters and let the healing power of all this beauty touch my broken heart.

Miss Stella died last night.

She kissed me goodnight, went to bed, and that was the end.

Her last day on Earth.

I knew something was wrong when I awoke to the smell of nothing.

No coffee, no warm buttery toast in the oven. It was frightening to creep out of my bed and cross the hall to her room. I saw the large shape of her lying still in the massive pineapple bed that she used a step-stool to climb into each evening. I couldn't go to her, though. I had to call our old friend Chuck Wilson, who was on the police force now to see if I was right and she was gone.

After he told me, I felt my entire body go numb. I collapsed onto the couch as tears fell onto my cheeks, but I took a deep breath and held on long enough to answer his questions. After everyone left, I walked outside, all over her beautiful grounds as the tears flowed unstoppable from my eyes to my cheeks, down my neck. This was my home, where I grew up, and as the memories flooded back, I leaned against the wooden trellis, closing my eyes to feel the soft petals and smell the warm perfumes that wafted on the sea breeze.

Spring had been our favorite time of year, and I had so many memories of Miss Stella joyfully planting and harvesting the flowers in her garden.

As bad as it sounded, I was glad Miss Stella was in a far more beautiful place. I would miss her forever, but I was relieved she'd never know what I'd done. She was always so good to me. She always encouraged me to make the right decisions.

I had really let her down this time.

*May 21, 19 –*

The funeral mass was held at Our Lady of the Gulf and many local residents came to pay their respects. Gigi, Meg, and Bill sat with me on the front row, and I had chosen a long black veil in anticipation of their presence. I kept my eyes down, away from him, through the prayers and communion and the Stations of the Cross.

Meg met me at the limousine that was to drive us to the burial site. Miss Stella would be laid to rest on her family's land an hour north of here in Lake Pinette. Meg held Lucy, and Bill stood a few feet behind her, hands in his pockets, also looking down. It was the first time I'd seen him since the night I told him I was pregnant. He was handsome as always, but I wouldn't allow my eyes to meet his.

"Oh, Lexy. I want to ride with you," Meg said. "But I've got the babies."

"It's okay," my voice was quiet, "I understand."

"What if Billy rides with you?"

My body tensed. "No," I answered too quickly.

Bill stepped forward to take my little namesake from her mother's arms. As he walked away, I watched him kiss her baby head, and I closed my eyes, fighting the urge to reconsider. Alone in the car, he could hold me and make this pain go away. I shook my head. I had no right to that kind of comfort.

Gigi stepped forward. "I'll watch the children if you'd like to go, Margaret."

"That's okay," I interrupted. "If you don't mind, I'd really just like some time alone."

"I want you to call me the minute you get back," Meg said, reaching forward to squeeze my hand. I nodded and climbed into the large black vehicle for the long ride north.

Miss Stella was the last of an old southern family that owned a plantation just north of Lake Pinette, and the property was adorned with beautiful live oak trees and dilapidated structures. At her gravesite, I left a bouquet of fresh flowers I had taken from our garden back home. Eventually, it was time to say goodbye, and I went back to the limo for the long drive south.

When I returned that night, Gigi was there to meet me. "Are you okay, Alexandra?" she asked.

"Yes, ma'am," I nodded, not meeting her eyes.

"I wanted to meet you when you got back and be sure you had something to eat." She showed me a casserole dish covered in foil.

"Thanks," I nodded. "I'm not really hungry. I think I'll just go to bed."

Meg's mother leaned against the kitchen counter, looking down at her pumps. "I'm sure Stella left you this house in her will. She loved you so much. She always said she didn't want to leave you homeless."

Fresh tears filled my eyes. "She was too good to me."

"You were like her own daughter."

"I can't live here without her," I blinked up at Gigi. "Do you think it would be wrong of me to sell it and just get something smaller further in?"

"I think you should rest and then decide what you want to do. You've had a lot on your mind today." She walked over and pulled me to her. "I'm sure you'll make the right decision. You've always done the right thing."

I nodded. She had no idea how wrong she was. "I'm so tired. If you don't mind, I'll just go to bed now."

She left, and I slowly climbed the stairs to change and lie down. After showering, I went to Miss Stella's armoire and pulled out one of her long, white nightgowns. It was way too big, but it smelled of her, which was just what I wanted. I climbed into her huge bed and curled into a ball as tears spilled over my eyes.

"Oh, Miss Stella," I whispered. "I still need you here. I need you to help me. I'm so lost and alone."

As I lay there in silence listening to the sounds of crickets and katydids, I noticed another sound, tires on the gravel drive and a door opening and closing.

I climbed out of the tall bed and went to the window to look out. Bill was standing beside his truck in the moonlight. Without hesitation, I ran down the stairs and out the front door to where he was.

"Why are you here?" I asked, breathless.

"I don't know." He stood there looking at me, dressed in jeans and a white tee, his hair blowing in the constant ocean breeze. "I was just driving, and I kept going until… I'm sorry, I know you said to stay away."

I rushed forward into his arms, and instantly he was holding me close. He hugged me tightly as I pressed my cheek to his chest, listening to his heart beating fast, breathing in his warm scent. I couldn't move for the longest time, until I felt his lips on the top of my head. Then I lifted my chin, and he kissed me softly, just pressing his mouth gently to mine and smoothing my hair back from my face. My body flooded with comfort.

I tucked my head against his chest again, and we stayed that way for several minutes. Just me in his arms feeling his strength. He inhaled deeply at the top of my head, and I closed my eyes, wondering how long I could hold him and pretend nothing bad could ever happen, that everything would work out and we would all be happy.

Finally, reluctantly, I lifted my head and stepped back. "I'm sorry." My voice was thick, so I cleared it. "Thank you for coming. I… I needed that."

"Wait…"

I shook my head. "You should go."

He looked down, and I turned to walk back to the house. But he caught my arm and pulled me to him finding my mouth again and kissing me, this time with passion and need. Our mouths opened, and in that moment my arms were around his neck. I was kissing him back because I needed him, too. I loved him.

Then I remembered.

I pushed against his arms, but he was stronger than me. He wouldn't let me go. "Don't," he said, his voice breaking.

Pain twisted in my chest as tears rushed to my eyes, but I pushed harder. "Bill, stop."

He immediately released me, and I stepped back, pulling the sleeve of the too-large gown back onto my shoulder.

"I'm sorry," he said, seeming dazed. "Did I hurt you?"

"Of course not."

"It's just… I feel like I'm going crazy." He pushed both hands into his hair. "And I hurt all the time. I need to be with you, Lex." He stepped toward me again, but I put my hand out, keeping us apart.

It was exactly how I felt, and I knew if I touched him again, I'd be taking him inside. "You've got to go home." My voice broke on the words. "And you can't come back like this again."

He nodded and turned to the truck. I barely heard him say, "I know."

I turned slowly, aching, all the way back to the house as he started the engine behind me and drove away. I walked through the huge, empty living room, making it as far as the stairs before I collapsed on them and wept.

*July 24, 19 —*

Time is passing, and my body is expanding and changing.

Now when I sit out on the shore with my eyes closed breathing in the salty air, I'm also listening, waiting, feeling for some indication little Julian is experiencing it with me.

Meg is right. His name is like the ocean, soothing and calm. Maybe I'm ashamed of how he came to be, but I can never be ashamed of him. I can't wait to see him, and these final months can't pass quickly enough.

Not seeing Bill during my pregnancy has been one of the hardest things I've ever done in my life. But I've carefully, oh so carefully, avoided any signs of him. I never go past his office, and if there's a book or magazine containing his picture, I don't look at it.

Other than that one night after the funeral, I've done a thorough job of separating myself from him. I've had to. Something happened to me that day on the boat, and I can't shake it. My eyes were opened, and I now see that I love him all the way to my core.

But he belongs to Meg.

Still, I've never felt this way in my life, like my body is independent from my brain, and it only wants one thing: Bill Kyser.

Some nights I lie on my bed and see his eyes. I pull the pillow over my head, and I can hear his voice. I get up and walk around the room, and I can taste his skin.

Everything inside me hurts, and I want to cry out and scream and throw things. Anything to distract myself, to make this longing for him stop.

I'd give anything to be able to drive to where he is and pretend I've never known Meg or anything about her and just be with him, wrap my body around his. Love him until the pain goes away.

But I can never do that. I've already done enough.

Our business arrangement now is that I'll stay. I'm still on the team, but I only meet with Bryant and I never see Bill.

Bryant and Donna were married a few years back, and Donna is expecting their first child as well. She and I are at about the same point in our pregnancies. We're all starting our families. Just in time for the ship to come in.

I made sure Bill was out of the office the day of Donna's shower so I could give her my gift, a painting of their future home in Springdale. Bryant had chosen to build a large home on several acres between Fairview and the ocean instead of the exclusivity of Hammond Island, and I admired his preference.

Not that I judged Bill and Meg for their choices. Meg was made for the trappings of wealth, and this whole development plan had been motivated by Bill's desire to be the most prominent man in South County. They were right where they'd always wanted to be.

When I was in the office, Bryant asked me to attend the huge ribbon-cutting event to celebrate the grand opening of Phoenician I. They were moving all our offices to the penthouse of that massive concrete structure directly on the Gulf, and Bryant wanted me at the ribbon-cutting to take pictures as head of design and marketing. Their dream had come true.

I remembered Bill in high school timidly approaching me about drawing up his ideas. His face had been so young, his blue eyes so round, when he'd asked. I think he was expecting me to bite his head off, but I'd said yes without hesitation. Was it possible I'd always been in love with him?

Now I would be front and center at the grand unveiling for his dream. The media would snap pictures of all of us cutting the ribbon and sealing the fate of our once-peaceful stretch of beach. A fate I'd always fought against—until he'd asked me to stop fighting.

Apparently there was no limit to what I'd do for him. I smiled bitterly and told Bryant I'd be there.

*Dec. 21, 19 –*

How can I write what happened here on paper? My hands still shake, and my heart is like lead in my throat when I even think of how it went down. When I remember the warning signs I completely ignored.

The ribbon cutting was the first big neon warning sign that I needed to go, to get far away from here, and I ignored it. Somehow at that event I'd ended up alone with Bill. We were in the elevator, and I'd simply touched him, caught my balance by holding his shoulder, and that was all it took. I kissed him in a way that... god, I probably would've done it right there in the elevator with him. I was just so weak and tired from fighting my feelings. He looked so good, and I wanted him so badly. We were nearly caught by Bryant and a crew of media professionals.

The whole situation still makes me cringe.

And I can just see how it would've played out in the news—me in a clench with my boss, the most important developer on the coast, my best friend's husband, and the father of my illegitimate child. It would've been the scoop of the decade, and it would've ruined us all.

Yet I still didn't leave. I still stayed.

A few months later, Julian was born...

I wouldn't even allow myself to remember that night, Bill's visit, the things he said and how I felt. It evokes a whole new level of pain. I forced myself to dismiss it as a surge of paternal emotion on his part. I simply had to.

Instead, I focused all my extra attention and energy on my little boy. The sleepless nights filled with longing and tears finally passed, and I managed to get myself under control again. Julian was a beautiful little boy, happy and energetic. He was dark like my dad. My mother had been fair, but my father gave me my dark hair and eyes along with my fantastic name. He had flair, the sisters at Little Flower had said. But Julian's eyes were all Bill's. Bright blue and sparkling.

For two years, I'd reported exclusively to Bryant. It was a good arrangement, and I regretted the unkind things I'd said about his boisterous personality in the past. Bryant was a good guy. I didn't know what he thought about my going from working so closely with Bill to reporting only to him and coming in strictly after hours. I suppose he accredited it to my "artistic temperament," but he never said a word and was always cheerful and upbeat. He also never asked about Julian's father, and as far as I knew, he was content to work with me in whatever way I chose. I found myself appreciating Bryant more and more as the years passed. I'd underestimated him.

So when I arrived at the company Christmas party, I was disappointed he and Donna wouldn't be there. They were home with their little boy, who had a fever. It wasn't anything serious, but Bryant fussed over his little son like he was the only baby in the world. It was endearing. Bryant decided to name him Brad because it closely matched his own name. He didn't believe in

215

juniors, he said. He'd also been telling us all about Brad's future as a football star, and I hoped the little guy was prepared to live up to his big daddy's expectations.

I wore a red dress in honor of the season, and my hair was pulled back from my face. Meg had suggested I take Julian to stay with the twins at Gigi's, but I'd opted to get my own babysitter at my house instead. I wasn't planning to stay late, and though Gigi was a dear, I didn't feel right leaving Julian with her.

I'd resolved to pretend like nothing had happened between Bill and me, believing that as time passed, I would forget him. It was the only solution that might work if I weren't going to leave, and I actually thought maybe it would protect me.

Meg ran straight to me when she and Bill arrived, and she looked like a snow angel in a light blue dress and white cashmere sweater. Her long blonde hair streamed down her back, and it was pulled up on each side in sparkling silver combs. I was glad to see her happy. Bill hung back, but I smiled and gave him a small nod. He responded with a tight smile, and I watched him take a scotch off a passing tray.

Phoenician I had been our first project, and we were so cautious back then. It had the most conservative design of them all. Inside it could've been any fancy hotel in any major city throughout the United States, but I was still proud of it.

Tonight, the enormous ballroom was decorated with twinkle lights, gold and silver. Tables were piled high with elaborate decorations and all varieties of finger foods. Waiters were circulating with small trays of hors d'oeuvres and champagne. A jazz band played swinging Christmas standards, and many of the guests were dancing.

After making the rounds a few times and grabbing another glass of champagne, I decided to visit my office. When we relocated everything, the guys had given me an office with a gorgeous view of the ocean. They called it repayment for bringing their dreams to life, but I think that overstated my involvement. I simply sketched out what Bill described.

I stood by my table looking at the interiors I'd been working on all week. The final phase, a large conference center with two hundred meeting rooms and a patio area facing the ocean. I'd decided it would be the last thing I did for Kyser-Brennan Equities. I had to get out of this rut. I needed to do different things, meet different people. I was considering my next move when I realized I wasn't alone.

"Who's there?" I strained my eyes to make out the figure, back-lit in the bright hall lights. It was Bill.

"Sorry," he said, clearing his throat. "I saw you leave, and there was something I wanted to give you."

I was instantly on edge. Despite my resolve, I didn't trust us alone together, and the uptick in my pulse at having him so close was the primary reason. "Can whatever it is wait until Monday? I was actually heading back to the party."

"It's just... I have a little gift for Julian." He'd been walking toward me, and now we were standing by my drawing table facing each other. "I don't know what he likes, but I picked this up the other day."

I took the small package from him, my eyes growing warm. "You didn't have to do this."

He nodded, and his eyes moved to my sketches. "They're perfect as always. I wanted to let you know you captured the exact feel we were trying to get with the conference center. Not too stuffy and business-like. Professional, but still at the beach."

I smiled, looking down, pleased as always and glad to change the subject. "I guess I've known you guys long enough to be able to read your minds."

"Bryant said you were making this your last job with us." I looked up and he was watching me, studying my face, his eyebrows pulled together. "I just wanted to know why. Did you get another offer? Are you moving? Do you need more money?"

"No," I shook my head, looking away again. "It's nothing like that. I want to get back to fine art. All this corporate stuff… I've been doing interiors so long, I feel like I'm stifled, and well, that's all. I'm not moving far. I was thinking Darplane or something like that."

He nodded. "I'm glad. I was afraid you were going to take Julian away. And, well, I know I don't see him much, but I'd like to keep up with him. He's a cute little guy."

"I wouldn't take him away without telling you first," I said quietly. "Giving you a chance to say goodbye."

We didn't speak, but he leaned forward almost imperceptibly, inhaling. "It's been a long time since we've seen each other," he said.

Instantly, my skin was humming, and I knew it was time to go. "That's for the best, I think."

"I miss how we would talk." I could hear his smile, but I wouldn't meet his eyes. "You said something about smell and memory once. For a while, I was afraid I'd forgotten the scent of your hair, and I thought if I could just get close enough one more time…"

My eyes flickered to his face, and I saw him smiling sadly. It twisted the pain in my chest. "I'd better get back to the party," I said.

"I didn't mean to make you uncomfortable." He straightened up. "I just wanted to say Merry Christmas."

I nodded. "Merry Christmas."

He leaned in for a hug, and I should've run away. But I moved in the wrong direction. All the time that had passed, almost two years, yet the instant we touched it all came rushing back. He kissed my head, and I pulled him closer pressing my cheek to his chest. The warmth of his body filled the space in my heart that had ached for him for so long.

He leaned back and gently cupped my face in his hands. So much tenderness in his eyes, it broke my heart. I couldn't stop him as he bent down to kiss me gently. It would have been too cruel. I kissed him back. Our lips parted, and it was like a sip of cool water after a long day in the hot sun. Such a relief. He moved closer to kiss the side of my face, my neck and my hair. I tightened my arms around him, resting my head on his shoulder and inhaling deeply.

So sweet, so sad. I wished with everything in me there was a way to change things. And when I opened my eyes, there she was.

Meg was standing motionless in the backlight of the hallway watching us.

My eyes flew wide as I pushed Bill away. "Meg! It's not what you think."

She didn't move, and even in the backlight I could see the betrayal on her face, her body trembling. I took two steps toward her, and she backed away.

"Meg…" I could barely whisper her name as I took another step.

She turned and ran, and I stopped at the door, trying to catch my breath, reeling from the shock.

*Dec. 23, 19 –*

My body is strangely calm as I write this. It's almost like I knew, that day in March, when I documented the events that led us to this place, this day was coming.

Just like on that day, I can look back at what happened and see every time I should've done something different. Each moment when I could've stopped how it ended.

After Meg ran from me in Bill's arms, I left the party and drove home. I decided to let Bill find his wife, and instead I would pack like I should've done after the ribbon cutting. I would get Julian and take him far, far away from here, and we would never come back as long as I lived.

I thought maybe I would write her a letter and try to explain. Maybe I could tell her she never had to worry about seeing my sorry face again because I would never, never come back to ruin her life.

She could go back to her palace and live with her prince and forget an evil witch had ever come and tried to destroy her life. She could pretend I never existed at all.

She could hit me.

Maybe she wanted to throw things at me. I would happily stand and let her hurl a piano at my head if it would make her feel better. Maybe she could hit me so hard I would forget him. Maybe there was a pill I could take that would stop me from touching the thing that wasn't mine.

The thing that belonged to the one friend I loved most in the world. My sister.

Once Julian's sitter was gone, I went to my bedroom and pulled out my suitcase. My little boy was sleeping, but I planned for us to leave first thing in the morning.

That's when I heard the car door slam.

I went to the window and only one streetlight shone on the driveway. Meg was standing by her car waiting for me. She still wore the light blue skirt and white sweater she'd had on at the party, but the skirt had a tear. And it looked like there was blood on her sweater. I went out and stood in the driveway facing her. She was swaying side to side, almost like she was drunk as she stared me down, anger and hatred burning in her eyes. Occasionally, a shudder passed through her body.

"You stole everything I loved." Her voice was hoarse, and her face was streaked with tears.

"Please come inside." My voice was shaky.

"That baby." Her voice grew louder. "Who is the father?"

"Meg, please." I held out my trembling hand. "Please let's just talk about it."

"WHO is the father?" she screamed.

Tears were spilling down my cheeks now, and I could feel my insides ripping to shreds. "I just need to explain… I'm leaving. You don't have to—"

"There is NOTHING you can explain!"

My head dropped as the tears took over. "Oh, god, Meg. Please. Please let me try. I'm so sorry—"

"You took EVERYTHING I ever cared about," she shrieked through the pain.

My body wrenched with sobs. "I never wanted to hurt you."

She staggered back against the car, opened the door and fumbled to get in.

"NO!" I rushed forward to stop her. "You can't drive!"

"Don't you TOUCH ME!" She screamed again and threw what turned out to be an empty scotch bottle with such force, it knocked me back and to the ground as it glanced off my temple. Blood instantly flowed into my eye, and sand flew in my face as her car shot out into the night.

I rolled onto my hands and knees, watching as the tail lights disappeared into the darkness. "Meg!" I cried, my shoulders breaking as my head dropped to my hands.

When Gigi called the next morning, I wasn't sure if she was going to curse my name or try and help me solve the problem. I wasn't sure if Meg would confide in her mother something as horrible as what I'd done, and if she did, I wasn't sure where I stood with Mrs. Weaver.

I'd known her twenty years. She'd watched me grow up. She was a mature woman. Maybe she'd have some insight into how we could work through this problem. Or at least know some way I could fix it so Meg didn't hate me. At least not forever.

"Alexandra? It's Gigi."

"Mrs. Weaver. I'm so sorry."

"What do you mean?" I heard her frown.

She must not have known what had happened, I thought. "I guess I was still dreaming," I said. "I'm sorry. What is it you need?"

"I need you to come to my house," she said in a strangely flat tone. "Do you think you could bring little Julian to my house this morning?"

"Sure," I said, unsure what this meant. "I'll be there in an hour."

I staggered to the bathroom and froze, stunned. The cut on my forehead looked dreadful, even though I'd done my best to tend to it. I probably needed stitches, but I hadn't been able to go to the hospital last night. Julian was asleep, and it was too late to drag him out.

I cleaned the cut and re-dressed it. I had some old butterfly bandages, and they helped close the gap. Then I slipped on my faded jeans and a long-sleeved black tee. I put Julian in one of his little fleece jogging suits and a little hat on his head and carried him to the car. He was almost two and getting heavy, but he still liked me to carry him. I liked holding his warm little body close to mine. His sweet face was the one bright spot in my otherwise disaster of a life.

We arrived at Gigi's in time for me to see several cars in the driveway, one of which was Bill's. I did *not* want to see him today, but Mrs. Weaver was waiting for me. I went to the door, and she opened it looking solemn. I walked inside, and Bill was sitting in a chair staring at the rug. He didn't even look up when I entered the house. The twins were sitting on the floor talking to each other, and Will was trying to get on his emotionless daddy's lap. The whole scene made me dizzy and slightly nauseated; something was very wrong here.

"Alexandra, come in," Meg's mother said, taking my arm.

"What's going on? I don't understand." I lowered Julian to the carpet, and he instantly ran to where the twins sat.

"I'm afraid we've got some bad news," she continued. "Meg was in an accident last night."

I must've fainted because the next thing I remembered, I was lying on the couch with Mrs. Weaver attempting to give me a sip of brandy.

"Lexy?" Her voice was a strained whisper. "Are you okay?"

"I'm sorry." I held her arm. "Where's Julian?"

"He's fine. He's playing with the children upstairs. You fainted, and we didn't want him afraid."

I couldn't stop shaking. I was the one afraid now. "You said something about Meg in an accident. Is she okay?"

There was a long pause as her mother looked down. I could tell now she had been crying, and as she looked at her hands, her tears started again. She whispered the words that stopped my heart. "Meg is no longer with us."

I rolled onto my side as the pain hit me again and again. I had no breath, and I curled into a tight ball, my hands over my face.

"I'll put on a pot of coffee." Gigi left the room, but I couldn't unclench. I simply wrapped both arms around my knees and squeezed, pressing my face into them.

After several minutes, I felt a hand on my side and looked up. It was Bill. I slowly pulled myself to a sitting position, away from him, hugging my knees to my chest.

"It's my fault," he said. "She would never have been in that car if it weren't for me."

My throat was so tight, but I managed to say it. "Or me."

"I haven't told her mother anything," he continued. "I haven't told anyone, but from the state of the house… Chuck could tell something was up."

I blinked up at him. "What was at the house?"

"Smashed pictures. All your paintings were torn and thrown in the yard."

I clenched back into my knees again, and a fresh stream of tears slid down my cheeks.

"She found the note," he continued. "She knew about Julian. About us."

I nodded. "She told me."

His eyebrows pulled together as he studied my face. "You saw her again?"

"She came to my house. She said she knew about Julian. She hated me, and I took everything she ever cared about."

He exhaled deeply, looking again at the carpet. "She would've forgiven you. One day."

"She would never have forgiven me. Not as long as I lived." I was sure of that.

After a few moments, he turned his palm over, studying it as he spoke. "Did she seem like she wanted to kill herself?"

I shook my head. "She wanted to kill me. And I was ready to let her. She was very angry and very drunk. I tried to stop her, but she hit me in the head."

He glanced at my eyebrow. "You need stitches."

"I can't take Julian to the hospital right now," I said. "It'll have to wait."

"Leave him here. I'll take you."

Gigi agreed to watch Julian while Bill took me to the hospital. I lied and said I'd hit my head last night and didn't realize how bad it was. I wasn't sure if the police would be able to tell Meg had been at my house, but the last thing I wanted was for people to know she'd been drinking or the reason she was there.

Bill took me to the emergency room in Fairview, and they led us back immediately. He sat with me while I waited for the numbing medicine to take effect.

"How did it happen?" I asked. "What did the police say?"

"Lightpole. Smashed into it at about 100 miles per hour."

"Oh, god." I closed my eyes as fresh tears filled them. He reached for my hand, but I pulled it away. "Don't. I can't take comfort from you. It's hard for me to even look at you."

He nodded, clasping his hands in his lap. "What will you do?"

"I don't know." I couldn't think for the pain in my chest, the storm swirling in my brain. "I can't go to that office again. I'm never going back there."

"You've got to do something. What about Julian?"

"I've got enough money saved to last a little while. I'll figure something out."

"Please let me help you." His blue eyes were so full of pain, but there was no way I could ever allow myself to be near him again. We'd have to find comfort elsewhere.

"I'll let you know if Julian needs anything. For now, just leave us alone."

The doctor repaired my head and even gave me something to help me sleep, as if I could take it with a baby in the house. I collected Julian from Gigi's and went home. He was tired from playing with the twins and Will, and I pulled him in the bed with me and closed my eyes.

I hoped to sleep for a long, long time.

# Anna – *December*

She hadn't written any more after that. I put the book down feeling weak and completely drained. Tears had filled my eyes over and over reading the pages, and I was sure it was because I knew what happened next.

For the next seventeen years Alexandra LaSalle lived alone with her son, she stopped painting altogether, and she withdrew from society. She shut Mr. Kyser out, and it wasn't until six months ago that Julian's near-fatal car accident drove them back into each others' arms. That was where I came into the story.

From what I could tell, it was also the start of Mr. Kyser's renewed efforts to coax her back to him, but her resistance was so strong. Even that day at her house when he'd practically begged her to tell Julian, when he'd pulled her into his arms and kissed her, she'd pushed him away.

I looked up at my window and thought of Julian. He was so happy and carefree all the time. I wanted to call him and ask him to take me somewhere. I wanted to pull his arms around me and make him hold me close. I wanted him to kiss me again. I wanted to be ready for us.

I studied my phone several minutes before deciding to send him a text. *Thinking of you*, I typed.

I didn't have to wait long for his reply. *Meet me at the beach?*

*Sure*, I replied.

In less than ten minutes, we were walking side by side in the growing dusk. I still wore my jeans and tee with the black cardigan from earlier. He was similarly dressed, but in a black hoodie. Every few seconds the sky would light up with a lone firework. The city was preparing for their New Year's Eve celebration, and apparently the producers were testing a few explosives early. We were walking by the shore with only the street lights breaking the dark and the occasional glittery rocket.

"I love nights like this." Julian's eyes twinkled in the light from the fireworks. He looked into the distance, and from where we stood, the glow of lights seemed centered over the ocean.

I studied his face. What would Julian say if he knew what I'd just read? I wanted to tell him so much, but now I understood his mother's fears. Maybe keeping this secret was the best thing after all.

"What were you doing tonight?" I asked instead, sliding my bare feet through the cool sand as we walked. I'd left my flip flops back at the pier.

"Welding, forging. Lyon's Share asked for a few smaller pieces, and I'm trying to make something they can sell."

Lyon's Share was a small, family-owned art gallery in downtown Newhope, and they had several of Julian's pieces on display. They were even writing a recommendation for him for SCAD. He was definitely following in his mother's footsteps—at least professionally.

"Have you sold anything yet?" I glanced over at him, and he smiled.

"Not yet, but once I do, we're going on a real date."

"Julian." I shook my head.

"Right," he nodded. "You're still in mourning."

I punched his arm. "I'm not in mourning."

"Good, because that guy was a loser."

I bit my lip. "He wasn't. It was just… complicated."

"Well, he was definitely stupid." He slipped an arm across my shoulders and pulled me into his side. I hugged his waist and thought about what I'd read of his dad at his age. Good genes.

"Tell me what you made," I said as we walked.

"Just generic stuff. Hummingbird feeder with vines and leaves. A dancer."

"A dancer?" That had me curious.

"Like one of those ballerina pieces? Just trying to make stuff people like to buy."

"I'd love to see it," I said.

He stopped walking and faced me, our arms still around each other. "Then come over now."

The fireworks testing seemed to have ended, and we'd circled back around to where my car was waiting. "Can I get a rain-check?" I said, stretching up to kiss his cheek. "I've got some work to finish."

"But we're on break." He smiled and I studied his lips. If I went back with him to his studio, we would most definitely end up making out, and I really wanted to do that again very soon.

But I shook my head, stepping out of his arms. "I can't. I have to finish this project this weekend."

"Is it for school?" He caught my hand.

"No… it's for the paper. Research. Historical stuff."

"Wow," he laughed, "am I that boring?"

"Of course not," I said, squeezing his hand that now held mine. "It's actually really fascinating stuff."

"Then bring it over. You can read it to me while I work."

"No." I shook my head. "I mean, I can't. It's… not really something you can read aloud."

I pulled my hand back and fished in my pocket for my key. Julian watched me for a second then he leaned forward and kissed my forehead. His lips were warm against my skin in the cool night, and his breath whispered against my lashes. An involuntary shiver moved through me, and my eyes blinked to his. I thought of New Year's Eve and midnight and kisses.

"Tomorrow's the big night," he said. "Want to come back and watch the fireworks show with me?"

I smiled and blinked down again. Then I nodded. "I'll call you."

* * *

The quiet in my empty house was like a presence. The last journal waited for me upstairs, and it was almost as if Mr. Kyser stood up there waiting with it, waiting to tell me his side of the story.

I poured a glass of water and took a few sips before going to the stairs. My phone lit up with a text from Lucy, telling me about a New Year's Eve party tomorrow night. I nodded, but didn't reply to it. Instead, I turned my phone off and dropped it in my bag. I was almost finished here. One journal left.

I walked slowly to my room, not sure if I was ready for more intensity, but I had to know the final side. Maybe it would help me understand the end, where we were today.

I shut my door even though I was home alone and reached under the bed to retrieve Mr. Kyser's leather-bound journal. As I held it in my hands, I thought about what I knew of him. Cold, distant, rude at times, completely withdrawn from his children. Well, except for Jack.

Yet, there had been moments when I'd seen a flash of something. I wanted to say vulnerability, but it was more than that. It was desperation, like he couldn't keep waiting. Something had to change for him. I'd seen him with Julian's mom, and the feelings he had for her were still so strong.

I opened the cover, and a letter dropped out. It was old, and I recognized the handwriting as Ms. LaSalle's. Pulling the sides of the envelope apart, I saw inside was a folded note along with the small slip of paper on which she'd written she was pregnant. I slid it under my pillow to read at the end.

First I had to take my last trip down this dark memory lane.

# Book 3 – Bill

*May 31, 19 –*

*Getting married right out of high school was <u>not</u> in the plan.*

Meg gave me this journal for graduation. She said I should document my journey to success. I like that — the idea that one day I can look back and remember our story, how we made it.

I think it's important to start there, with that fact. I did *not* plan to get married at nineteen.

Bryant and I had our whole career path mapped out. We even ran it past the retired veterans at the small business center in Newhope. They were impressed. Said if we could convince farmers south of Fairview to stop planting sweet potatoes and cotton in the sand and sell us their land, it could work.

It was all coming together. And then Meg told me she was pregnant.

I couldn't believe my luck, and after how careful I'd always been.

Mardi Gras. That was when it happened. We'd all been drinking, and Meg was dancing around in that little short dress. We got back to Dad's truck, and I couldn't wait to pull her on my lap. It's not easy to remember protection every single time when your girlfriend looks like Meg — and when she's always so ready to go. I kept trying to get her on the pill, but she said it would make her fat. So it was up to me.

And I'd been careless. Lost focus.

Bryant is going to flip, and after two years of planning.

We got our big idea one summer in Florida. We'd spent the first two months working on my uncle's farm in Corona, driving combines and stacking hay bales. It was hard work and in the South County heat, I hated it. I swore to Bryant we were going to get the farms out of here if it was the last thing we did. He laughed, but Bryant's a good guy. We've been friends since we were kids.

Bryant's grandparents own a house in South Walton, and for ten years developers have been going down there, taking forgotten beachfronts and finding investors to purchase lots for luxury resort communities. Some are full-time residents and some are rentals.

I decided we could do the same in South County. We'd turn those swaths of open sand around East End Beach and Hidden Pass into tourist dollars with our names stamped on every one. It was going to work, and it was going to work big.

Now it felt like it was all slipping away.

Meg said nothing has to change, but I know she doesn't understand how much I'm going to be working.

Meg.

I'd never seen a girl like her when I started at Fairview High School. She caught my eye the first day with her long blonde hair and long, tanned legs. She walked right up to me and introduced herself, and we've been together ever since.

She'll make the perfect wife for what I'm planning, and even better, she believes in it as much as I do. So maybe she's right. Her mom can help with the baby while I'm at school, and we can keep moving forward.

But she has to understand, until we make it, work has to come first.

Bryant and I decided since I'm more of the salesman, I'll get the business degree at the university in Sterling, the county over. I'm hoping with summer school and intersession courses to finish in less than three years.

Bryant's dad is in construction, so Bryant will handle the site research and finding the best engineers and contractors. Then, when I finish school, we'll travel to Atlanta to start courting investors. And even though she claims to be against the whole thing, Miss Alexandra LaSalle is drawing up the elevations and landscape plans for us.

Lexy. That's a whole other story.

I'd also never met anyone like her before Meg introduced us. She's like some of the horses on my dad's ranch, wild and skittish and stubborn and beautiful all at the same time. She's a painter, and she likes to go out on the beach and close her eyes and just sit there. She says she's meditating, drawing inspiration from nature. I always thought she was crazy like her mom, but she's Meg's best friend. The two of them are inseparable, and that's a good thing. Lexy's part of the plan, even though I haven't told her yet.

She leaves for art school in the fall—the big one in Savannah—and I'm glad. She'll get the credentials she needs, and then I'll convince her to come back and join my team.

She might always try to fight with me about what we're doing, claiming she's against our ideas, but she drew up the first elevations for us for free. Said she just wanted to see if she could do it.

I don't know about that. All I know is when she unveiled those sketches for Bryant and me, it was incredible. There it was—the whole thing on paper. It was real, and I was so excited, I almost kissed her.

So let her go to Savannah. I'll finish up in Sterling, and once everything is in place, we'll have a first-rate team ready to bring it all home.

In two weeks, I'll be a married man with a baby on the way. That's a lot to swallow, but I don't plan to mess up again. We're going to do this just like we planned it, one step at a time.

It's going to work. I've made myself that promise.


*June 11, 19 –*

I've never done this, just so you know. Kept a journal, I mean. I'm not sure how to start this. I guess where we are now: Two months, and we start.

Bryant and I are so ready, it's hard to keep our focus on following the steps.

I'll do the wedding, get settled in the house Dr. Weaver is giving us in Fairview, and then I'll hit school running.

I signed up for twenty-one hours first semester, and if I'm able to handle that, I'll up it to twenty-four in the spring. Summer school max is eighteen, but I don't expect that to keep me from finishing in three years or less. They'll let me take up to six hours during intersession. That's how we mapped it all out.

It's going to be a lot of work, but I'm not afraid of work. I've been studying every book I could get my hands on for two years, starting with Warren Buffet's autobiography and working my way down. Accounting will be key, economics. We'll have all the details ready when we make our first board meeting in Atlanta. We might look like kids, but those suits won't know what hit them. Sledgehammer.

The hardest part was coming up with the name. We tossed around ideas for what to call the set of nine monster complexes, complete with a massive conference center, for almost two years before settling on Phoenician. We went Greek because it was smart, but tough. That was the image we wanted to convey. A force to be reckoned with. Solid towers, clean lines, and unmovable.

After Hurricane Frederick wiped everything out down here, Bryant and I agreed that in addition to economics, making these complexes strong enough to face down any storm was our top priority.

We also decided on the name of our company: Kyser-Brennan. I was worried my name first might ruffle feathers, but Bryant didn't mind. Like I said, he was a good guy. He and I were meant to do this together. Bryant was dependable and a worker, and he wasn't bothered by insignificant details like whose name was first on a piece of paper. All that mattered was making it to the end and coming out on top.

Everything starts in August. Until then, I plan to give Meg as much attention as possible. She says she understands what's coming, and she says she's fine with how hard it's going to be, with how much I'll be working. But I don't believe her. And if it all starts coming undone later, I want to be able to say I tried. I want her to have something happy to look back and remember.

I suggested we all go sailing last night because I knew she liked being with Lexy, and I was still planning to get The Artist onboard to lead our design team in a few years. It'd just be her to start, but Lexy's very good, and she knows us well enough to translate our ideas into images we can sell. Once we all finish undergrad, I'll convince her to come back here and join us. She might not get paid right away, but we'll take care of her once everything's up and running.

Bryant brought Donna Albriton. He's been talking about her a lot lately, and I'm pretty sure they're getting serious. I've never heard that guy say more than two words to any girl, so I expect him to pop the question before it's all over. It's cool with me. I like Donna. She's sweet, and she'll make him happy.

Some girls are crazy. Always getting into trouble or pulling stunts to get attention or make guys do what they want. Neither Meg nor Donna are like that. And Lexy's so focused on her art, I've never even seen her date.

Heck, one summer she set up an easel down at the marina, and she must've made five thousand bucks in three months. People would come down and watch her sit there quietly painting boats and pelicans, and she was making money hand over fist.

Yep. That's what we need on our team.

The girls arrived for the cruise about the same time. I couldn't take my eyes off Meg, she was so fine. I helped her onboard and gave her a kiss. She smelled like candy, and I was thinking about later, when we'd be alone. One good thing about getting my girlfriend pregnant, I could forget all the safety precautions and just enjoy myself for a few months.

Lexy looked pretty. I'm not sure why she's always pissed when I'm around, but I'll win her over soon enough. When Meg and I are married, Meg can help with that. And I'm sure she'll be glad to help if only to get her best friend back home. Meg's funny about having all the people she loves in the same place.

Lex likes to accuse me of wanting to destroy the beauty of our hometown. She just doesn't get it. It's not about destroying anything. It's about enhancing what we already have, and it's about getting in on the ground floor of what's coming. She'll understand soon enough. You can't stop progress.

Meg also told Lexy I knocked her up. Whatever. I'm glad. I was ready to tell Meg's parents the minute she told me. She's already three months along, not that you can tell it. She's hid that pregnancy well.

I don't like hiding, but she says we needed to wait until after our honeymoon.

I understood keeping quiet until after graduation. School officials were pretty uptight about stuff like that, and I wasn't jeopardizing my diploma. But now that we're out, she needs to let her parents know. With her dad's connections, he can probably pull strings or whatever and get her special treatment. But Meg wants to wait, so I agreed. It's her deal anyway.

Lexy looked at me with those brown eagle eyes of hers and made some crack about being nervous. I just shrugged her off. I'd worked this all out in my head. The baby was Meg's project. The plan was mine. Maybe it'd even be good for Meg to have a baby to occupy her time while I'm at school. And her parents will help her. She doesn't have to work or anything. Just stay home and play Mama while I take care of the rest.

I studied the five of us as I steered the boat. It's a good group. I imagine at some point there'll be six of us. Hopefully, Lexy'll hook up with someone we like. Maybe Meg could set her up with Rain Hawkins. His dad owns some prime farmland we could use for a base of operations, and maybe he'd throw in some capital.

It doesn't matter right now. Those details are the least of my concern. The girls are talking about the wedding, but I'm looking ahead to our future.


*June 30, 19 –*

Wedding, done. Honeymoon, done.

Honeymoon. That was a nice surprise.

I'd suggested we wait until after college to get married, but Meg wouldn't hear that. Then after she got pregnant, she was all, "Why create a scandal that would just turn into a reason for some uptight investor to vote against us?" She had a good point.

After our honeymoon, I was pretty happy I caved. If those seven days were any indication, our home life promises to be… pretty damn hot. I'd always heard guys joke about pregnant women being horny, but Meg surprised the shit out of me. First, she'd bought this underwear – crotchless and whatever – I expected that, but then she took it a step further by knowing exactly how to work it in her sexy panties. It was like I'd married an undercover porn star. She said she'd been studying some of her daddy's old magazines, and I started wondering what the hell Dr. Weaver was reading and shouldn't he be worrying about having another heart attack.

Sure, I already knew she was comfortable with the standards, her on my lap, doggy style, dining at the Y (I take care of my girl), but then she turned it around. She put on one of her little garter outfits and then wiggled her perfect ass against my fly. Working it backwards, shaking her long blonde hair, and winking at me over her shoulder. I almost blew it on the spot.

Naturally, I suggested we practice all her new tricks several times so I'd be sure she was enjoying it as much as I was. I was glad she hadn't started that behavior in high school. You'd be looking at one sweaty horse-rancher for sure if she had. We wouldn't have made it to senior year without her getting pregnant. Maybe twice.

You see, Dad had offered to let me take over the ranch when we announced the wedding. It was a good offer, but it would just be more working in the heat all summer long. And ranches were going the way of the dinosaur. No, I was going to college and Bryant and I would carry this ball all the way to the goal. I'd never have to work outside an air-conditioned office again.

Anyway, back to the honeymoon. One night after we'd followed Meg's preferred method — me on top, a little higher to hit the angle right… Okay, I confess, it was one of my favorite ways to go, too, because I could watch her beautiful face go all pink and her smooth brow crease when it happened for her. Anyway, after that I'd cuddled her in my arms and started thinking about August and how much I'd be gone. I wished again I'd had more self-control at Mardi Gras, but she just insisted she wasn't worried about it.

Actually, for the first time she suggested she was worried about me. Me? Something about me getting involved with another woman. That was when I knew she didn't have a clue how busy I'd be. I'd be lucky if I could muster the energy to sleep with *her* much less have time to worry about keeping some extra woman satisfied. Or under wraps. The thought of how much added time and labor that would require almost made me laugh out loud, but I didn't. I tried to be sensitive to her fears. I kissed her and assured her it would never happen.

I never thought someone like Meg would be insecure about anything. She was gorgeous, and her parents always took good care of her. Now they were expecting me to do the same. Marriage might not have been in the plan, but I wasn't going to let anybody down.

Not being around for my kid was going to suck. My dad was always there for me. He taught me to care for the horses, and I remembered being a little guy riding the tractor with him. I knew he loved me. Mom took off before I started kindergarten. She wanted to be a singer and moved to Branson. I barely even remember her. All I remember was being with Dad. Just the two of us. I hated that I wouldn't be around much for my little guy. I'd always thought I'd be a good dad like my own...

But that's spilt milk. No use crying over it now. My kids will learn who I am when they never had to worry about money or their future.

*Aug. 1, 19 –*

Two more weeks and I start school. Meg's dragging ass telling her parents about the baby, and I'm trying not to push her.

We moved into the small house in Fairview her parents gave us. It's tiny, but I'm not complaining. Everybody starts somewhere, and it won't be long before we're building that home overlooking Lost Bay.

I spent the rest of the summer with Bryant going over the details of what he'd be doing while I finished my degree. He's not much of a scholar, but he has great trade sense. He knows just about everyone in the business down here because of his dad's work. He already has a job with Cade Builders, and after three years as Mr. Cade's apprentice, he can apply for his Master Builder's license. Once he has that, it'll give us clout with the subcontractors in the area. He'll also get a good feel for the best specialty guys, the electricians and plumbers. We need good people who can assemble top crews.

Most of the workers'll be migrants, but that doesn't bother me. Those guys put their heads down and got the job done. I just need bosses who can deliver the goods on time. That's all Bryant's department, and he assured me again and again he's on top of it. I trust him. We both want the same thing.

He and I drove out to South Walton one week and surveyed the work they're doing off 30-A. Some of the developments stretch for miles inland, going way back into the pine trees with trails and lakes for canoeing and fishing. I hadn't considered something like that, but it's worth keeping in the idea file.

For now, we're working off the assumption that if vacationers are headed to the coast, they want to be on the beach. So our focus is on the Gulf. But I'll be watching to see if those places become popular with the tourists. There's plenty of good wildlife and hunting in South County if we want to develop north into Evangeline and Corona.

Starting out, though, we're focused on the beachfronts from Dolphin Shores through East End Beach, down to Hidden Pass. The nine Phoenician complexes will line the water like a wall, and each one will be five-star, ultimate luxury with a Gulf view.

We'll court the high-end retailers to set up shops in them and help market the different locations. Each one will have a different feel and theme, along the lines of what they're doing over in Vegas. It'll take about ten years to build them all, but after the first two are up, the rest will be the gravy that sees us through retirement.

*Oct. 5, 19 –*

Classes are going strong now – once I got over the logistics nightmare. It didn't occur to me to drive over and map out how far apart the actual rooms were when I stacked all my classes back to back. After being early for my first class, I was late for everything else, and I'd have to hustle if I planned to graduate with honors. Professors are not impressed by tardiness.

But the coursework is a piece of cake. I pretty much covered most of the subject matter in my own independent research. Now the trick is giving the profs what they want and getting myself noticed. So many of them are retired businessmen, and I want them to pass their connections on to me.

At home, Meg is turning into a cute little pregnant lady. I was worried about her getting too attached and being lonely, but surprise, surprise – I'm the one having problems. She's stayed tiny except for the basketball under her robe, and she'll pull her blonde hair into pigtails and waddle around our little house making breakfast and bringing me the paper. I lie in bed and watch her, grinning like an idiot, but I don't care. She'll smile and kiss my head, and I try to let her leave the bedroom occasionally.

Twice I entertained the idea of letting my plan go. I could take Dad up on his offer and run the ranch. It's a ready-made setup, and I wouldn't have to push us so hard. I wouldn't have to leave my family. But that isn't what I want, and I know it isn't what Meg wants. She's happy to make these sacrifices now because she knows I'll get her that house on Hammond Island. She'd never be satisfied being a rancher's wife in Midlind.

Nope, I'm sticking to the plan, and having a baby on the way makes me more focused than ever on getting the job done.

When we finally told her parents last month, I made a bunch of big promises to her dad about how I wasn't going to let them down. I meant them, too. Dr. Weaver really raked me over the coals that night, but I was expecting that. Meg dropped the bomb right in the middle of dinner, and he got up and took me from the table for "scotch and cigars." Meg said she had a nice little conversation with her mom about how they planned to bankroll everything, but that was not the conversation I had with her dad.

I followed him into the living room preparing for what was coming. It was good practice—I'd be facing guys like him soon enough in the board rooms. Old suits who underestimated me because I was young, who were just waiting for a reason to say no.

"Baby on the way," Dr. Weaver said frowning.

"Yes, sir."

"So you and Meg were together before the wedding?"

Give me a break. Meg and I dated four years. He knew the score. Still, I played along, acting regretful. "Yes, sir," I said, looking down.

"I don't approve of that sort of thing, but I guess that's neither here nor there at this point." He took a sip of his scotch. "Did you know about her pregnancy before you got married?"

"Yes, sir," I said, holding my tumbler. I was still underage, but I guessed we were past that now. "I wanted to tell you, but Meg said we should wait."

"I thought you were a smart man, Bill. This doesn't give me much evidence to support that belief." He walked over to the fireplace. "Are you planning to let Meg make all the decisions in your marriage?"

"No, sir," I said. "I just wanted her to be happy, and well, I hadn't planned for this to happen. We were being careful, but... I'm sorry."

"Sorry doesn't unspill milk."

"No, sir."

He stared hard at me, and a line ran straight down the center of his forehead. "What are you going to do now?"

Here goes. "I've thought about that a lot, sir. I'm hoping I can still follow my plans."

For a moment he didn't answer. Then he said, "I understand you were planning to take a pretty heavy course load. I guess you're expecting me to step in and bail you out."

"No, sir," I said quickly. "I mean, I hoped Mrs. Weaver might be able to help with the baby, and I hoped she could provide some company for Meg. I wasn't expecting you to bail me out. I'll work and go to school. It just might take longer than I'd originally planned—"

"I don't think you have longer," he interrupted. "I think your idea's a good one, and I think the longer you take to get it in motion, the more likely it will be that someone else comes in and beats you to the punch."

You could've knocked me over with a feather. "Yes, sir. I've thought of that."

"That's why I am going to help you. But I'm doing it for my daughter and my grandson. You got careless, young man, and I don't believe in rewarding carelessness."

I nodded, keeping the relief off my face. "Yes, sir."

"Lucky for you, I also don't believe in letting my only daughter suffer because of your poor judgment." He set the tumbler down, the stern face back. "But I don't expect to see you mess up again. No coloring outside the lines. Personally or professionally."

I looked him straight in the eye that time. "I'm committed to seeing this through, sir."

And that was it. It was all on me to live up to my end of the bargain—which was exactly how I wanted it. I'd made my plan, and I intended to deliver. It helped Meg was covered now. I could focus.

That night in bed, Meg said she wanted to name the baby after me. It was really cool—made me feel kind of important already, even though I didn't have anything to show for it. I kissed her, and we ended up doing it all over again.

After Round 2, she started talking about us having a John, Jr., for her dad and a Lucy for Lexy. I told her we had to wait. She got pouty, but her saying all that shit nearly gave me heartburn. It was like I kept telling Bryant, one step at a time. We'd get there, but we had to get on our feet first.

She could have all the kids she wanted once we made it.


*Dec. 12, 19 —*

First semester down, four more to go.

Will came a month ago. I was right in the middle of an accounting exam. I didn't know if that was a sign, but

I managed to make it across the bay and spend some time with the two of them in the hospital before I had to turn around and drive right back.

He's a cute little guy. I had a week before intersession started, so I spent every day watching Meg feed him and change his diapers. That was about all she did, but it was still fun to watch. I helped with bathing, but it was mainly because we were both scared she'd lose hold of him. He was like a slippery little noodle in the water, and even though she used a tiny tub with a ramp, it was nerve-racking.

Naturally, the first time Meg bathed him, he sprayed her down. She screamed, and I laughed. You can't get a little guy naked, wet, and cold like that and not expect to get soaked. I thought about all the things she wouldn't know about raising a boy. This could be pretty funny in a few years. Even if I do have more time then, maybe I'll hang back and see how some of the situations play out.

Dr. Weaver came over a lot to visit, and Meg officially quit her job at the hospital. After he and I had our conversation, he eased up on me, and I was pretty sure he realized I meant business when he saw how many courses I crammed into each semester.

I noticed he looked kind of tired. Something around his eyes seemed not quite right. Weary or something. I'd be the last person to say anything to him, but I wanted to mention it to Meg. He might need to cut down on the hours now that he was a pawpaw.

Bryant was keeping up his end of the bargain. He recruited the top two contractors in South County to work with us on the developments, and working with Cade had him in the mix of specialty guys and suppliers. Just as we'd planned, all our crews would be in place when we were ready to make our pitch.

Lexy even came home for Christmas. She was having a little adventure at SCAD, I overheard. I stayed out of their conversation, but she and Meg spent hours discussing some professor she'd taken up with.

On the one hand, it was *not* great because I was still hoping she'd come back and work with us. Her getting mixed up with a professor could turn into her deciding to stay in Savannah permanently.

On the other hand, it *was* great because Lexy was just a kid. If this professor wanted to date her, no matter how hot she was, something wasn't right. And it might make her more ready to come back and work with us.

Either way, I kept my opinion to myself. Everything would work out in its own time.


*May 1, 19 —*

Yeah, I know I'm not the first guy to say this, but I will never understand women.

It started a month ago. I got home from class all ready for a relaxing evening with my family before I had to hit the books, and Meg blindsided me saying she wanted me to slow down.

Slow down. Like that's even an option!

We went over this a million times last year when she told me she was pregnant. I told her it was going to be hard, and we should wait to get married, but no. She wouldn't hear that. We were getting married right away, and she would never say a word about my working or being gone so much.

Now she's changed her mind. Well, guess what? It's too damn late for that. I've already committed myself to too many people, her father included. She'll just have to deal with it.

Then, I agreed to have a dinner party with those Hayes people she met—I was happy to do it! I don't know where she got the idea she couldn't have or go to parties, and Travis and Winifred Hayes appeared to be a very nice couple, if a bit older than us.

Meg took Will to her mother's house for the evening, and after the initial cocktails and small-talk, we all sat down for dinner. That was when the fun started.

"So, Bill, I hear you're in the development game," Travis said.

"Trying to be," I answered, being friendly. "At the moment I'm up to my neck in classes, getting my business degree."

"How long do you have left on that?" he asked, like it was his business.

"The goal is three years, but I'm hoping to shave that down to two and a half. So far, I'm on track."

"Two and a half years!" He looked stunned, which I liked. "That sounds like it might be a record."

I shrugged. "I don't care about record books. I'm just focused on getting it done."

"And you're working with someone?" He stabbed the carrots Meg had made, and I noticed the ladies weren't talking. That was my first clue something was up. Still I played along with his twenty questions.

"My friend Bryant Brennan," I said. "His dad's got connections in the construction field, so he's working on making contacts there and getting crews in place while I finish up at school. So far he's ahead of me."

"Very interesting. I find that line of work fascinating." Dr. Hayes chewed a bit, and I figured we were done. Not quite. "Is this project of yours something you came up with on your own?"

I nodded. "Pretty much, but it's nothing new. You only have to look around to see development approaching us on all sides. We're just trying to catch the wave."

His eyebrows rose. "I guess that's the sense of urgency."

"I'm so impressed by how committed you are to this project," his wife jumped in.

I glanced at her before answering. "Our commitment is what's going to determine how far we go."

Meg joined the conversation now, seeming a little nervous. "Billy's been planning this out since we were juniors in high school. He and Bryant have it all mapped out."

"Isn't that something!" Winifred said. "And Meg, you said he basically puts in 60-hour weeks? How long can you keep that up, Bill?"

Mrs. Hayes was starting to annoy me. "I'll keep it up as long as I need to," I said. "For now I'm looking at two more years."

"Winnie, don't pester the man. He's got a plan." My eyes went to her husband, but I couldn't tell if he was patronizing me or not. Meg looked uncomfortable.

"This pasta's great, Meg." I decided to change the subject.

"Tell me about your boy, Bill." Travis sounded like Dr. Weaver now.

"Not much to tell. He's about six months old, so he's not doing much yet."

"I thought six months was when all the magic happened," he smiled at his wife.

"When they start doing all sorts of things."

"You're the doctor," I replied. "I guess you would know."

"Yes, but you're here with him. Has he smiled at you yet?"

I shook my head. "Not really. But he goes to bed early, so I only see him about an hour every night. And then he's usually eating or bathing."

"That's too bad." Dr. Pompous Douchebag said. "Can't get those days back you know."

I'd had enough. "You're an intern, right, Travis?" I asked.

"That's right," he said, looking smug.

"So you guys are waiting to have children?"

"Well, we're not waiting on purpose," he said. "We've just been having a little difficulty."

"What's the matter, Travis? Shooting blanks?" I was being a dick, but I had a reason.

"I'm sorry?" He put his fork down.

"I guess that's none of my business," I said.

"I'd say it's not."

"Kind of like what's going on in my family's none of your business."

That shut his interfering mouth. The rest of the dinner was dominated by the girls' discussing their upcoming DAR functions and Art in the Park. When they finally left, I was more inclined to talk to Meg.

"I'm sorry," she said after we'd gone to bed. "Travis was way out of line tonight."

I pulled her onto my chest ready to make peace. "It's not your fault. I just don't like you being influenced by people like that."

"Influenced is the wrong word, I think."

I combed my fingers through her soft hair. "What would you say?"

"Enlightened?" She sat up and faced me then.

I frowned. "I don't get your point."

"Well, they *were* meddling," she looked down, "but I do agree little Will should've smiled at you by now. I worry you're missing a lot of time we won't get back."

"We went through this last month," I said, getting angry again.

"But you didn't let me finish," she pressed. "You just shut me out."

"I'm not shutting you out. You're not listening." I paused to soften my tone. I didn't want to fight with her, I wanted to help her get her eyes back on the prize. Remind her of the things she wanted, the things I was working so hard to give her. "We've got to keep going like we planned. Don't you want the big house on the island? Aren't you excited about being married to the most important developer in South County?"

"Of course," she said, studying her hands in her lap. "But your plan is not going to disappear. You could still do it and spend time with us."

I reached over and covered her hands with mine. "That's where you're wrong, Meg. If I slow down, someone will come in and beat me to it."

She didn't like it, but I knew I was right. And I hoped this phase she was in would pass. I didn't like the pressure she was putting on us, and the more she pushed, the more I saw us growing apart.

*June 22, 19 –*

Asking Lexy to attend Meg's second dinner party was a stroke of brilliance. She was definitely a positive influence on my wife, and she was deceptively tough. Those Hayes jackasses didn't stand a chance against the two of us. We shut their stupid mouths.

Watching her maneuver her way through Travis's thinly veiled barbs solidified my decision to get her onboard with Kyser-Brennan. I'd had a few brushes with investors so far, and they lived to eat your lunch and test your strength. I'd learned to be on my toes, and Lexy seemed to be a natural at it. Where she got it from, I didn't know, but she could definitely hold her own. I imagined Bryant, Lex, and me entering a board room and smiled. We might look young and inexperienced, but those suits had better be on their toes.

Her trip home for the summer was also taking the pressure off me being in school. Lexy and Meg spent almost every day together, and as a result, Meg completely stopped nagging me about my course load. I imagined Lexy must've talked some sense into her. If we were going to do all the things we'd planned, somebody had to bust his ass.

The only problem with summer was that it ended. Fast. It was so much easier for me to concentrate on my classes knowing Meg had someone keeping her away from that Hayes woman. I was sorry Lexy was heading back to Savannah, but we all had things we were working on.

Bryant and I decided to have a meeting to see where we stood and what still needed to be done, and I was pleased with our progress.

"My dad's got some good ideas for roofers," Bryant said, flipping through the small notebook he always carried. "And he's found this guy in Destin who's working on a way to reinforce the walls to get them to Cat 5 zoning cheaper. I'm going to meet with him next week."

"Sounds great," I said.

"How's school coming?" he asked.

"Getting there." I had my calendar out, counting off the months until I was free. "I think eight's my limit, but that still should put me finishing in two and a half years. And I've had a few professors give me names of potential investors in Atlanta. You and I should go out there by Christmas and start feeling them out."

"I'm in. Just tell me when and where." He folded his book, and put it in his front pocket.

I figured I'd run my other idea past him now that we were close to starting. "What do you think about bringing Lexy onboard to head up marketing and design?"

"Lexy?" His brow creased, and he rubbed his chin. "I thought she hated our ideas. What changed her mind?"

"Well, I don't know if it's changed or not," I said, my hands going to my pockets. "But I was thinking about approaching her with an offer. If you're in agreement."

"You know I trust you, Bill. Need me to do anything?"

I smiled. "Doubt it. I'll let you know. For now, I'm just pushing through as fast as I can."

"We'll get there," he said.

That's what I like about Bryant. He's straightforward, cut and dried. You always know where you stand. He isn't trying to pull any fast ones, and he's always ready to offer a hand. Partners like him aren't easy to find. I'm lucky our dads were friends.

I couldn't remember not knowing Bryant, and I was looking forward to the day when these preliminaries were done and he and I could show this town what we could really accomplish.

I drove out that evening to the Romar Beach Pavilion and parked the truck. To the east there were a few old motel buildings. What was left after Frederick flattened this place a few years back. They were low-end and crummy, typical South County fare. People didn't expect luxury down here, they just wanted to bring the kids and flop out on the sand. Drink beer and fire up the grill.

I got out and walked down to the shore. The sun was setting to my right, and the sky was lit a brilliant pink color. With the help of these blue waters and shimmering white sands, I was going to change all of this. Those rednecks could stay up in Dolphin Shores or Port Hogan, but East End Beach was going to be different. The Phoenician complexes would be replete with luxury and high-end opulence.

But the clock was ticking. I knew I wasn't the only one with these ideas. We had to get here first. I had to be the one to stake that initial claim on these acres of sand just begging to be developed. In ten years' time, you wouldn't recognize this place, and it would all be the result of one man's dream.

I grinned. One man's dream. Bryant would love that. Okay, one man's dream and the belief and support of his best friends. We were all working hard, and it was going to pay off. Patience was the hardest part.

*Sept. 7, 19 —*

The death of Meg's father was an unexpected blow. First week of classes, and I got the call to come home right away. Luckily, since it was the first week, I wouldn't get too far behind, and a death so close in the family warranted a few days off.

Naturally, Meg and her mother were a wreck, so I took over all the business arrangements, settling up the finances, and making sure Mrs. Weaver was taken care of.

I liked Dr. Weaver, but he was always more like the wrath of God waiting to hit me over the head if I screwed up than a kindly father-in-law. I didn't think he ever approved of me dating Meg, even when we were in high school, much less our getting married. Still, I liked to think I'd begun proving myself to him toward the end. He didn't seem to scowl at me so much, although that could've been Will's doing. He softened up a lot once that little guy made his appearance.

Dr. Weaver was originally from Birmingham, so many of his relatives would be driving or flying in for the funeral and then heading back out almost immediately after. Luckily the old Magnolia Hotel in Fairview was still in operation. It needed restoring badly, but it would do for the large group we were expecting.

Meg called Lexy, and she was coming back for the funeral. I was surprised she could get the time off from school, but it was her first week of classes, too. She probably had plenty of time to get caught up on what she'd miss.

Once the day came, I was pleased at how many people packed Our Lady of the Gulf Catholic Church for the funeral mass. The family all sat in front, but Lexy and Miss Stella were in the row behind us. Lex sure cried a lot. I never realized she was so close to Dr. Weaver. Or maybe it was sympathy for her friend.

Later that night when we were all back at the cottage, I heard the girls talking about that professor she'd been dating. Seemed he'd taken up with some new student since school started back, and Lexy was considering dropping out of art school. I thought about approaching her with my plan for working with us but decided to wait. She might say no without even considering the offer just because she was upset. I'd give her a chance to get over that loser then we'd talk.

*Oct. 23, 19 —*

Looking back on my academic career, I'd have to chalk this semester up as being the hardest. Even more so than my first when I was dealing with all the logistics and trying to get to class on time. Even more than last spring, when Meg started hanging around with Winnie Hayes and wouldn't stop nagging me to slow down and be at home more.

For starters, Dr. Weaver's funeral almost killed my schedule. I lost two weeks helping wrap up his business and supporting Meg and her mother. I'd hoped the two of them would lean on each other, but instead Mrs. Weaver took off for Arizona. She went to stay with a friend in Sedona for several weeks, and Meg was left home alone with the baby.

Meg said it was her idea, but then I found her crying and trying to sort through old papers and pictures. I finally convinced her to leave all that to her mom. Mrs.

Weaver might be out of commission now, but she'll come around. And it's still her business.

We had just put that behind us when Dad called to say he intended to sell the ranch and move back to Opelika. My grandfather's Alzheimer's had gotten worse, and Dad wanted to go home and take care of him.

I hadn't spent much time with my dad since I started school, but knowing he was there was reassuring. Although I wouldn't admit it, the ranch was my safety.

I took a Saturday and drove alone to Midlind to visit him. I found him in the barn brushing down one of the horses. It was so familiar being back, I could almost hear the sounds of tractors running and men whistling and shouting back to each other in the distance. It had been years since this place was up and running at full capacity, but Dad still kept a few horses. I leaned my arm on a mare and scratched her neck as we talked.

"Been a while since you made it out here," he said, pulling the hairs out of a brush.

"I've been working pretty hard at school," I said, patting the red-brown beast beside me, inhaling the sweet-sharp scent of hay and manure and horse sweat.

"I figured as much," Dad said, going to the tack wall and stowing the brush. Gonna make a name for yourself."

"Trying to."

He walked back and leaned down, patting the front of the horse's lower leg, prompting her to lift her foot. I watched as he inspected her hoof then lowered it and moved to the next one. I hadn't thought about what I wanted to say when I'd decided to make the drive southeast to see him. Now all I could do was stand and watch him work.

"How's Grandpaw?" I finally said.

Dad's lips tightened as he slowly shook his head. "Not so good. Keeps calling me Stuart."

My lips pressed together. "I'm sorry to hear that." My great-uncle Stuart had died ten years ago.

"It's pretty bad," Dad nodded. "I hate to tell you, son. Don't think he'd know you if you made the trip." He exhaled and walked to the door of the stall. I followed him slowly.

"I figure if you don't want the ranch, it's the only thing holding me here. And he needs me now," Dad continued.

"I hope you don't think I didn't love it here."

His smile was tired. "You just never were into ranchin. That's something you got from your mama. That itch to do something big. Make a name for yourself."

I wasn't sure what to say next. We didn't talk much about her. But I'd always wondered, so I asked. "After Mom left, did you ever think about trying to go get her? Make her come back?"

"Nah," he breathed. "You can't make somebody love you if they don't."

I nodded at the familiar words. "I'll miss you, Dad. It meant something to me knowing you were out here, and I could come home if I ever needed to."

"You can still come home if you need to, son."

"But you know what I mean."

He stopped walking and clapped my shoulder. "You were always a good boy, Bill. And you're smart. You'll do fine."

We spent the afternoon cleaning up the place. He gave me an old photo of him and my mom when they were younger, and I looked at my blue eyes staring back at me from the face of a stranger. All I remembered of her was she ran off when I was little, broke Dad's heart, and left everything a wreck for him. He never saw another woman, and on those bad nights when he started drinking and missing her, he'd usually pass out around nine. I'd take a horse and ride down to the creek. The water there fed into Coyote Bay and eventually made its way to the Gulf.

I didn't know that just like her, one day I'd leave this place for good, too.

*Nov. 28, 19 –*

Dad's leaving hit me harder than I expected, but I buried myself in schoolwork. And when I looked up, we were almost through November. Only two semesters to go and I'd have my degree. Nonstop coursework had paid off, and I was finishing in record time. Two and a half years, with honors.

My professors had been extremely encouraging, and one of them introduced me to Abe Mitchell, the president of the college. He put me in contact with Rex Harding, chairman of Peachtree Investments. They were a fat-cat investment group in Atlanta that Abe said was always looking for new blood to throw money at. A few of the board members were heavily involved in some South Walton developments, so they knew how hot the market was down here.

Bryant and I decided to drive north and meet with them. To feel them out. It was a dead week for everyone, and I had a few days before finals started. It was a good time to talk about future plans and places to throw money. So we made an appointment to speak to their board after their regular meeting.

It was our first meeting with investors, and I was more than ready to go.

*Dec. 1, 19 —*

I don't remember who said it first, but I love it when a plan comes together.

That trip to Atlanta was an incredible success from start to finish. There was even an unexpected perk — I got to teach a prickass art professor a lesson about mistreating one of my future team members.

But backing up, the whole thing started with our meeting at Peachtree. We agreed I'd lead the charge because I was more comfortable talking to groups. Bryant tended to ramble when he got nervous, and while he was very good at handling crews of burly construction workers, these sharks in suits threw him off. He preferred to sit back and answer any technical questions while I painted the picture of what was coming in their minds.

Peachtree Investments was located in the penthouse suites of a forty-floor office building in Buckhead. We booked hotel rooms at the Winfrey directly across the street, and I spent the day going over our charts and projections. I had Lexy's drawings in my briefcase, and I was ready to show them our plans, discuss their opportunity and give them a glimpse of South County's future.

We also made dinner plans with Lexy for after the meeting, and I decided it was time to make the big pitch to her as well. I should say to Alex now. When I called and talked to her, she said she preferred Alex since she'd started her career. I kind of liked it, too. Sounded more grown-up or something.

She'd been up here working for some advertising company, and I didn't want her getting so entrenched that she wouldn't want to come home. That professor was supposed to help me. Instead he'd sent her flying to Atlanta with a school friend. But you couldn't keep successful people down. I just had to link her success with ours.

Rex Harding could've been the same age as Dr. Weaver, and at our first meeting he was already sizing me up. It paid to be good-looking when you asked people for money — something about investors wanting to be associated with attractive people — but my face was a major drawback with these old guys. I looked too young, and it meant I had to work extra hard to be taken seriously. But I was ready, and it helped that Bryant was an ex-football player. He towered over most of these guys, and he outweighed them by about sixty pounds, too.

"Mr. Kyser, Mr. Brennan, welcome to Atlanta," Rex said, shaking our hands. "I hope you're having a pleasant visit."

"Thank you, Mr. Harding," I said. "It's always a pleasure being here."

"Call me Rex," he said, holding my arm and motioning toward the door. "We're looking forward to hearing your proposal. Doris, I see Bill has handouts for everyone, please pass these out. Can I get you a drink?"

"Just water," I said, following him into the room. "And since it's late, I'll go ahead and start. I know everyone's ready to call it a day."

The board consisted of nine silver-haired men in glasses and three younger guys ready to eat me for lunch. I walked to the front of the room and placed our first elevation on the easel that had been set up for me. Doris lowered the lights, and I switched on the projector.

"Gentlemen, I know there are several of you here who've worked in beach development in the past and who are currently involved in such projects now." I started the presentation. "You know the markets are changing, consumers have more disposable income than ever before, and populations are migrating to the water at rates that are unmatched in history, both for recreation and to live.

*Next slide, map of development trends.* "Up until now, the panhandle of Florida has been the most popular destination in our area, and we've watched development creep westward from Panama City to South Walton to Destin, Fort Walton, and now Pensacola. It's only a matter of time before it crosses into Alabama, where the first stop is Hidden Pass followed closely by East End Beach.

*Enter Kyser-Brennan.* "Our proposal is to meet that demand with a series of luxury high rises that feature a mixture of time-shares, rentals and outright ownership condos complete with amenities such as indoor tennis courts, high-end restaurants, shopping, a convention center, even nightclubs. The complete, five-star experience."

"I don't know about this," one of the younger members interrupted. "Aren't there plenty of high rises in East End Beach? And I haven't heard the market there is changing so much. When most people think of beach luxury, they think of Sandestin, Tiger Point, places like that."

"It's true, they do. Right now," I said, undeterred. "Those places were specifically developed to attract the executive golf and country club market. But they're not going to be enough." I pulled up the graphics, Lexy's drawings of the Phoenicians. "These areas are just taking off, and two developments won't hold the numbers that are being projected for the next ten years. That's why we're ready to break ground as soon as we've got the investors in place."

"But south Alabama isn't thought of as high-end. It's more Redneck Riviera," an older member chuckled.

"Dolphin Shores is proudly the heart of the Redneck Riviera," I smiled, pulling them back to me. "But East End Beach and Hidden Pass are just getting on the board. They're waiting to have their reputations established. I'm saying if we jump on that, we can shape that image and have people thinking of it as the more refined next door neighbor."

"Sounds risky," the gentleman to Rex's left spoke. "We've got more security in Florida. People know about Florida, and there's still plenty of space to add more developments when we're ready to do so."

"Of course it's risky," I said. "What investment doesn't come without risk? I'm asking you to look ahead. In the packets you'll see all the numbers. We've had the best market analysts in Newhope and Sterling look at them, and at our projections, and they all agree this is a sure thing. For someone. I'm suggesting that someone be you."

"And you, of course," the old man laughed.

"I've heard enough," another young member spoke. "Who is this kid? And we're supposed to trust him with millions of dollars?"

"With all due respect," I said. "You don't look that much older than me, so I take it somebody must've trusted you at some point when you were younger. Our numbers are sound. Just read our proposal. Run it through your own analysts."

"Don't worry, we will," he said. "And when I ask someone to take a chance on me, I have the credentials to back me up."

Rex stepped in at that point. "Bill comes to us well-recommended, Troy. I had a personal call from Abraham, who's very impressed with his performance so far."

"Thank you," I said. "Gentlemen, we've got a great location. We've got friendly residents and a beautiful ocean. I grew up in this area, so I know most of the workers there, and my partner here has lined up the best engineers and crews who are ready to make the jobs happen. What more do you need besides location and people with the determination and know-how to make it succeed?"

The member to Rex's left spoke. "Young man, are you attempting to educate us on how a successful business deal is made?"

"No, sir," I said, nodding in his direction. "I'm attempting to reassure you that *I* know how a successful business deal is made."

He raised his eyebrows and leaned back in his chair. "Rex?"

Rex's lips pulled tight, but it felt like I had them. "I'll take this under advisement. Thank you, Bill. We'll look over all your materials, and I'll let you know where we stand on Monday. If we have any questions, we'll ask."

Bryant and I left the building walking on air. I couldn't stop smiling.

"I'll be damned. Shit," Bryant said, clapping me hard on the back. "You nailed it at the end there. Where did that come from?"

"Two years of concentrated thinking," I said, buzzing with adrenaline. "Everything I said in there is just what I've been saying to you since that summer on the farm."

"I've never heard you say it like that," he laughed. "And in front of that kind of audience."

"Bullies is what they are. Just trying to make us sweat." I unbuttoned my coat and loosened my tie. I was ready to cut loose. "But they know a good thing when they see it, and we're handing them the opportunity of a lifetime."

"You got me convinced." Bryant was still shaking his head.

I glanced at him. "I thought you were onboard from the beginning."

"Oh, I was. But I've always had working with Dad to fall back on."

"Well, so did I. But this is going to happen, Bryant. I haven't been bustin my ass all this time for nothing." We stopped at my rental.

"So what now?" He said. "Recruitment meeting number two?"

"Yeah, I'll give Alex a call and tell her we're out. Her office is up in Roswell, so we'll beat you to the restaurant. Grab Donna and head over as soon as you're ready."

He hailed a cab, and I pulled onto the freeway. We'd agreed to have our pitch meeting and celebratory dinner at Ray's on the River. It was a fancy restaurant, and I wanted to impress our future design leader.

Lexy's new company Stellar Advertising was a high-end firm, and I'd have to pull out all the stops to get her to leave them and come work with us. Especially since we were starting primarily on faith. On top of that, I had to overcome her prejudice against the idea. But that Board meeting had me feeling more than confident.

I almost didn't recognize Lex when she walked out of the massive office building to meet me. I hadn't seen her since the funeral when she was so upset, but tonight she was all business and very professional in a grey suit with her long dark hair hanging loose down her back. We exchanged a casual hug, and I drove us to the restaurant as we made small-talk about advertising, living in Atlanta, seeing old friends.

I figured Bryant would be a half-hour behind us at least. He had to get back to Buckhead to pick up Donna at our hotel and then drive back to meet us. I suggested we wait at the bar, but as we entered the dim-lit room, she froze.

I caught her arm as she shrank back. "What's wrong?" I asked.

"I can't..." she looked down and away fast. "I don't want to go in there."

"Why not?" I quickly scanned the low tables to see what had caught her eye. I saw a dark-haired fellow sitting at the bar with a young blonde. "That guy? Who is that?"

"Can we just go?" she whispered, her dark eyes pleading. "Let's get a drink somewhere else and meet Bryant for dinner later."

I was in no mood to run from anybody. "This is the nicest place around," I said. "Just relax, you're with me."

"You're not my date, you're my best friend's husband."

"He doesn't know that. Be cool." I slipped my arm around her waist, hoping to boost her confidence. She straightened up at least, but I could feel her body was tense.

"What are you going to do?" she said quietly.

"Order us a few drinks. What do you want?"

She stopped walking. "Anything. I'll sit at this table back here.

"You're coming with me." I took her arm and led her casually to the bar, finding an open space right next to the fellow and his blonde date.

Of course he noticed us. He stood and approached Alex, and I could feel her draw back as if she were going to run. I tightened my grip on her arm.

"Alexandra?" the fellow said. "I can't believe it! You take my breath away! So grown up."

"Nick, what a surprise." Her voice was higher than normal. "This is... my friend, Bill Kyser. Bill, this is my old professor Nick Parker."

It was that guy. I'd never seen Lexy so intimidated before, and it pissed me off. He'd really hurt her. "Nice to meet you, Nick," I said. "Let me buy you a drink. Two Glennfiddich please, and what will you have?"

"Scotch? I thought you only liked champagne." He smiled at Lexy, and her cheeks turned dark red.

"That can be for you two," she said. "I'll just have a glass of wine."

"So you two are friends?" he asked me.

"More than that." I decided to deliver the good news to him before my newest team member. "Alex has just agreed to become the new head of my design team."

She blinked but played along. "I didn't agree. I said I'd think about it."

"Right." I smiled, slipping my arm around her waist and giving her a squeeze. "But I won't take no for an answer. You're the best."

"You look very young," Professor Asshat said. "Design team for what company, if you don't mind my asking."

"Kyser-Brennan Equities. We're building the Phoenician resorts on East End Beach? Surely you've heard of it."

"East End Beach?" His brow creased. "Can't say that I have."

"Well, if you were in development you would have." I took a sip of my forty-dollar scotch and returned his unimpressed expression. "And you're in education?"

"I was Alexandra's professor last year. Remember, sweetheart?" He put his oily hand on her lower back. I saw her stiffen at his touch.

"I guess those that can't, teach. Right, Parker?" I clapped him on the back hard, and pulled out my phone to keep from punching him in the face. "Excuse me. I need to check on our flight."

I turned my back but spoke loud enough for him to hear. "Bryant? Is the plane ready? Give us an hour, and we'll be there."

"We'll have to finish our drinks another time," I said, turning back. "We've got a plane to catch."

"A plane?" Lexy frowned at me.

"Remember earlier when we were discussing escargot?" I smiled, pulling her away from the slimeball and back to me.

"Uh... yes?" We hadn't, but she was a great actress.

"I wanted to surprise you. Surprise!" I said. "I thought we could get some. How does l'Escargot sound?"

"L'Escargot?" Parker butted in. "As in Paris?"

"Then you've heard of it." I turned back to Lexy. "The sky's the limit for my best girl."

270

"You want us to fly to France tonight," she said.

I put my hands on her waist and kissed her nose. "You've been saying you wanted to go. If we leave in an hour, it'll be dinnertime when we get there. I've got it all set up, private jet. We can sleep on the way. Or not…"

She was doing everything in her power to hold her expression neutral, and I had to confess, I was struggling not to break character myself. I placed a stack of twenties on the bar and pulled her to the door leaving Professor Nick Parker staring after us.

We left the building cool and collected, but in the parking lot Alex fell against the car, dropping her head in her hands. "Oh my god," she exhaled loudly.

"Get serious," I hissed, pulling her up so I could open her door. "He might be watching."

She complied, and in a few moments we were headed back into the city. I glanced at her a few times, but her face was a mask under the flashing streetlights.

"He kept calling you Alexandra," I finally snorted.

She cut her eyes. "Grow up, Billy."

"I'm sorry. I'm sorry," I held up a hand, still grinning. "It's just that guy was a real piece of work."

"You're the piece of work," she said turning to the window again. "Was any of that for real?"

"The eighty dollars worth of scotch sure was. The rest was all a bluff."

"Eighty dollars for two scotches?" She looked at me disapproving.

"We can cover it."

I'd called Bryant and told him to meet us at Ray's in the City. It was an easier drive for him, so he didn't object. Then I turned to Alex who was still quietly looking out the window. "That was the jerk you were crying about to Meg wasn't it."

Her expression changed to irritation. "She told you about that?"

"Meg doesn't tell me your business. I just heard you two talking is all. He needed to be taught a lesson."

She looked down and I noticed her shoulders relax. "I've got to hand it to you, you do have the whole white knight thing down. Meg was right."

"I don't know about knights," I said, watching the streetlights pass. "I just don't like my friends being treated that way."

"Nice touch with the job offer."

At that opening, I took a deep breath and charged in. "That was actually real. It's why I wanted you to meet us for dinner tonight."

"Bill…" I could hear the protest coming, but I wasn't letting her finish.

"Just hear me out. I was thinking about how you did all those elevations for us back when we were in school. You're really good, and I want to make you an offer you can't refuse."

"To work for you."

"To join our team. Kyser-Brennan Equities. Bryant and I are putting together a core group, and I was thinking you could be head of design and marketing."

She was quiet a moment, which I decided was a good sign. "Are you already that far along?"

I took it slow, letting the vision take hold as I said it. "I'll graduate next year, and we've already started approaching investors. If you helped us, we could do a whole line of brochures and mock-ups. Really come out strong."

"I don't know, Bill. I mean, I've got a great gig here, and I hate developments. I wish a hurricane would blow them all away."

"It won't happen with us," I said, still careful. "Bryant's been working with the best guys to make the Phoenicians tough enough to stare down a Cat 5 storm."

"That's what you said to Nick."

"That's what we're calling them. Phoenician one, two, three and so on. Our goal is nine and a two-hundred-room, stand-alone convention center with a ballroom and patio extending out to the ocean. It's all going to be five-star." Then I paused, just a beat. "But I need your help bringing it to life."

She exhaled and looked away. "You can hire somebody to do that. Somebody who believes in what you're doing."

"I want a friend." I hoped that still carried weight with her. "And you've been with us from the beginning. C'mon, Lex. You're who we want. I'll pay you more than you're making here."

"How?"

I exhaled a laugh at her cutting to the chase. "Just have a little faith. We'll get there, I promise. Give it a chance. For me?"

"Nope." She shook her head. "I'm not doing it for you."

It stung, but I had to expect that response. "That's gratitude," I said with a grin. "And after the way I stood up for you back there? How come?"

"You're too ambitious. If I hitch up to your wagon, no telling where I'd end up." She looked at her hands in her lap. "I'll do it for Meg. She's so convinced that you're going to conquer the world. I'd hate for her to be disappointed."

I was on fire tonight, but I resisted doing a victory shout—or gesture. "One year," I said calmly. "Give me one year, and you'll be well-compensated."

"I'm only working on contract. And I set my own hours."

"Done." I nodded. "Whatever it takes."

A sly smile crossed her face. "Hmm… you might not be such a bad boss after all."

I loved that look, and winning her over was as big a rush as impressing Rex at the Board meeting. It was going to happen. We were going to make it.

"You let me know if anything makes you unhappy," I said, "and I'll change it."

"Including you?"

Then I laughed. "No promises there."

*May 15, 19 —*

*Pushing, pushing, pushing… Don't give up. Keep going…*

*Almost there…*

*Almost there…*

*Almost there…*

*Done.*

Finishing school was like running a marathon. I knew if I could make it to the twenty-mile mark, I could finish. But about half-way through, I started getting tired. The funeral, the disbelief of investors, Meg's complaints, Dad's leaving, that ass Travis Hayes…

Every part of my brain was telling me this was crazy, and I was going to fall flat on my face. What made a nobody-hick like me think I could ever accomplish something this big? What qualifications did I have? It was an insane idea and only ignorant people who liked to believe in fairytales would have faith in me. And I was missing so much. My wife, time with my little boy…

I fought those voices back by telling myself nothing comes without hard work and that this was the hard work that was going to pay off big. Why shouldn't I be successful? Who else had worked as hard or spent as much time preparing? I had to keep my eyes on the goal and not get distracted.

Then the doubts would quietly creep back. *But what if you lose? What if you fail? And in front of all these people who are depending on you to succeed.*

The only solution was to put my head down and keep pushing. Put the blinders on and just look straight ahead. The journey of a thousand miles began with a single step. The road to hell was paved with good intentions. Intentions were not actions. It was the action that puts you on the other road. The road to heaven. The road to winning.

And the next thing I knew, I was done.

Graduation day, and the investors were lined up. I was ready to put on a hard hat and get out there with Bryant directing the workers, monitoring our progress.

Actually, I had already started. We broke ground on Phoenician I three months ago. I decided we should keep it low-key, opting instead for a big ribbon-cutting ceremony once the building was complete and we had a better handle on how successful it was. Perhaps I was in the throes of an internal struggle when we made that decision, but looking back, I still think it was the best approach.

Watching them lay the foundation on what would become a massive, twenty-story high rise was an awe-inspiring event. The size of the concrete pilings they dropped to anchor the huge structure drove home the potential force of nature that could hit these big boys. And watching the trucks come in and compact it all, seeing the steel girders and the rails, it was impressive. I felt a surge of confidence. This was what I had done. This was the product of our labor.

*June 28, 19 —*

We were renting office space for the time being from one of the local realtors. We managed to get a good deal and our offices overlooked the intercoastal waterway between the mainland and Dolphin Shores.

Since Alex came back, we'd gotten in the habit of a daily meeting around mid-morning to go over our status and determine where we stood and what needed to be done. Often Bryant met with us, but just as often he was out on the site meeting with contractors or troubleshooting and problem solving.

Those meetings were the best part of my day — going over where we were and where we were headed, making measurable steps forward. They made our plan feel as strong as those concrete pilings, and it was great talking to another person as eager for this dream to be a reality as I was.

It was an encouraging contrast to Meg's increasing complaints we were taking too long and begging for another baby. Her constant nagging made my stomach burn. I wanted her to be happy, but I barely saw Will as it was. Just a few more months was all I needed. Then I could stop working so much. I could be around more… be a better dad.

But Meg couldn't seem to hear that.

When I arrived at the office, Henry Austin was waiting to fit me for two new suits. He was the best local tailor, and I'd decided after the last two board meetings I needed a more polished edge. It was an extravagance, but after seeing how the younger partners liked to show off, I decided it had to be done.

"I've brought over the fabric swatches for you to flip through while I take your measurements," Henry said. I slipped out of my coat and pants while he pulled out the tape measure.

"What's the latest thing in Atlanta?" I asked, not really up on fabric choices.

"This dark brown with the plum pinstripe is flying off the bolts, and with your coloring, it should do nicely."

He took a swatch and held it over my shoulder as I stood in my boxers waiting to finish being measured. It seemed silly to spend this much time on clothes, but I knew it could pay off with a contract.

"Sure," I said. "And I guess I should have a dark blue or grey?"

"Yes, sir. The darker fabrics are toward the back. Just select one you like. May I suggest the petrol?" He pulled out a dark grey worsted wool sample as Alex tapped and entered carrying two coffees.

Our eyes caught, and she quickly turned on her heel so her back was to me. "I didn't know this was going to be formal," she said.

I laughed. "Don't you knock?"

"I tapped. That's the part where you shout 'indecent' or something."

"Give me a second."

She left the room and Henry finished taking measurements. I was dressed and putting my coat back on when I stuck my head out the door to find her leaning against the wall flipping through one of Henry's catalogs.

"A thousand dollars for a suit?" She glanced at me with an eyebrow arched. "I'm trying to think if I spend that much on clothes in a year."

"Get in here." I took the catalog from her hands.

She breezed into my office wearing one of those flowy dresses she preferred. She'd given up the power suits except for official business, and I didn't object. Lexy always looked beachy and beautiful, just like my plan.

"What's the deal? Did I get a raise and you forgot to tell me?" she asked.

"Do you need a raise?"

"No, but if you're buying thousand-dollar suits, I'm starting to feel underpaid."

I went around and took my spot behind the desk. "It's for board meetings. You don't know how those guys act when I walk in wearing a hundred-dollar off the rack number."

She leaned back, sipping her coffee. "I thought they forgot all about your lack of fashion sense after you wowed them with your big dreams brought to life by my artistic renderings."

"It helps," I said, taking the lid off my drink. "But there's always some guy close to my age who's sizing me up, and what I'm wearing is a big part of his evaluation."

"Hmm. I think you're just rationalizing a nice suit. And don't get me wrong, I get it. It's fun being treated like a princess."

"Prince?"

"Potato, potahto," she grinned.

"So what are we looking at today?" I watched as she pulled out her portfolio and spread it across my desk.

"I've put together what we talked about last week for Phoenician VI, the lobby and the outside patio. Were you wanting to do something different for the penthouse atrium and fitness center?"

I looked over the drawings, amazed how they reflected exactly what was in my head. "What did we do with five?"

"Calypso," she groaned. "Against my better judgment. You don't remember that?"

"Oh, yeah. I really liked that with the steel drums and all. Very nice."

"Hmm. Thanks, I guess." Her nose wrinkled. "You know, I've never actually been to Jamaica, but I've seen pictures."

"We should take a research trip," I said, thinking how it might work. "Visit other high-end resorts in different locations. It would be a write-off if we were scouting ideas."

Her eyes widened. "Sounds great! Who do you know with high-end resorts in exotic locations?"

"Right." I leaned back in my chair again. "And there's the catch."

"Talk to some of your investor-friends," she said, going back to her sketches. "Where's Bryant? I want a second opinion on this."

"Some problem with the frameworks at Phoenician I. He told me, but I can't remember the details."

She straightened and tossed down her pen. "You don't remember what Bryant said. You forgot my loud objections to the Calypso theme. What's with you these days? You're so distracted. Is it the suit?"

"I don't want to talk about it," I said, not looking up.

"Trouble at home?"

My tone grew impatient. "I don't want to talk about it."

"If it's something with the development, you'd better tell me. I could probably still get my job back in Atlanta."

I glanced up then. "It's nothing with the development. Everything's going great there, and I'm scheduled to go back and meet with another investment group in a week. I'll follow up with Peachtree and then I'm meeting with Aspen Equities. Your job's secure."

She nodded. "Aspen. That's a big deal. So if it's not the development, then what is it? Battle fatigue?" She leaned back in her chair, crossing her legs and retrieving her coffee.

I followed suit. "Maybe. Probably. Since school's been out, it's like what do I do with all this extra time? Normally I'd be either in class or up here working all hours. Now it's like… I feel like I'm forgetting something all the time."

"I bet if you wanted to take a few days off no one would have a problem with it. We all know how hard you've been working."

I shook my head. "I can't do that. I'm finally here full-time. Bryant's been carrying the ball on this end almost three years."

"It's not like you've been sitting on the sidelines doing nothing."

"I know, but I need to be here. I need to establish my identity in the office."

She smiled. "Time for that portrait?"

"Nah, you were right." I gave her a little smile back. "We should probably wait a few years before I start declaring the coast conquered."

"How does Meg feel about all this?"

"I don't know," I deflected. "She's not really interested."

She narrowed her eyes. "I'm sure she's very interested in talking to you about your feelings. Did something happen?"

I snapped the lid back on the now-empty cup. "I'm not talking to you about her."

"We talk about everything else," she said, leaning forward and sliding her sketches back together. "I mean, heck. I just saw you in your shorts ten minutes ago."

"I'm not giving you ammunition to use against me. I know you two. You would never take my side against her."

"I didn't know there was a side to take."

My eyes met hers. "I'm not discussing this with you."

She heaved up her portfolio case. "Fine. I'm going to start on our Small World theme. That's what we're doing, right?"

"I was thinking more greens and turquoise. Emerald city."

"If you only had a brain," she called.

"A heart."

She rolled her eyes, pushing through the door. I grinned. It was pretty awesome having someone who really understood my vision and could still make me laugh on the team. I never expected it would be her.

*Jan. 16, 19 —*

Taking the gang to Mexico was a stroke of luck I couldn't pass up.

Rex called from Atlanta saying he wanted me to meet with a good friend of his, Marco Dominguez. Marco owned Tango Sol, a high-end resort right on the Pacific, and while I suspected Rex meant for me to go alone, my chat with Lexy had been on my mind ever since.

Things with Meg were escalating, and we'd all been working hard. I figured we could use some personal and professional bonding time. We were moving past our status as high school friends, and with the first Phoenician so close to opening, I liked the idea of us having a more jet-set image, regardless of how it was funded.

Marco and I were instant friends. He was a smart guy, and like me, a native of the area he developed. The difference was his family had owned the property and had given him the money to help him get started.

He put us up in his best accommodations, but since it wasn't quite his high-season yet, I figured it wasn't setting him back much. Once Meg and I were settled in our private cabin, I walked down the hillside to his office to meet him.

"Bill." Marco shook my hand. "Rex says you're the next Gerald Hines."

"Rex exaggerates," I said, opting for humility with my peers. "I'm just a salesman. But we have some great engineers on the team."

"Well, it's good to meet you at last." He motioned me to a chair. "The last time Rex was here, you were all he talked about. The up and coming star. He wanted me to fly over and see what you were doing on the Gulf Coast."

"The door's open," I said, taking a seat. "Once we have the sites online, you owe us a visit."

"I'll take you up on it," he said, sitting as well. "How do you like the place?"

"It's gorgeous. You've done too much for us."

"Not at all. Only the best for a fellow visionary."

"So Rex said you had lots to share. Where should we start? A tour of the grounds?"

Marco grinned. "Let's start with the problem of finding a good manager. One who can take all the work off the owner."


*Jan. 18, 19 —*

Most of my days in Mexico were consumed with meetings and touring the property, but I wasn't complaining. Bryant and I were learning things that would otherwise have taken us a lot of trial and error to figure out.

The resort at Tango Sol was much larger than I expected, and it included a full golf course, a spa, a restaurant with a bar out on the beach, and private cabins separate from the main hotel building.

Marco took advantage of the hilly topography by incorporating it into the architecture and the landscape of the grounds. Waterfalls flowed over paths that connected most of the main buildings and cliffs looked out over the Pacific. And while I was preoccupied with work, the girls seemed to be enjoying themselves.

Meg was happier than she'd been in a while. She even wanted to revisit a few of those sex positions we hadn't tried since our honeymoon.

Her body is rocking as ever, and both of us are experts now at getting each other off. But here's the deal—and I know this is going to sound all New Age and shit—even though our nights were hot, I couldn't seem to connect with Meg the way I used to. Something was wrong somehow. It was like a separation as wide as the Gulf had spread between us, and sex didn't fill the void.

I wanted to shake it off. I figured it was the stress or all the damn baby talk. She brought it up again, but I managed to change the subject. I told her this trip was supposed to remind her of what we were working toward, what I wanted to give her. Once we were over the mountain, we could sail into the sunset, relax, and have fun. And she could have all the babies she wanted.

I just feel like I'm talking to myself half the time.

Making my way down the hillside to the kitchen area I looked out toward the ocean. The effect of the view and the sound of the waterfalls made me eager to get back home, back to planning. I wanted this ambiance for our sites, and I needed to talk to Lex about working up some sketches based on what we were seeing here. She was taking pictures of different elements. We'd look at what she had at our next meeting back home.

I was at the pool when I glanced up and saw her alone sunbathing. I slowed my pace, surprised by my response. I'd seen Lexy in a bikini before, lots of times growing up. But somehow it was different today. She was simply lying on her stomach on a lounger reading a book, but she looked... very sexy.

I tried to compartmentalize my reaction. So she was sexy, so what? I was glad we could contribute to the pretty scenery.

"Laying out alone?" I asked, sitting on the sand beside her chair. "Where's Suzanne?"

She looked up and smiled at me, and suddenly I couldn't remember what I had wanted to tell her. When had she started looking so good?

"On her way," she said. "I just didn't feel like waiting back at the room."

I watched as she slid her robe over her smooth shoulders, and my fingers itched to touch her skin. "You don't have to cover up," I said. "I'm not staying."

"You're very dressed," she sat up, and I watched her torso flex.

What the hell was wrong with me? Every single movement was hitting me inexplicably hard.

"Meg says we shouldn't be tanning anyway," she said. "It ages our skin or something."

I looked down trying to focus on Meg and not how disoriented I felt. Lexy and I were together all the time. I'd never felt like this around her, like I was tense, anticipating her every move.

"I know, you couldn't care less," she continued, misreading my silence. "But if it weren't for Meg, I'd be a complete fashion misfit."

"I'm sure," I looked up and forced a smile.

"So what's the deal? You haven't been down here once this whole trip."

I shrugged. "Marco's really thrown open the doors. I'm learning a lot."

"Like what?"

"Management stuff, troubleshooting, staffing problems. Things I hadn't really thought about before." Things I was thinking hard about now because they were the exact opposite of anything sexy. "The day-to-day details of running a high-end resort. We'll hire most of these functions out, of course, but I like knowing how to do every job."

She exhaled and leaned back again. I kept my eyes focused on my hands and not her body. "Sounds terribly un-exotic," she said. "But I'm proud you're making this an honest-to-goodness business trip, even if we never see you."

I stood and tried to joke. "Nobody wants to see the boss in a swimsuit."

She slanted an eye at me, and even that was a turn-on. Shit. I needed to get out of here.

"I've seen you in a swimsuit practically every summer since we were kids," she said.

"That was before I was signing your checks."

"Oh, so it's like that now. Well, you can let Bryant sign the checks for this weekend."

"It's really just a stamp of my signature," I said, backing away and trying not to come across as weird as I felt. "I think Millie does them all at her desk..."

"So you're seriously not going to spend any time with us?" She propped up on her elbows again.

"We've been having dinners together," I said looking down. "Speaking of, we're touring the kitchen today. Wanna come?"

"Not even a little bit," she laughed. "Oh, here's Suzanne."

Lexy's friend from Atlanta was very nice, if a little plain. She was also very smart, and I felt her sizing up what was going on with me. I dusted off my palms and held out a hand. "Suzanne."

"William the Conqueror," she said, shaking it.

"That's a new one," I said. You ladies have a fun day. I think the guys are hitting the links after kitchen duty."

"Nice seeing you for five seconds," Lexy called.

"Same here. Use sunscreen."

I walked away feeling my control slowly returning. Maybe I'd gotten too much sun yesterday.

That night Lexy and Suzanne didn't join us for dinner. Meg said they'd decided to take the bus into town and have a girls' night out, which suited me fine. I wanted to get my focus back on reconnecting with Meg. I decided to start getting home earlier in the evenings once we were back. Learn when to stop working and see if I couldn't make her happy again, get our marriage back on track.

We had a great dinner with Bryant and Donna, and after the evening was over, I let those three walk back to the cabins while I stayed behind to finish my drink.

I was slowly making my way up the hill in the semi-darkness when I noticed a figure wobbling toward me. Lexy. She was looking down and ran straight into me. I caught her before she fell, her flowery scent wrapping around me with her soft hair.

"Whoa, are you drunk?" I asked, holding her arms and trying not to feel anything toward her.

"Bill! Shh!" She held a single shoe in my face, eyes huge. "I've lost my shoe!" Then she snorted.

I couldn't help a little laugh. "Where's Suzanne?"

"At the cabin. I was there, and I looked down, and... Poof! No shoe!"

I shook my head. "Where did you lose it?"

"I don't know! I was trying to find it, but it's so dark!"

She turned and dropped to her knees, squinting down the path.

I reached down to pull her up. "Know what? It'll be easier to find in the morning. Let me help you back to your room before you fall in the pool."

She leaned back and frowned, then nodded. "That's a good idea," she said. "You're very smart. Have I told you I think you're very smart?"

"You just did."

"You're very smart."

"Thanks. You usually are, too."

Her dark brows pulled together. "What does that mean?"

"It means you're drunk."

"Oh my god!" She softly cried, holding her head. "I know. It's terrible."

Her exaggerated gestures made me grin. I'd never seen her like this. "And you can't find a shoe on the side of a hill in the dark when you're drunk."

"See?" She poked my chest. "You're very smart."

"Come on." We started making our way up the path.

She wrapped her arms around my waist and rested her head on my shoulder. Gone was the wall between us. Tonight she was only soft and beautiful and holding onto me. I thought about kitchen tours and finding band-aids in soup. Resort concerns that were severely unattractive.

She started giggling again.

"What now?" I asked as we reached her room.

She sniffed and lifted her head, looking in my eyes. "I didn't like you in high school."

"I know," I said softly.

"I thought you were bad for Meg."

"Yep."

"But I was wrong, and I'm sorry."

"I'm not holding it against you."

She planted her feet and turned to face me. Then she put both hands on my shoulders. "I never thought I'd say this, but you're a good guy, Bill Kyser. And I consider you my friend."

I raised my eyebrows. "Uh-huh."

"That's it." She dropped her hands, still staring at me.

"Well, I'm glad we cleared that up," I said with a little smile.

"Yes. All clear." She waved a hand between us. "Goodnight, friend Bill."

"Goodnight, friend."

I shook my head and walked back to my room still smiling. I wasn't sure what prompted that declaration, but I figured it would make for good blackmail later.

Yes, we were friends. Only friends. And Meg was waiting when I crawled into bed. It was our last night on the island together, and I wanted to get started on my resolution to focus my attention on her. I kissed her shoulder and slipped my hand around her waist. My wife. She wasn't wearing anything, and my hand moved from her bare midriff higher to her soft breast. She stirred and rolled into my arms looking for my mouth. I kissed her again, sliding my hand between her legs, finding her most sensitive spot and gently massaging, coaxing. I kissed her slowly until her soft moans told me it was time for me to replace my hands with my body, rocking with her, into her.

This was right. This was me remembering what I was doing, why Meg was here. This trip was my first step in trying to make things better between us.

*March 10, 19 —*

She lied to me.

Over and over. She looked me in the eye, kissed me, let me make love to her, pretended to care about my feelings, and every time it was a lie.

The more I thought about it, the more I wanted to break something.

Even worse, she completely ignored my feelings, my reasons for waiting. What I'd said about missing Will growing up. How it made me feel guilty. She didn't care about that. She didn't care about any of it.

And now we're going to have twins. Two more mouths to feed and bodies to clothe. And where will we put them?

Nevermind. Those details we could've worked out—if we'd made this decision together. Her mother would've let us move into her big empty house if we'd asked. And we had the money. But none of that mattered.

What mattered was she made the deliberate choice to ignore how I felt, to completely ignore me. And not just once. She'd done it every time. <u>Every time</u> I'd been loving her, trying to make things better, she'd been lying to me.

We'd talked about this so much. I'd given her good, solid reasons why we needed to wait. I was encouraging. I told her there would be plenty of time for more babies. As many as she wanted. I didn't say no. I only said wait. Just wait.

I'm so angry, it's hard to put my feelings into words.

My head felt like it was pounding, and every time I looked at her, a fist of anger tightened in my chest. She tried to make up, to smile at me, but all I could see was a little girl who never grew up. A little girl who wanted to play with dolls and wear her hair in pigtails while she dressed in her favorite play clothes and fixed her play husband meals.

I've been busting my ass trying to make these last pieces of the plan come together. I'm dealing with old men in suits who treat me like I'm a kid. I'm working overtime to be taken seriously. And then she goes behind my back and does this. In my own home, in my bed. The one place where I should feel safe.

Twins.

John and Lucy.

She said their names as if that would make it all better. As if I would forget that we'd been having this conversation nonstop for almost nine months.

I did everything I could to make her happy. The Mexico trip—she was probably doing it even then, pulling out all the old positions, using me like one of the stud horses on Dad's ranch. The thought made my fist tighten.

Then when we got back, I stopped working late. We started eating out more. I'd listened to what she'd said about how she was feeling, and I tried to make it better. But she couldn't do the same for me.

I couldn't even look at her now. I didn't want to touch her. If Lexy hadn't been in the other room when she told me, I'd have thrown something. I had no intention of hurting Meg, but I didn't know how to get her attention. I didn't know how to get her to wake up and understand I was being serious. After Lexy left we said a lot of things, and I meant every one of them.

I kept my voice calm, focusing on what she'd done. "I can't believe you lied to me."

"Billy, I—"

"No." I didn't want her excuses. "Nothing you can say will make this right."

She blinked and looked down. "I'm sorry."

"I appreciate you saying that, but you lied to me. I trusted you. I explained everything to you, and you said you understood."

She was crying now, but even her tears didn't move me. "I know," she said. "I don't have a leg to stand on. I just… I just wanted…"

"Please stop talking," I said, my jaw clenching on its own. "There's no way you can make this right."

Her blue eyes blinked large at me, but all I saw was a selfish little girl. "Don't you want to have more babies?" she said.

"That's not the point," I shook my head. "That was never the point. The timing wasn't right, and I told you that."

"What if it was an accident?" she cried.

"But it wasn't an accident, was it."

"You act like I robbed a bank. I got pregnant. That's all." She crossed her arms and turned her back. "You get to run around playing with your skyscrapers and building your towers, and I just have to sit here and do nothing. Wait for you to have time for me."

My voice was quiet. "I said it was going to be this way. I wanted to wait."

"And I could wait three or four years, but we're up to five years now, Billy." She was crying again. "It's never going to change is it? You're always going to be working all the time. You never know when to leave that office."

"We're right in the middle," I argued. "I never said how long it would take, but you knew how much we had to accomplish. We're still living in this damn cottage for Chris' sake."

"I can't help that. All I know is Will's in kindergarten, and he'll be in first grade before long. He won't even know his little brothers and sisters if we wait for you to finish conquering the world and come home."

"So that's it," I said. "You're giving up on our dreams?"

She threw out her hands and began to pace. "When were they ever our dreams? It was always your big plan and what you were going to show everybody."

"And the house on the island?" I said, reminding her of what she had wanted. "The money, the prestige. Those things never mattered to you?"

"Not enough to give away my family. Or wait until I'm too old to try and have another baby."

I groaned through an exhale. "You're twenty three. That's younger than most girls who've even *started* having babies. And this is all way off the point. You lied to me."

She rolled her eyes. "And you just insist on making this the worst thing that could ever happen to us."

"Lying to me is pretty bad."

"Fine!" She cried. "I get it. I'm a terrible wife. So what do you want to do? Divorce me?"

"Don't be dramatic."

"I don't know what else to say. It's done now."

"And I just have to deal with it." Saying the words made my stomach burn with anger. "Why couldn't you just get a part time job? Work at the hospital again? Volunteer at school?"

"I didn't want to work at the hospital. It reminded me too much of Daddy."

"What about volunteering at the school?"

"I didn't think of that." She looked down and pushed her hair behind her ear, and it was clear she still wasn't taking this seriously.

"I can't talk to you anymore," I said, going to the door. "I'll be at the office if you need anything."


*March 15, 19 —*

I've slept at the office a week now.

Alex came in the second morning and saw me, and I have to give her credit. I half expected her to rush to Meg's side immediately, ready to tell me how unreasonable I was being. But she didn't. Instead she sat on the couch beside me, two coffees in hand.

"Sleeping at work?" Her voice was gentle. "That's terrible for those thousand-dollar suits."

I sat up and took one of the steaming cups. "Thanks. I haven't felt like going home."

"Don't be mad at her," she said softly. "I mean, it was wrong of her to do that, but she's going to get her share of payback when those twins arrive. I think she's just as worried as you are now."

Her dark eyes blinked to mine and she smiled. I studied her pretty face. First we were friends, and now we were allies?

"It just really burned me," I said. "I specifically asked her not to do it, and she did it anyway. It's like I can't even trust her now."

"Well, she can't get pregnant again. You should go home and kiss and make up."

I shook my head and looked down. "I'm too angry."

"But you love Meg, right?" She leaned down and tried to catch my eye. "Those babies won't be here for at least six months, and a lot of these projects are almost done. It'll work out."

I glanced at her. "Maybe they can stay at your house."

"Whoa, hang on," she laughed. "I'm being supportive over here. I'm not crazy."

I smiled then, but I was still mad. At least I wasn't brooding anymore.

Still it didn't make a difference. I tried, but I couldn't go home. I thought about our conversation, and Alex was right. I had to forgive Meg. I just couldn't figure out how when she didn't seem to understand how much she'd damaged my ability to trust her. To love her.

Maybe I was thinking about it too much.

Last night Alex stayed late to talk to me again. She tried to take the blame for it all. She tried to convince me it was her fault that Meg had tricked me — that she'd told Meg to do it.

At first I was angry at both of them, but when I saw Alex's worried face, the tears in her eyes, I knew the truth. She might've said the words, but she could never have acted on them. The thought might've crossed her mind in a moment of frustration. But she would never have actually done it herself. And she was stunned by the knowledge that Meg would. That Meg did.

I looked into her tear-filled eyes and I knew. She would never have held me in her arms, kissed my lips, and lied to my face.


*April 5, 19 —*

It's been more than a year since that night in the office.

It's been less than a month since that day on the boat.

I never expected it to happen when I gave everyone the afternoon off, but looking back, I should've seen it coming a mile away. I should've realized it could happen after Tango Sol. I should've known it could happen after the showdown over the twins.

I set myself up for the fall, and I walked right into it.

I was furious with Meg and carrying the twins had been difficult for her. We hadn't slept together since she told me. Even after they were born, when she was feeling better and we might've made up, I just couldn't do it. I couldn't let it go. I wasn't trying to punish her, but whenever I looked at her, resentment burned in me.

A year had passed.

One year.

That amount of time makes you wonder what it's all about. It makes you feel like a free agent or something. Like nobody even cares any more. Meg was back to her old self, but I wasn't back at her side. I didn't want to be.

Then I thought about how it happened. About Alex on the boat, wearing my shirt over her bikini. Her long, brown hair swaying in the breeze.

What was I thinking when I'd suggested we go for a sail, just the two of us? I don't even know now. It seemed like I thought it would be innocent. It was the first time we'd been out on the boat as friends. Back in the day, we'd always been at odds, and she'd always been frowning on my boat with me. Now everything changed.

I loved the water so much, and any time I thought of relaxing, it was there. I wanted her with me, smiling this time. When I'd playfully grabbed her, I never expected the look in her eyes. Her brown eyes that were so deep and warm. She wanted me. And in that look, all the feelings I'd been fighting for her swept over me, pulling me under.

It was hard to think about what happened next. I was always so controlled, but I lost it then. I took her, and I could still feel her soft skin against my lips, her legs wrapped around my waist. She was as passionate and sensual as I'd imagined. With her on my lap, my hands moved from her silky hair down her smooth back to her waist and up to her small breasts. My mouth followed suit, tasting every part of her body I could find. I lay her back on the bed with my brain on fire. I didn't even hesitate in exploring her, and when we'd come together, it happened too fast. We were both satisfied, but I had to hold her again. I had to go slower, to remember.

The second time changed everything. She looked at me with those serious eyes, stroking my forehead, my face. I couldn't tell what she was thinking, but I could see it in her expression. She loved me. And I loved her. I covered her mouth with mine and kissed her deeply, again and again. We truly made love. And we fell asleep wrapped in each others' arms, my lips pressed to her forehead.

I woke up and she was gone. And now she won't see me.

She's right. I know she's right. We can't see each other. Not now. It had been too easy to pull her to me, and it could too easily happen again.

I can't lie. I want it to happen again. I find myself envisioning things…

Things that would never work.

I should never have lost control. Now the knowledge of what it was like to be with her, the memory of us together, is always in my thoughts.

I should've let her go to Atlanta like she suggested. But I couldn't. Somehow the knowledge she's still here keeps me going.

Driving to work this morning, I surveyed the massive structures going up all across Dolphin Shores Boulevard. It was the product of Bryant's and my big gamble. We knew it was a sure thing, and now we were getting interviews from business magazines and leaders across the industry wanting our advice. A few more months, and we'd have more money than we'd know what to do with. We could even move the offices from that Brown Jones rental to the penthouse suites of Phoenician I.

I noticed a white sheet on my chair as I unlocked the door and walked into my corner office. It was a cool morning, and I looked out across the intercoastal waterway as I opened the note. I recognized her swirling script. One sentence, and I dropped it to the floor.

I'm pregnant. –A.

*April 6, 19 –*

I stayed late last night to see her.

I'd agreed she wouldn't see me again, but not after that. When she walked in the door, I was struck by her beauty. It seemed even more intense, despite her apparent exhaustion. I wanted to take her in my arms and comfort her. I wanted to smooth her hair back and make love to her. I wanted her to say she missed me as much as I missed her, that her insides ached like mine now that we never saw each other.

But I couldn't do that.

She'd asked me to stay away, and I was taking a big chance being here now.

"Alex," I said softly.

Her dark eyes flicked up. "I guess you got my note."

"I did." I took a step toward her, but she turned to her desk and started unpacking her bag.

"I didn't want to see you. I just wanted you to know."

I tried to keep the desperation out of my voice, but I wasn't sure I was successful. "What can I do?"

"Nothing," she answered quickly. "Or... I don't know. Help me figure out what to do."

My heart beat a little faster at the invitation. "I'll help you any way I can," I said. "I'll give you money. I'll give you anything—"

"I don't want your money," she said, looking down. "I don't... I don't know what I want. You needed to know, but I can't have you in my life like that."

"I want to be in your life. I want us to be together."

She faced me then, eyes blazing. God, she was gorgeous. "Are you crazy? Have you completely forgotten about your wife and three children? What's wrong with you, Bill?"

I cleared my throat and looked down, rubbing my forehead. "I haven't forgotten. I'll take care of them. I'll take care of them forever, but... I can't stop thinking about you, about us. We have to be together."

"Because of what happened on the boat?" She shook her head. "That was nothing to base anything on. You were still angry, and I was drunk. Or stupid. Or both."

There was no way I was letting her dismiss it that way. I knew better. "It was a lot more than that and you know it."

"Well, that's too damn bad. It's too late for that. Years too late. There's Meg." She took a quick breath and shoved her hands in her hair. "Oh, god, I can't stop thinking about Meg. But even if it wasn't for her, you're my boss. You're married and you have three children. Can't you see how this looks? It would ruin you. Have you really worked so hard to just throw it all away like that?"

"I don't care about those things."

"Yes, you do." She dropped her hands hard. "Don't even say that to me."

"Okay, yes, I care about my work and what we're doing here. But before you came back that was all I cared about. I didn't even know I could care about anything else until you." The pain in my stomach made me reflexively touch my midsection. "God, Alex. Just seeing you makes me happy."

She squeezed her eyes shut. "Stop it! It doesn't matter, and it's not going to change anything."

I took another cautious step toward her. I was ready to beg. "Really? Do you really mean that?"

"I am not going to be the person who destroys Meg's home." Her eyes glistened with tears. "She's my best friend. My sister. I could never be happy if I hurt her like that. I could never be happy with you knowing what it cost her."

I released the breath I didn't realize I was holding and slowly turned away. I walked to the windows to stare out at the darkness. I was beaten. I could never win this fight with her.

"I know," I said quietly. "I knew you would say that. I've been going over and over it in my mind, but I knew in the end you would always say those words."

Her voice was small. "I do care about you, and if things were different…"

"But they're not."

"They're not," she repeated.

I turned back and tried to smile through the pain. "So what now? What do you want from me?"

She tried to smile back, but a single tear hit her cheek. It ripped me in two.

"Nothing," she said. "I'd like to have this baby if that's okay with you. You don't have to do anything. I can take care of us, and you won't ever have to worry —"

"I'm not worried," I said. "Whatever makes you happy."

"I'm sorry if you're angry," her voice broke. "I'm sorry if… if I've hurt you."

"There's no need to apologize. You're right. Of course, you're right. About everything." There was only one thing I wanted. "I just… I hope you'll stay here. I'd like to be able to see you. Both of you. Even if it's from a distance."

Her brow creased. "I'm not sure that's a good idea."

"I won't force you, but I wish you would. That way I could help you if you ever needed it. You wouldn't even have to ask, just let me know somehow."

She nodded. "I'll think about it."

I walked slowly to where she stood and reached down to take her hand. I looked at it a moment, thinking how precious it was to me now. "I want to know that you're okay."

She slipped her hand away. "You should probably go now."

I nodded and turned to leave. My whole body ached with the knowledge I could never change her mind. She would never allow me to be anything other than Meg's husband. It was right, but the pain was far worse than I'd imagined it would be. For a whole day I had allowed myself to hope a baby might change things for us. But I knew it never would. She was right, we were years too late.

*May 13, 19 –*

At twenty-five, I'd lost interest in everything. I was married to a beautiful woman who was devoted to me, and I had three beautiful children of whom I was very proud. My business was booming, and our dreams were turning into reality. But I couldn't seem to care about any of it.

I tried to put what happened behind me. I tried to focus on my work and think back to the good days with Meg. I tried to remember our happier times.

But I longed for Alex. I missed seeing her every morning and talking to her. I missed laughing at her expert way of keeping me in my place, of reminding me who I was. I missed my friend.

Every day when I arrived at the office, I looked anxiously for signs she'd been there the night before. At times she'd leave finished sketches on my desk with notes asking for approval or direction, and I'd trace my finger over the strokes of her pen imagining the touch of her hands. The scent of her hair.

The days were piling up behind me. The twins were smiling and holding their little heads on their own, working to sit up. I usually arrived home after all of them had gone to bed, but that night I heard one of them awake as I walked through the quiet, dark house. I slipped into their room to look in their little cribs.

Jack was watching me with my own blue eyes, his soft white hair like a halo around his little head. He was such a quiet baby, so alert and attentive, like he was analyzing my every move. I put my hand on his small body, and he smiled. Lucy was nearby sleeping peacefully. Lucy, who was named for her mother's best friend.

In the bedroom, Meg was sleeping on her side. I looked at her golden hair spread across the pillow. She was always so beautiful, but I could see the sadness in her face. It had been a long time since we were as happy as we'd been on our honeymoon. We'd had it for a moment in Mexico, and even in the few weeks after that. But so much had changed between us. We'd grown up and apart. And I wondered if it were even possible for us to get back to those days, those feelings.

I took off my clothes and slipped into bed beside her. She stirred softly and nuzzled into my chest as I slid my arms around her. She tilted her face up to mine and kissed my neck. A few more kisses and experienced strokes and our long separation was over. Making love to Meg was familiar and comforting, from her smooth skin and sweet scent, to the way she clung to me and the little noises she made as we finished.

My heart ached at what had become of our marriage, and I clenched my jaw thinking of Lexy's words. Meg needed me. I had to try and make this work.

With enough time, perhaps I could forget what had happened on the boat. I could forget what Meg had done and remember how things used to be with us. I'd conquered the coast. Surely I could conquer this problem, too.

I drifted to sleep with my wife in my arms, a line of determination creasing my brow.


*May 17, 19 —*

When I joined the Kyser-Brennan team full-time, after college, I'd always been the lead guy in the office while Bryant headed up the construction crews in the field and out on the job sites. A month ago, I abruptly changed that arrangement, asking Bryant to handle certain office matters, design in particular, and in return, I'd taken over meeting with the survey teams and handling site research. It was part of my deal with Alex, and while Bryant was cooperative as always, I could tell he was suspicious.

"I just don't understand why you're out in the field now," he complained. "I don't mind going, and you're better at being cooped up in an air-conditioned box all day."

I smiled at my restless friend. "You're a co-owner here, Bryant. If I'm the only person in the office, it starts to look like you're working for me. I don't want it to be that way."

"I appreciate your concern for my image," he said, shoving a stack of papers on his desk. "But you don't know anything about site surveys, and I don't know anything about design. How is this an improvement?"

I looked out the wall of windows. "Maybe I need to get out of the box more."

He studied me a moment. "Was there some problem between you and Alex? I know you guys cross swords, but I always thought it was in good fun."

My arms dropped, and I turned back to his desk. "There was no problem between me and Alex. I'd just been working with her nonstop, and you needed to get in here and put your stamp on some of these images."

"My stamp? More like my X on the line. You know I'll just go with whatever she says."

I breathed a laugh, knowing how to convince him. "Look, if you want me to double-check anything, just leave it on my desk. But you'll get the hang of it. And half the time it *is* just going with whatever she says. You're an extra set of eyes."

"I don't like it. Something's up."

"Nothing's up. I just need to get out more, and you need to be seen in the office more." I went to his door. "You've been in enough buildings. Trust your instincts. If something doesn't feel right, ask her about it."

He wasn't completely onboard with the change, but I was out of the design loop. Except for the occasional written note, I wouldn't be involved in any more dealings with Alex. I hated it, but I had to make these changes if I were going to live up to my promise to make my marriage work.


*May 22, 19 —*

Miss Stella's funeral was another test of will.

The dowager's death was unexpected, and I knew Alex would be devastated. I remembered when Dr. Weaver died without warning, and how it had impacted Meg and her mother. Mrs. Weaver had completely withdrawn, and if it hadn't been for her friend in Arizona, she might've stayed that way. I ached thinking of Alex alone and suffering, especially with the baby coming and our secret still fresh in our minds.

She was hidden behind a black veil the entire service, so I couldn't see her expression or know how she was handling it. But Meg was a good friend. We were with her throughout the event. At the limo, I was stunned when Meg suggested I take the long ride with her to the burial site. Of course, it was exactly what I wanted, but Alex closed that door. Frustrated, knowing she was right, I took Lucy from her mother and left. They could work it out.

But that night I couldn't sleep. It was a perfect spring night, cool but not cold, the moon almost full. I decided to take a drive and headed down to the water. Without really thinking about it, I turned west where McKenzie Street met the beach road. The bright moon threw everything in contrast and lit the black waves with silvery tips. After several minutes, I turned north over Little Lagoon then west again down Port Hogan Road.

When I got there, I wasn't sure why I'd driven to the house or what I expected to happen. It was completely dark, and I had no intention of waking her. I was here and she was there. It was close enough. I climbed out of the truck thinking I'd walk down to the little spot of beach where we'd talked her first day back. The garden looked enchanted in the moonlight, with all the flowering bushes lit white and grayish blue.

I heard the screen door slam and looked up to see her running toward me like a ghost in a long, white gown, her dark hair streaming loose behind her. My stomach tightened at the sight of her, and adrenaline surged through me. But I wouldn't touch her — not without her asking.

She stopped right in front of me, panting and glowing in the moonlight. I was afraid to speak or even move in case she changed her mind and ran back inside. But she didn't. Four little words, and she was in my arms. I held her so long, feeling her warmth and listening to her breathe. I never wanted to let her go.

I pressed my lips to the top of her head, inhaling the soft perfume of her hair. Too soon she stepped back and thanked me for coming. It was absurdly formal, and I couldn't tell what she was going to do next. She turned, but I couldn't let her leave that way.

I caught her arm and pulled her back to me. I needed to kiss her. I needed to give her my love. Instantly her arms were around my neck holding me close. She was kissing me back, and I held her cheeks, her shoulders, wrapped my arms around her body as our mouths opened. Hope swelled in my chest, but without warning, she started pushing away, breaking the spell.

"Don't!" It was all I could think to say, to make her stop. Then I realized she was struggling to get away from me, but I was holding her too tightly. I let her go and apologized. She said something about how I had to leave, but I was already going.

I walked back to the truck and climbed inside, my insides torn to pieces. In the brief moment I'd held her, she'd kissed me back. But even then I knew she would never let it go for long. Not now. And god, it hurt so bad.

I arrived at the house and went inside. There was a decanter of scotch in the living room, and I poured a double. Standing by the fireplace drinking it in, I looked at the pictures of all of us from years ago. As I studied them, I pondered the unique manner in which alcohol could take searing pain and turn it into a dull ache. A few more sips, and I didn't even feel it anymore.

I thought about my dad looking at pictures of my mom, and I remembered his words about not forcing her to come back. He couldn't make her love him.

I wasn't going to turn into him. I wasn't.

A few days later, a letter appeared on my desk from Alex. She wanted me to help her sell Miss Stella's old Victorian home on Port Hogan Road and find something smaller near the beach. I dove into the project as if it were the beginning of a new series of high-rises, and soon I'd found her a quaint little cottage on West Street that was on the market after some Snowbirds had decided against relocating.

It was a great deal, and I was able to buy it for her while still shopping Miss Stella's place. I imagined the old Victorian could be sold for the land alone and should fetch a high enough price that she wouldn't even have a note.

Her decision to sell was smart. Whoever built that old wooden structure in the middle of constant salt breezes wasn't thinking of things like mildew and rot. Alex would've gone broke keeping it in repair. I wasn't sure how the old widow did it.

After she moved into her new place and signed all the paperwork, I received a formal thank-you letter, and that was it. Through the entire process I never saw her. It was infuriating, and I had to fight the urge every morning to drive to her new home and make her talk to me.

Instead, I kept the car straight on the road to our offices in Homeport. She wanted it this way, she'd have it this way.

*Aug. 20, 19 –*

The ribbon-cutting ceremony was envisioned as our big introduction to the coast. Sure, everyone knew who we were, and we'd been on all the up and coming lists for a few years now. But this was our official presentation to the world. We'd invited local media, all our investors, civic leaders, chamber representatives, the works. After the obligatory photo of the core group cutting the ribbon, we'd planned a reception and an afternoon of showing off.

It turned into an incredibly close-call with Alex. She'd arrived at Bryant's request as head of marketing and design, and at six months pregnant, she literally glowed. It was the first time I'd seen her since that night, and she'd changed so much. Meg had mentioned she was having a boy, and I couldn't focus on the interview questions as she stood beside me with my son in her body. I wanted to hold her and tell her she was beautiful, ask her how she felt, if she needed anything. My whole body was tense, but I managed to appear calm and professional. It wasn't until we were alone in the hallway together that it happened.

My head was burning with all I wanted to say, but I tried for a neutral compliment. "You're looking… healthy."

She actually laughed. "Are you saying I look fat?"

I blinked, stunned. "Not at all! You look very fit and six months pregnant."

"You're good at timing it," she said, staring at the silver doors.

"I have a good memory." As soon as I'd said the words, our conversation halted, and we stood in awkward silence waiting for the elevator to arrive.

I wasn't sure how we'd managed to be alone like this together, and I clenched my fists to keep from touching her. The thought of being this close to her and at the same time so far apart was almost unbearable. Six months ago she'd been wrapped around me, and evoking that memory caused a sharp pain in my temple. There was no one here. No one would see…

The doors opened, and I stepped forward to hold them just as she stepped forward to enter. Her balance shifted in my direction, and I released the door to catch her waist as her hand caught my shoulder. It was too much, too close. I leaned forward and kissed her, pressing my palm lightly to her cheek. A tiny whimper came from her throat, and I felt her fingers slide into my hair just above my collar, pulling my face closer. I kissed her deeply, tightening my arm around her, trying to pull her against me but at the same time being gentle with her midsection. She inhaled sharply and both her hands were in my hair now. Oh, god, were we doing this? Would she let me take her like this? Here? Our kisses grew desperate, and I was more than ready.

Just then, I heard Bryant's big mouth coming up the passage. She stepped away quickly, turning and smoothing her hair, her dress. I reached up to wipe my mouth. Bryant and the crew were soon with us, but instead of getting in the elevator, Alex said she was feeling tired and went home. For a brief second, I thought I saw a bit of the struggle I was feeling reflected in her eyes.

That was the last time I saw her before Meg got the call from the hospital.

*Nov. 21, 19 –*

When Alex called Meg to say she was in labor, I didn't even think about staying home. We brought the kids to Bryant and Donna, and I waited while Meg helped her through the delivery. I couldn't sit in the lobby, and the hospital staff knew us well enough that they let me stand in the hall outside her door. It was a mistake. Every cry twisted in my gut, and it took all my strength not to go inside with her. Once it was over, Meg went with Julian to the nursery, and I slipped into her room. I had no idea what I would say, but I had to see her.

I sat by the bedside and gently lifted her hand into mine. "He's beautiful," I said softly. "How are you feeling?"

She let me hold her hand. "Tired, sore, happy." Then she blinked her dark eyes to mine. "I didn't talk to you about his name. Is Julian okay?"

I smiled. "I like it. It's something you'd come up with."

Her voice was hesitant when she spoke again, but her words soothed me like a warm embrace. "I'm really glad you're here," she said. "I was afraid to say anything to Meg, but I wanted you to see him."

"I couldn't stay away. You have no idea how hard this has been for me."

Then she tensed. "Please don't. Don't say anything about that now."

"Oh, Lex. Isn't there any hope for me?"

She pulled her hand away. "I will never hurt Meg like that."

"But what if she realized what I know. That we were too young, we shouldn't have gotten married, we made a mistake." God, I was desperate.

She smiled, but it wasn't happy. "You really can't see how wrapped up her life is in you? Only you. She would do anything…"

I stood up hard then, turning away. "What about me and my life?"

She took a deep breath. "I think if you tried, really tried, you could remember how you loved her, and go back to how you used to be."

I faced her then, anger clenching my jaw. "How can you say that? I know you don't want that. You want to be with me. Admit it."

Her eyes closed and a tear slid down her cheek. I fell at her bedside, pulling her to me and kissing it away, tasting the salty drop. She placed her palm on my face for a long moment, and I leaned back, looking in her eyes. Then she lowered her hand and squirmed to loosen my embrace.

My arms fell away, my whole body weak from fighting. "God, Lex, don't you know how much I love you?"

More tears glistened in her eyes. "Why are you doing this?" she whispered. "You're breaking my heart."

"*I'm* breaking your heart?"

Just then Meg returned, and I stood, quickly stepping into the small bathroom. The light switch was connected to a loud fan, so I was confident no one heard as I collapsed against the wall, sliding to the floor, my head in my hands.

*Feb. 21, 19 –*

Three months have passed since that night, and I haven't seen Julian since his birth.

At his mother's request, I've worked very hard to put my feelings for her aside and do the right thing. I threw myself into work and building our new home on Hammond Island. Meg is happier than I've ever seen her planning it, and I'm doing my best to focus on her and the children alone. They're beautiful and sweet, and they're depending on me. If I keep waiting and working, those old feelings will pass. Julian will always be my son, and I'll help them any way I can, but I've made promises to Meg, and I'm doing my best to keep them.

Peachtree became our biggest investor in the Phoenician developments. Our meeting with Rex had turned into a close friendship that opened doors with bigger groups and introduced us to other money men. Real estate had become a hot investment option, and our popularity was snowballing.

I traveled to Atlanta periodically to meet with Rex, and through him, I became acquainted with Jennings Grant, who was chairman with Aspen Equities. In a few short years, I'd become well-versed in the language of investment banking and real estate development, and it was a great distraction from other, more personal matters.

"It's been fun watching you grow, Bill," Rex said, pouring scotch into three heavy crystal tumblers. We were meeting with Jennings to discuss the status of the first rollout of buildings and to get his group involved in the next series of developments. "The first time you came in here, I was strictly meeting with you out of courtesy to Abraham, but you held your own. I was impressed."

"I had nothing to lose back then but pride," I said, taking the tumbler.

"There's a lot to be said for fearlessness." He clinked his against mine.

"Would you say you're not so fearless now?" Jennings asked, studying me.

"Fearless is the wrong word," I said. "Being in the mix of the day-to-day routine takes the edge off enthusiasm."

Jennings frowned. "So you're less enthusiastic now?"

"Not at all," I said quickly, tilting the tumbler of scotch I held. "It's just more a foregone conclusion now. Less like something that has to be sold and more like an inevitability that you can either be a part of or left behind."

"There's the old arrogance," Rex laughed, slapping me on the back.

"I'm sorry if that's how it comes across," I said. "It was just what was bound to happen, and we want you to be a part of the team, Jennings. I'd rather work with people who come recommended by friends."

Aspen was onboard shortly after that meeting, and I was starting to feel like everything I touched turned to gold. In my professional life, at least. So business was good, but I was having a hard time caring about anything.

Working with the elevations and planning out design had been one of my favorite aspects of the job. Now it was all bricks and mortar. I tried to put it in perspective. I'd wanted to build buildings. I needed to be out where the rubber met the road. Meeting with the survey crews, looking at the empty lots, this was where it all began. But walking on the empty tracts of land reminded me of sitting out on Port Hogan Road looking out at the sea with Alex. I remembered her long hair drifting into my face and talking about portraits and the future.

The ribbon cutting ceremony was done, and we had moved our offices from Homeport to Phoenician I. That development was soaring, and every day a new high rise was on its way up. The Gulf Coast looked more and more like the elevations we drew senior year. I always knew we could do it. Sure, there was an element of luck involved, and it kept me on my toes. But now it was here, the massive framework in the sky, lining the Gulf like a wall. We simply had to sit back and watch it all come together.

*Dec. 20, 19 –*

She knows.

I have to find her because I don't know what she'll do.

I'd only intended to give Alex the gift for Julian, but I couldn't do it in front of everyone without arousing suspicion. It had been a lucky break when I saw her slipping out of the party in what looked like the direction of her office. A friendly conversation, Merry Christmas, and the gift. That was all that was supposed to happen. I was still trying to piece together where I got off track.

It was still there—that invisible pull between us. I was still in love with her, and the closer I got, it was impossible to fight. She was so beautiful in that red dress, and I kept thinking if I could only smell her hair one more time. If I could only hold her in my arms one more time...

Meg had appeared out of nowhere, and Alex had run after her. I knew she would go back to the house, but I didn't have a car and Bryant was home with a sick kid.

I never wanted to hurt Meg.

She would never believe that.

I had worked so hard to do right by her. I had to find her. I had to apologize. I had to explain that I couldn't keep going like this. She could have anything she wanted. She could have everything, the house, all of it. I would give it all to her if she would just let me go. Set me free.

"I need a cab."


*Dec. 22, 19 –*

I'll never forget the first sight of our house after the cab dropped me off at the end of our driveway. It was clear she'd been here. The front door was wide open, and the entire house was lit. I paid the man, and he pulled away as I slowly picked my way toward the entrance. Paintings were smashed all over the flagstone drive. Our family portrait was in shreds, and as I went through the doorway, I saw shattered frames and torn pictures scattered all around.

Inside, windows were broken and the plate-glass mirror was in fragments. Framed pictures were all over the floor. By the fireplace, the picture of the three of us was pulverized, and another picture of the two of them on my boat had a hole in it that looked like it had been made with the heel of a shoe.

"Meg?" I called loudly looking up the stairs. No answer.

The light was on, so I went to check the bedroom to see if she was there. My bedside table was emptied and papers were scattered everywhere. What was she looking for? I saw the note on the rug and picked it up, slipping it into my pocket. Just then I heard voices downstairs. I saw her journal on the floor and picked it up, sliding it between the mattresses. I would look at it later.

I ran to the doorway and out onto the balcony. It was the police.

"Bill?" It was Chuck Wilson, our old high school friend and now chief of police in East End beach. "The door was open... Are you okay?"

"Hey, Chuck," I called back. "Yeah... just a little misunderstanding."

His face was lined with worry. "Bill, I'm afraid we've got some bad news. You'd better come down and have a seat."


*Dec. 24, 19 —*

Two days have passed. It's Christmas Eve, but nobody's celebrating. I haven't seen my children. Gigi has taken them somewhere.

I have to think hard to recall exactly what happened after Chuck broke the news to me. I was picking through the rubble of torn photographs and paintings. The last thing I'd heard him say was, "She didn't make it."

Meg didn't make it. Her car had wrapped around a light pole, and her little body didn't bend in the same direction as the twisted metal. They estimated she'd been going about a hundred miles per hour on impact. I imagined her putting her head down on the wheel as she drove.

They asked me if I had any reason to believe she'd wanted to kill herself. I wanted to tell them they were looking at her Number One reason. The man she'd built her life around. The one she'd decided at fifteen she would devote herself to. The one who callously tore her heart out and threw it on the ground. The one who slept with her best friend.

I didn't say any of that. I simply said no. I didn't believe she would kill herself. She was devoted to her children. And as I said the words, I knew they were true. I'd simply hurt her so badly, she wasn't thinking straight.

I'd killed her. It was the same as if I'd driven the car myself. It was my fault. They should arrest me.

I shook my head as we all absorbed the loss. The beauty queen. The prettiest girl at school. The sweet one who'd only wanted to marry me and have my babies and volunteer in the community.

My wife was dead.


*Dec. 28, 19 —*

Only two people know the real reason Meg was behind the wheel the night she died, and we have no intention of sharing it with anybody. Ever.

Alex stays far from me now, which is right.

It was as if both our hearts had gone into shock following the loss of Meg.

Hundreds of people turned out for the funeral. My wife had known almost everyone in South County it

318

seemed, and those she didn't know personally knew her parents and came to pay their respects. She was buried in the Weaver plot near her father. Her mother watched with composed resolve as she bid her only child goodbye. I convinced her to stay with us to help with the twins, and then I threw myself into work.


*Aug. 15, 20 –*


It's been many years since that last entry. I feel like I should round out the story for this autobiographical record no one will ever read. I should probably burn it. But for some reason, I can't bring myself to do that. Yet.

Gigi stayed with us until the twins started kindergarten. I worked all the time, hoping I would wake up one day and find it was all just a horrible dream. I withdrew from everyone, including Bryant. Eventually we dissolved the development firm of Kyser-Brennan Equities, and Bryant went into some other line of work. We still held all the ownership rights, and our future was secure. I just couldn't find a reason to keep moving forward.

Development in South County carried on, and as hurricanes came through and wiped out older places, developers came in to plot out and build new ones. The only structures that stood the test of time and the weather were the Phoenicians. We had done our job well. I was satisfied to run the existing business and provide consulting services to start-ups. I'd accomplished all I'd wanted, and we were financially secure for a long time.

Alex eventually opened a little art and souvenir shop down on the beach road, and from what I could tell she was pretty successful at it. She stopped painting altogether and dropped out of all social circles. I only heard from her if Julian needed something she couldn't afford, and then I'd deposit a check into her account. I always doubled what she asked for.

She never told him who his father was. Ten years after that night, the one time I'd suggested coming clean, she'd told me no. The fallout would be too great. She was probably right, and I've never brought it up again.

Now, except for the occasional, accidental crossing of paths, I never see her. I heard about Julian growing and becoming interested in art. He isn't a painter like his mother, but I read he's developing an impressive body of work in sculpture.

Time is passing and I'm watching my children grow and evolve. Meg would be pleased that they're all fine-looking kids. Of the three, I'm closest to Jack, and I'm grooming him to take over my role in the business. He's controlled and mature for his age, and his instincts are good. Lucy is impossible to manage and is always getting into trouble. I don't know what to do with her, so my one hope is I can pay for whatever damage she causes.

Will has been the most troubled. He inherited my drive to take the business world by storm, but he's ruthless and cold. There's a cruelty to his approach that I don't like. He doesn't want to produce a legacy, he simply wants to win. I blame the loss of his mother, which hit him hardest since he was old enough to remember her well. At times it feels like he blames me for her death, as if he somehow knows, which is impossible.

I hang back and observe my children as they find their way in the world. Perhaps they won't make the same mistakes I've made, but they probably will. The hole I created in their lives when I drove their mother away is gaping and apparent, and I never want them to know what really happened.

In the evenings, I walk out on the patio and look out at Lost Bay. I stare at the darkening skyline as the misty stars light up one by one. South of me I can see the product of my years of dedication and focus, and I wonder how it can be possible that I accomplished something so enormous and yet repeatedly failed at something so simple.

I started out on one path, and then I discovered I was lost. I reached out to change direction and took a life. There was a time I sat and wished it would all be over. But the end is a long way off.

When I'm feeling honest, I'll admit I'm not ready to acknowledge my defeat. I've never failed when I've been truly determined to win. I think about the night I'd been ready to give it all away, everything I'd devoted my life to achieving, if I could just be free. That level of motivation and focus has always served me well. This time will pass, and I will have what I want.

We will be together.

# Anna – *December 31*

I sat back and exhaled deeply. It was all so sad.

They hadn't been much older than I am now in the beginning, and by the end, they were all so far off track. I didn't know whether to cry, to be angry, or to be disgusted with all three of them. How could they be so selfish and blind to the ones they were supposed to care about? At the same time, I could see them making these mistakes, and I could also see why. And how easily it all fell apart.

Ms. LaSalle's reasons for wanting to keep these dark facts a secret were understandable. Julian would have to deal with the knowledge that his entire existence was a product of a betrayal that ultimately led to a death. But I couldn't understand what Mr. Kyser wanted. Even though their marriage seemed doomed from the start, I couldn't believe he'd put his family through this revelation, even if he did want to know Julian as his son.

So why had he given me these books? Why did he want me to know all of this?

I leaned my head against my bed. Mom and Dad would be home in a few hours. I needed to do this now. Scooping up the three journals, I grabbed my jacket and my bag and headed downstairs. I scribbled out a quick note for Mom, telling her I was meeting Julian and wouldn't be much after midnight, that I had my phone. In minutes, I was speeding down the familiar, two-lane beach road in the direction of Hammond Island.

He'd be there alone. I knew from Lucy's text she was at the party with B.J., and Jack and Will were in

New Orleans. The sun was dropping fast, but one glance at the clock told me I had time. And I needed answers.

I parked in the large, circular driveway and stepped out onto the flagstone. Everything was different now as I looked up at the massive stucco mansion. I was different. I wasn't afraid anymore.

Bill Kyser had pulled back the curtain, and everything made sense, from his rude question about birth control that first night to his separation from his children to the things he'd told me during our interview in his office. Not to make plans at my age, feelings change.

The side door was unlocked, and I let myself in, walking through the mud room into the kitchen. The house was quiet and dimly lit. I continued into the open living area and looked out toward the large patio that faced the bay. There he stood.

He was just outside the doors with his back to me, dressed in khaki pants and a long-sleeved shirt. The wind pushed his light-brown hair around his head.

"Mr. Kyser?" I called.

He didn't turn immediately. His hand lifted, and I watched him take a drink first. Then his back expanded with an exhale, and when he did turn, I was impressed again by how much both his sons were like him in different ways.

His blue eyes went from my face to the books in my hands and he nodded slightly. "You finished."

"Yes, and I wanted to bring them back. I knew Lucy was out." Somehow I couldn't just charge into what I wanted to know. I felt the need to be more formal, which didn't make any sense, given all I knew about him now.

"Thank you," he said, not moving. "You can leave them on the counter."

But I didn't move. I wasn't going anywhere yet. It was strangely liberating to know so much about a person, and even if we weren't exactly friends, my old fear of him was gone.

"Why did you give them to me?" I asked.

His eyes flickered down, and he entered the living room, going to the fireplace. He placed his tumbler on the mantle where pictures of Jack and Lucy as babies, him and Will, were arranged. He studied them a moment before answering.

"I wanted your help," he said quietly.

My brow creased. "How can I help you?"

He traced his finger down one of the frames before dropping his arm. "I want my family together. I want them to be in my life. I want this" — he looked up at the giant house, around the panoramic view with the Phoenicians rising faintly in the distance — "all of it to mean something." His last statement was almost a hushed afterthought.

I inhaled deeply before answering. "I don't know if that's possible. And even if it were, how can *I* help you with that?"

His eyes held mine then. "The day you said Julian needed to know his father — what made you say that?"

I shook my head, gesturing with the books. "I said it because I didn't know all this."

"Yes, but that day, why did you say it?"

I blinked several times, thinking. "Because he'd said something that... well, I knew it bothered him not knowing who you were." I paused, then quietly added, "And because it's not fair."

"Why?" I could tell he already knew my answer.

"You could give him so much."

"I want to give them everything," he said. "I want them to live here with me. I want Julian to know he has a father. To know how proud his father is of him."

I could tell by his tone he knew it was an impossible wish, but he was giving me a glimpse of his private pain. My eyes grew warm at that thought combined with what I knew. Julian believed his dad didn't want to know him, never cared about him, never gave a shit. He had no idea.

"But what about Jack and Lucy?" I asked. "And Will. What happened was so awful. I don't know if there's a way back from it."

He didn't speak. He turned to the mantle again, and I couldn't help feeling a twinge of guilt. But it was the truth. And it was a truth I knew he was well-acquainted with.

"I can never be forgiven for something that happened so long ago," he said softly.

His words made my stomach hurt, and I didn't know how to respond.

Then he glanced back. "Julian has an opening soon, right?"

I nodded. "He has a statue being installed at the Sports Center. It's kind of a big deal."

"Are you going?"

"He asked me to be his date."

His lips pressed into a tight smile before he spoke. "I'll be there. I'll come over and speak to you about our feature for the paper. I'll mention the possibility of using his art in some way at one of my developments."

"Ms. LaSalle would never—"

"Lexy's going to be the biggest obstacle." He reached for the crystal glass. "I'll talk to her, ease her into the idea."

"But you still haven't answered my question," I said, walking over to a wooden table standing beside the brushed, leather sofa. I placed the three books on it. "You didn't have to show these to me to ask for my help. Now I know all of this, and I can never tell Julian. I can't tell any of them!"

"I needed you to understand." Ice rattled as he tilted the glass. "Now you know why we can't have you talking about it."

"But I was never going to talk about it! I just wanted you to… " I shook my head. "Okay, maybe I *did* ask you to tell Julian the truth, but I meant you, not me. And if that's your ultimate goal anyway, how? When?"

"When Lexy says I can," he said.

"She's never going to say that!" My voice rose as I started to see what this really meant. "Julian and I are getting close. I think we might get serious, and now you've put this huge thing between us."

"Lexy will come around," he said, restoring the tumbler to the mantle as if he weren't even listening to me. "And in the meantime, you can help me find ways to help Julian, to know him better. Then perhaps he won't feel so—"

"Shocked? Betrayed? He's already angry that his dad's never shown up once."

His eyes caught mine, and I saw his determination. "That's why I need your help. I need to know these things about him. I won't let you get hurt."

I turned away, my chest burning with what I knew. "You can't promise that. And I don't know if I can help you. I don't know what the right thing is."

"The truth is always the right thing."

"I'll have to think about it," I said, picking up my purse and heading to the door. I needed to go.

The sun was quickly disappearing, and the sky outside the patio windows was a blaze of orange, gold, pink, and blue. I wanted to get out to the water and breathe in the salt air and listen to the surf. I wanted to be with Julian. They were the two things that always helped me find calm, only now I didn't know what I would find when I saw Julian again.

* * *

The whole drive back, I rubbed my lined forehead as I stared at the two-lane road. Everything Bill Kyser had said swirled in my brain. He wanted me to help him know Julian better, he was going to talk to Ms. LaSalle, he wouldn't tell Julian until she said yes, and now I was right in the middle of it.

I parked at the beach pavilion and ran out to the Gulf in front of the towering Phoenician I complex. Once there, I turned around to gaze at the massive high-rise, and my breath caught in my throat. He'd done it all right. He'd spent the last twenty years unfolding his big plan, and these monuments had withstood it all.

The faintest glow still lit the horizon. I shivered in the chilly air and pulled out my phone, quickly texting Julian, letting him know I was here. The moon was rising over the dark water, and everything was changing to silver, black, and white. Further down the beach, the occasional firework pierced the night, but the show hadn't started yet.

I stared back up at the dark tower standing tall behind me. Tall, unmoving, and alone just like the man I'd left behind on Hammond Island. What was going to happen now? Could I make it out of this current without being drowned?

My phone buzzed, and I looked down at the number Bill Kyser had given me with the books. I slid my finger across the face to answer.

His voice was stiff. "A letter was in my journal. It's missing."

"Oh my god!" I squeezed my eyes shut. "It's under my pillow. It fell out, and I forgot to put it back."

The squeak of feet on sand caused me to jump around. A figure was jogging in my direction. Julian.

"I'll get it to you. I have to go," I said, just barely hearing his father's voice as I turned off my phone.

Julian slowed down as he reached me, smiling curiously. "Important call?"

I shrugged, smiling back. "Just checking in with the parents."

It wasn't a total lie, but I still cringed inwardly. Lies were what had led to the end of their story, and I hated bringing lies into ours. My damaged emotions had been one problem, but what I knew now was a far bigger one.

He stood in front of me, the wind pushing his dark hair around his handsome face. "It's funny," he said. "I was thinking about you, and right then you texted me."

"I was thinking about you, too." I glanced back in the direction he'd come. His house wasn't too far from where we stood, from Mr. Kyser's offices. I'd never considered the proximity before. "It must be nice to live so close."

He shrugged. "Except when the storms come."

We were quiet again, listening to the noise of the surf. I thought of his father back on that island, in that huge house alone. My dilemma was heavy on my mind, but more than that, I didn't want to wait anymore. I'd read too much about people in love being kept apart. I was terrified of us getting closer and him finding out what I knew, but in this moment, with him standing right here in front of me, I didn't want to think about Bill Kyser anymore. I didn't want to worry about the past. I wanted to think about my future.

"School starts back Monday," I said. "Are we still doing everything?"

A little grin flickered across his lips. "Correction. Everything *together*."

I looked up at his blue eyes, and I couldn't resist. I stepped to him and put my arms around his waist. He quickly wrapped me in an embrace, and soothing calm flooded my body. As if on cue, the fireworks show went off behind me, and I looked back at the green, red, and gold glittering lights illuminating the ocean.

My cheek rested on Julian's chest, and we didn't say anything as we watched. I felt him gently stroke my hair, his chin on the top of my head. I listened to his heart beat during the pauses. His breath moving in and out, mixing with the sound of the waves roaring behind me. Before long the whole sky burst into a nonstop display of lights and explosions. It was the signal for midnight, and I tilted my head up.

He looked down, and I lifted my chin higher, meeting his lips. My hold on his waist tightened as my mouth opened and I tasted his minty-sweet kiss. Delicious warmth flooded my body just like before, and I felt his lips curve into a smile. Mine did the same. It was exactly what we both wanted, our bodies close, this bond strengthening between us.

His kiss moved to the corner of my mouth, then my cheek, and he looked deep in my eyes. "I know, you still want to go slow."

My face felt flushed with emotion. "I think we can pick up the pace."

The twinkle in his eye made me so happy. He gave me another little kiss, and we turned and started walking back in the direction he'd come. I was very aware of our fingers laced together. I never wanted to let him go.

"Want me to drive you home?" I asked when we reached my car parked at the pavilion.

He squeezed my hand. "I think I'll walk. It's only a few blocks."

"It's a great night."

"One of the best," he said, pulling my hand to his lips and kissing my fingers. "You'll wear my ring now?"

I nodded, thinking how the minute I got home, I would unwrap it, put it on again, and never take it off.

"Cool," he smiled.

I was a little breathless. He pulled me closer, pressing his warm lips to mine again, his exhale whispering across my cheek. It felt like we were glowing in the darkness.

"Happy new year," he said softly.

"Happy new year," I whispered back.

He leaned in again for a longer, deeper kiss. Energy sparkled through me, just under my skin, and instinctively I held him tighter, pulled our bodies closer.

It was a new year. Julian and I were starting something new, and I was sure we could face whatever was coming and make it through.

My mind was on the future. Us together.

It was going to be amazing.

~ ~ ~

If you enjoyed this book by this author, please consider leaving a review at Amazon, Barnes & Noble, or Goodreads!

* * *

Be the first to know about New Releases by Leigh Talbert Moore! Sign up for the New Release Mailing list today at http://eepurl.com/tzVuP.

* * *

*Watercolor*, Book 3 in the Dragonfly series, coming Oct. 2013!

### *Watercolor*
by Leigh Talbert Moore

*Finishing senior year is supposed to be the best time in a person's life.*

*Finishing senior year as Julian's girlfriend should've been the icing on the cake.*

*Knowing the secret that could change his whole world is the only thing threatening to spoil it all.*

*Until Jack returns.*

Anna and Julian are together at last, and it's as hot and happy as they knew it would be. The only problem is the truth. And Jack.

But while Anna is determined to fight for the guy she loves, she could still lose him when he discovers the secret she's been helping to keep.

# Author's Note

Writing a book that includes large portions of journal entries, my goal was to find a way to bring the recorded events to life.

With that in mind, I added dialogue and descriptions to make it feel like the reader was there, watching the events as they occurred.

Obviously, most journals aren't written this way, so I took some artistic license. I hope it enhanced your enjoyment of the story.

As always, *thanks so much* for reading!

# Acknowledgments

First, I have to thank my friend Kim Secord, who was the first person to read this book and say to me, "I read it in one sitting," way back in 2010. I knew right then this dream of mine might actually happen.

Thanks again to Magan, Jolene, Kim Barnes, Tracy, Sharon, and my sweet husband Richard for loving it from the start.

Special thanks to Jolene for the gorgeous cover design and for finding the *perfect* fonts.

Thanks to Susan and Tami for challenging me.

Thanks to KP for hanging with me through the down times and for saying you believed in me when I was so tired.

Thanks to my sweet daughters for trying to understand why Mom is always typing on the computer and saying, "One more minute!"

Thanks to my parents and my in-laws for tolerating my disappearing acts.

Thanks to the writing community for your unfailing support and encouragement.

Thanks to God for this blessing, and

Thanks to YOU — all my dedicated readers who keep me motivated by saying you love it and asking for *more*!

Here's to love conquering all. <3

# About the Author

Leigh Talbert Moore is a wife and mom by day, a writer by day, a reader by day, a former journalist, a former editor, a chocoholic, a caffeine addict, a lover of great love stories, a beach bum, and occasionally she sleeps.

**Also by Leigh Talbert Moore:**

*The Truth About Faking* (2012)
*Rouge* (2012)
*The Truth About Letting Go* (2013)

*Dragonfly*, Book 1 in the Dragonfly series (2013)

All of Leigh's books are available on Amazon, Barnes & Noble, iTunes, and Kobo.

**Connect with Leigh online:**

Blog: http://leightmoore.blogspot.com
Facebook: http://www.facebook.com/LeighTalbertMoore
Amazon Author page: amazon.com/author/leightmoore
Goodreads: http://www.goodreads.com/leightmoore
Twitter: https://twitter.com/leightmoore
Tumblr: http://leightmoore.tumblr.com

CPSIA information can be obtained at www.ICGtesting.com
Printed in the USA
BVOW03s1930080514

352982BV00004B/225/P

9 781490 970615